THE
ACHILLES HEART

Karyn Rae

KARYN RAE PUBLISHING

Visit Karyn Rae's official website at www.karynrae.me for the latest news, book details, and other information

Copyright © Karyn Rae, 2015

Date of first printing: January 2015

Edited by: Grace Labatt; Samantha March of Marching Ink LLC
Cover Design by: James, GoOnWrite.com
Ebook Formatting by Guido Henkel, www.guidohenkel.com

For all of my girls:
A life without friends is a cruelty I hope never to experience

The greater the power, the more dangerous the abuse.
-Edmund Burke

PROLOGUE
WEST POINT GRADUATION, 1992

JACK

With only two hours to go before commencements, the heavy knock on my barracks door was unexpected. The courteous silence that followed was telling: the person on the other side had to be a plebe. After four years at the United States Military Academy at West Point, a pervasive amount of invaluable information concerning the chain of command—as it applied to a cadet in the military—was entrenched in my psyche. The first and most ingrained lesson was that a cadet, whether a first-year plebe or a fourth-year firstie, was never at the top of the chain.

I opened the door to a scrawny and pimple-faced cadet whose uniform seemingly swallowed his adolescence, trapping him between a boy and a man. In some respects, I envied his innocent features and insecure demeanor. It seemed as though, even as a boy, I had always had to be a man.

"Superintendent Phillips requests your attendance in his office immediately, sir." Scrawny overcompensated by using an unnecessarily loud voice.

"Is there a message?" I asked hopefully.

"No, sir, no message," Scrawny answered. But, then, turning around, he whispered, "Good luck, sir" as he closed the door behind him.

The five-minute walk across the parade field known as "The Plains" gave me enough time to consider that the highly decorated staff at West Point had finally untangled my past. Beyond this field, no valedictorian speech would await me, and a dishonorable discharge was inevitable—along with the stench of jailhouse foulness to wake me each morning. I envisioned the handcuffs slapping my wrists as soon as I opened Superintendent Phillips's door.

What awaited me, instead, was an entirely different bombshell. It was the opportunity to start my life over *again*. And this time, it would be legal.

"At ease, Stallings," Phillips instructed as I entered his broad and stately office. It was covered in oil paintings, each depicting a different but equally gruesome battlefield scene. Flanking the four corners of the superintendent's bureau were four dark-suited gentlemen, all of whom wore tiny earpieces that resembled spaghetti hanging around their ears.

Even though the men were quite obviously Secret Service, full panic wasn't necessary yet. My ability to remain calm in problematic situations had set me apart from any other cadet in the academy, and it was one of the main reasons I was graduating first in my class. Deductive reasoning was another special skill I had, and since the vice president of the United States was our graduation keynote speaker, I was betting that the suits were part of his entourage.

"Jack," the superintendent started, flashing a look at the stonewalled men and giving a nod to the one standing closest to the door. "Is your valedictorian speech complete?"

"Yes, sir!" I answered confidently.

"Is it any good?"

"Yes, sir. I wrote an exceptional dissertation, which is not only thought-provoking but inspirational as well, sir!" This was somewhat of a fabrication. I never wrote my words down on paper, and only pulled them from the roots of my mind.

"Suppose I tell you, you won't be giving that speech today. Suppose I tell you, you won't be graduating today either, or that all traces of you will be eliminated from this institution. How would you accept that, Stallings?"

"Sir?" I asked, but I thought I knew exactly where this line of questioning was headed. The last headache West Point wanted was a scandal on its hands, especially one coming in the form of a valedictorian.

"You are about to be offered a unique assignment, Jack, and like most opportunities in life, it comes with a price. You have the ability to decline this offer and participate as scheduled in the day's events, to go on to serve this country, and possibly to make general, living out the rest of your days watching your grandchildren play on the lawn. Or you can accept this challenge with the courage and appetite that only the top graduates of the United States Military Academy procures. Only three cadets have been approached with this opportunity over the last thirty years of my career. With big rewards come big risks, Jack. Are you willing to risk it all to be number four?"

"Of course, sir. I took an oath to serve and protect my country no matter the cost. I will do so without question or doubt. The military has given me life, and I am prepared to give that life back, sir."

"Don't you want to know the assignment before you sign your life away?"

"Not particularly. If you feel I'm the man for the job, then I trust your judgment, sir."

"Well stated, Jack. Which family members would you like to call first? Do you have a mom or dad, aunts or uncles sitting in the audience, waiting to see you graduate? How about loved ones who would miss your presence if you disappeared for ten years? Is there *anyone* Jack, who would even know you were gone?"

What the hell is he talking about? I've made it until graduation day in the academy without any questions about my past, and now suddenly, he wants to know my family tree. Something significant is happening, and I should be smart enough to figure it out.

Before I decided on a response to Phillips's question, he broke my silence with the answer, and the unexpected truth. He came around his solid oak desk and lay a hand on my shoulder.

"Ease up, son. I know you have no one to call, and not a soul is in one of those seats waiting to congratulate you. I've known for quite a while, Jack, but today is not the time for an explanation. It's just one of the many reasons you are a perfect fit for The Odyssey."

The Odyssey?

Sweat began trickling down my heavily clothed back, and the certainty of his words launched like the silver sphere in a pinball machine, pinging each lie I had told over the last four years. A minefield of colorful lights and sounds flashed through my head.

How much does he know? Does it even matter at this point?

Turning to the largest suit, the one standing near the door, he stated, "We're finished here. He's ready to go." Then he squeezed my shoulder and offered some words, which have stuck with me over the last twenty years. "Jack, the military is now your forever home, and she will protect you as long as you protect her. God be with you."

9

As the Secret Service led me toward the office doors, Phillips yelled out, "One more thing. Can I find a copy of the valedictorian speech in your barracks? An outline to follow will give the next in line a jumping-off point, since he's just found out that he is now at the head of the class, and he needs to give a speech to five thousand people in a little under an hour."

"No, sir, I never write anything down. Paper always leaves a trail. I've trained myself to just remember, sir."

A slow smile swept across his face, as if he were watching the sun rise for the first time.

"I thought you might say that." He laughed, and his voice boomed through the corridor.

The thickness of the daylight heat swept over my face when the main doors opened, but strangely, I felt cold inside. Superintendent Phillips's words continued to replay in my head. *She will protect you as long as you protect her.* It almost sounded like a threat.

Two black Lincoln town cars were parked in the main entrance of the circle drive, one behind the other. The door opened from the inside as I approached the subsequent car. A man who looked to be the same age as me occupied the back.

As I lowered myself into the remaining empty seat, the driver cocked his head to the side and, without taking his eyes off the windshield, said, "Jack Stallings, meet Jamie Black. Best if you two get to know each other, because you're going to be spending a lot of time together." A simultaneous nod from both our heads was the only exchange. The caliginous granite of the neo-Gothic buildings cast a hazy shadow through my passenger-side window, and the car slowly pulled out of the drive.

My name is Jack Stallings, and those were the last moments of *this* life as I knew it.

PRESENT DAY
2013

ANNIE

I didn't want to believe Kessler would pull away from me so quickly, but the gates were already closing down around his heart, while his guard was going up. Six weeks had passed since my trip to Kansas City, and with the weight of our new circumstances, Kessler had swiftly retreated to the safety of his previous life—a life before me.

On the flight from Kansas City back to Nashville, I had contemplated how to tell Kessler that my should-be-dead husband was, in fact, alive. So alive that he had waited for me to visit his gravesite, thinking that would be the best opportunity to announce how alive he actually was. Jack was a living ghost, professing a grandiose fantasy of the future life and love we had yet to experience together.

What could I say to Kessler? How could I explain an unearthly phenomenon that hadn't fully manifested within me yet? People don't come back from the dead, not unless they've been in a daytime soap opera for at least a decade. Or, apparently, in Jack's case, not unless they're in the CIA. No matter how I said them, the words would break Kessler, and eventually, they would break us.

As it turned out, I was right.

The moment I uttered the impossible—"Jack is alive"—an afflicted look swept across his face, and suspicion settled like sand in the ocean blue of his eyes. The chafing silence that followed the torpedo clung to us like smoke from a campfire. Only, we couldn't change our clothes; this was not something we could wash out. We were not speaking in hypotheticals. This was a fact that we could not change. Jack was alive, and just as his death had brought Kessler and me together, his life had already begun to tear us apart.

During the first night after my confessional, I got the *real* Kessler, with his raw yet honest desperation about what was to come of us. And in the days following that night, he slowly began turning away from me.

"What did he say? Why did he fake his death?" Kessler softly asked in disbelief.

He hinted at several other details of the conversation Jack and I had, but he never fully asked the questions. He was constantly starting and then stopping, realizing—the same as I was—that considering the big picture of our current triangle, none of the details actually mattered. The only question of any importance still hovered around us, and that was the one that would either allow us to move forward or force us to part.

"Are you leaving me?" he finally whispered. His eyes dragged across the room, avoiding interlocking with mine until well after he had asked the question.

I couldn't respond, because I honestly didn't have an answer. My past heart and present love were clawing through me like lions in the Sahara, battling for control of the pride.

When dealing in human emotions, a person possesses certain levels of accountability, depending on the means of contact. Texting or emailing news to someone has a very basic grade of feeling. Such shorthand notation gets directly to the point, and because of the lack of human interaction, it sends your words and thoughts into virtual space, with no immediate backlash or response. A phone conversation has an intermediate level; it certainly heightens the connection between both parties. Confidence in thought and speech are more easily mustered when words are spoken into a receiver. The dial tone is a finite ending point, and terminating contact is easily done with the push of a button.

Speaking directly to someone while sharing the same physical space with him is incomparable to any other mode. All senses fire simultaneously. Hand gestures pair with speech, facial expressions accompany words, and the eyes reign over the entire conversation. Taking responsibility for inflicting emotional suffering is unavoidable when misery is painted on the other person's face and agony colors his stare. You cannot un-see another's torment, and unless you have psychotic tendencies, the image stays burned into you forever.

The next few hours scorched within me, creating an eternal Polaroid of Kessler's pain.

"Annie, answer me," he calmly insisted. The aching in his eyes grew with my silence. "No, don't. Your silence says enough," he mumbled as he turned and headed toward the bedroom.

"Wait!" I yelled, running after him and slipping in through the bedroom door before he could shut me out. "Kessler, please don't go." I touched his arm in an attempt to distract him from looking for his car keys.

"Why? Why should I *not* go? You are! I see it in your eyes, Annie. I hear it in your silence." He paused long enough to make sure I felt like a complete asshole. "I'll ask you again. Are you leaving me?"

"Let's not do this right now. Please, I don't know what to say," I pleaded as tears pressed against my cheeks.

"You don't know what to say," he echoed through gritted teeth, reaching into the pocket of a crumpled pair of jeans and pulling out his keys. "Do you love him?" He winced with the words, as though the fire imploding throughout his insides actually burned his skin.

Again, my lack of answer came too slowly.

"Do you still love him?" he screamed toward me, his face quickly turning from red to purple. He locked his hands safely inside his disheveled hair, where they could not shake the answer he wanted out of me.

"Please don't ask me that. It's a totally unfair question," I answered, startled at his behavior.

"Fair? You can't even answer a simple question, Annie! You want to talk about fair? None of this is fair!"

Then he went silent. A switch had flipped inside of him, and his face shifted. The round, black pupils occupying all the blue in his eyes now funneled down to pinpoints, like sand slipping through an hourglass. Pulling the keys from the antique dresser, he mumbled, "This is bullshit. I'm going out." He grabbed a bottle of whiskey from the kitchen counter. I heard the door to the garage slam shut.

I hadn't seen Kessler in this state before, and my heart broke from knowing that I was the source of his pain. His truck tires squealed against the concrete cul-de-sac. I had no idea when or if he would be back.

What does he expect me to say? It's not like I asked for Jack to rise from the dead. I don't think a little space is too much to ask for, considering what I've been through over the last year. I told Jack I was in love with Kessler, and I told Kessler about Jack. I'm not keeping secrets from anyone.

My life became a pendulum again. This time, I was swinging back and forth between two men—which, despite what daytime television glorified, was actually heartbreaking. How could I choose between a man who unconscientiously magnetized my body to his just by sharing the same physical space, and the man for whom I had handwritten my wedding vows over ten years ago?

Like a rock sinking to the bottom of a pond, the thought buried me.

Oh my God. Am I still married?

My first instinct was to grab the edge of the counter to catch myself in case of a fainting spell. But, the brittle woman of a year ago, who had crumbled with the onset of staggering news, no longer existed. Instead, I poured a glass of pinot and allowed the burgundy prophecy to pacify my anxiety. There would be no conclusion to this triangle tonight, and I wasn't going to force one. I hadn't felt this miserable since the day Officer Grady had told me Jack was dead. Now Jack was alive, and ironically, I felt just as bad.

KESSLER

Burning my tires into the pavement was childish but liberating. After watching the speedometer reach sixty on the straightaway, I hit the brakes, skidding into the open acreage at the forefront of our neighborhood. Dust from the field mixed with the cold night air and rose around the lights of my truck, like a swarm of ghosts.

"FUCK!" I screamed, pounding my fists on the steering wheel while laying on the horn. I floored the gas again, and the truck took off spinning and jumping like a rodeo bull on an eight-second ride. Gripping the wheel through dips and hills, I tore the hell out of the custom landscaping—and had fun doing so. When my tantrum ended, I wound up in the same tracts where I had started my tirade, slumped into my seat and feeling drained. I needed to get my anger and frustration out, without saying something to Annie I couldn't take back.

Goddammit! I knew better than to fall in love, and worse, get comfortable in it! This is why I never let myself get attached to a woman—it's all heartache.

Just as I was about to tell myself all of the reasons why I shouldn't love Annie, a knock on the driver-side window startled me.

Oh shit, I thought as I rolled down the window to Wade standing in the exhaust, wearing a giddy smile across his face.

"What?" I mumbled.

"Hey, buddy. I was just sittin' in my living room watching *Deadliest Catch*, when I saw some maniac tearin' down our neighborhood street. I figured, since we've got kids who live on this road, I should go on over and see what in the hell's wrong with this asshole. Only, once I got out here, I saw that asshole was you. Mind telling me what's pinchin' your dick?"

"First of all, it's eleven o'clock at night, and there aren't any kids running around the neighborhood. Second, I think I ripped my oil pan out from under the truck when I jumped the creek over there. I need you to help me look for it," I said, instead of an apology.

Wade busted up laughing as he opened the passenger-side door. Climbing into the truck, he asked, "What's your lady trouble, little buddy?"

"What makes you think anything is wrong at home?"

Through the lit-up windshield, we surveyed the extensive landscape damage I'd caused. Wade turned to me and said, "Kess, this has got *woman* written all over it."

Even though Wade was a bit of a handful at times, he always managed to remain rational when dealing in the matters of the heart. Just because he was rich and famous didn't mean he cared all that much for it. Wade was the essential blue-collar working man, the backbone of America, even in the temptations of a sinner's world. He'd come from a rice field in Arkansas and had never forgotten what it meant to be small town—a term that could be construed as simpleminded, but only by the people who hadn't lived in one.

No matter the problems I had, I could always go to Wade for the kind of advice I might not want to hear, but needed to hear. I guess that was why he and his mother-in-law, Mama D, were always fighting like kids on a playground, both of them competing to give the noblest advice.

"He's alive," I sighed.

"Who's alive?"

"Jack Whitman, Annie's late husband, or ex-husband, or maybe current husband. He's not fucking dead, Wade. He concocted this master plan over a year ago, and now he's telling Annie that his vanishing act was to protect her from some terrorists he screwed over."

"No shit?" Wade twisted the hairs of his handlebar mustache, staring at the floorboard.

"He's got her emotions all tangled up, playing on her loyalty to their marriage and his service to America. I don't understand why she can't see him for who he really is. Everything he's put her through over the last year has been a lie. Leaving a little trail of breadcrumbs in the hopes that Annie will clean up his mess, and then, once she's finally happy—happy with me—he gives her some shit about honor and duty to our country. He's a fucking con-artist wrapped in an American flag."

"You want me to kick his ass?" Wade asked with a cockeyed grin.

"Dammit, this is serious, Wade. Help me! I don't know how to keep Annie from leaving me for someone who's done nothing but lie to her throughout their entire marriage. I love her. I didn't mean to completely lose myself in loving her, but I did, and I need to figure out how to convince her to stay."

Wade unscrewed the top of my whiskey bottle and took a long swig before he spoke. "Kessler, you're all caught up in your emotions right now. The only logic as I see it is to let her go, not push her out the door, but give her the space to decide for herself. Annie loves you, and I can see it plain as day. She looks at you the same way Hope looked at me when we first met. You can't make her stay. If you go screamin' and hollerin' at her, she *will* leave, and you'll go back to being miserably alone in your big ole house."

"How am I supposed to give her space when we share the same home?"

"Ha!" Wade laughed. "That's somethin' us married men have been askin' ourselves since we lived in caves. I'll tell ya what, I'm fixin' to go out on tour next week. Why don't you play a few shows with me, like old times? Hell, you know the fans would love to see you, and this will give you something else to focus on while you're out of the house. We make some money, and Annie makes a choice."

The thought of making music on a stage gave me instant excitement. An anxious void had slowly crept up in me over the last month. I had tried my best to ignore my nostalgia for the butterflies that only a live performance could create, since I'd retired last year and thought I wasn't supposed to miss that part of my life. I shouldn't have been so quick to quit music, but like most life lessons I'd learned, this one had come the hard way. Always a black and white type of thinker, until only recently I had failed to notice all the different shades of gray in the world. Having stepped back from the music scene, I now saw that I didn't have to quit making music; I just needed someone to share in the experience.

Balance in life sounds like a simple achievement to check off a list, but really, it's a tight rope that takes skill to walk across, and you can only perfect it by practice. The opportunity to find balance is presented to us every moment of every day. The hard part is discovering the correct letters and numbers in the mathematical equation that fit your life, because the answer is different for all of us.

"All right, I'll make some calls tomorrow. I hope Annie and I make the right choice, and we both choose us." I followed this with a burning rush of whiskey down my throat.

Once again, Wade had come through with the good advice I didn't want to hear. But, I would do whatever it took to be the only man standing at the end of this fight. We sat in the truck cab for a few more swigs, and as I looked at the mess I'd made, with my truck and my girl, I knew it was time to get to cleaning things up.

As if Wade heard my thoughts, he broke the silence and lectured, "You know, Hope is gonna make you pay for the new landscaping. She's on the homeowners' association board, and she's gonna be all kinds of pissed when she drives by these sad little bushes tomorrow morning."

"Yeah, I know. Just tell her I'll write her a check. She can add it to the rest of them. Let's go find that oil pan."

ANNIE

The soft turn of the door handle pulled me out of a scanty sleep, but the smell of whiskey could have done the same. Kessler sat gently on the edge of our bed in an attempt not to wake me. He pulled his boots off, making soft grunting sounds upon the freedom of each foot. I closed my eyes and waited, hoping that if he thought I was asleep, he would talk to me, *really* talk to me.

He lowered his face down into the cradle of his hands, exposing a vulnerability usually hard to find in men. With a release of breath, he whispered, "Please don't leave me, Annie. I don't want to do the rest of this life without you."

I couldn't leave him hanging like laundry on the line, twisting and blowing in the wind. When I opened my eyes, they instantly connected with his.

I propped up on my elbows and promised, "It's going to be okay. Everything is going to work out for the best."

He sighed as he pulled his white cotton T-shirt over his head. "That's what I'm afraid of, baby." Kessler then extended his hand out toward me and whispered, "Dance with me."

"Here? Now?" I suddenly felt embarrassed.

"Yes, baby. Dance with me."

I rolled over and clicked the radio to an old country love song. A deep-throated voice sang about a woman and the pain she'd caused him by leaving.

He took my hand in his and pulled me into the warmth of his bare chest, the smell of whiskey wafting around us. We moved together in unison, my feet following his, and he led me around our bedroom in a slow embrace. The song ended and another one began, but Kessler stopped moving. I encircled him, running the tips of my fingers all over his skin and mapping out every brilliant muscle in his unforgiving body, replacing my fingers with my lips. But even though the moment was intimate, there was palpable distance between us. Our faces were touching, but he refused to look at me.

"Kessler," I whispered. "Please talk to me."

Tracing my arm with his fingers, up to my shoulder and down my back, he pulled my nightgown off of me, dropping it around my feet. I turned his head, until he had nowhere else to look except directly into my eyes.

I lay down on the bed, showing him every part of my naked body, and he stood stoic, taking me in with his eyes, as though trying to savor a mental image.

He lowered himself beside me, and the warmth of his chest against my skin lured my arms around his neck and our breath together. We'd already shared a variety of colorful boudoir activities, and he had taken me to heights I didn't know were climbable, but tonight he was different. There was a serious desperation in the strength of his momentum as he pushed himself inside of me. He was struggling with our imposing triangle, and his desperation had transferred into our sex.

Urgency washed over me. I felt like I was losing him.

As he rolled over panting, his hands running through his sweaty hair, I whispered, "I do love you, Kessler. I just need some space to sort through my head."

"I know, and that's what I'm going to give you," he answered, and then he kissed me hard before rolling back over and falling asleep.

Sleepless nights were something I'd grown accustomed to before I met Kessler, or before I really met myself. Being married to Jack was easy, *too* easy. During ten years of marriage, Jack had taken care of almost everything: bills, cars, finances. At the time, I'd thought that made me happy. Now, looking back at the woman I was, I felt sorry for her. When I was twenty-five and Jack had rode up on his white horse, I thought I was being saved—saved from a life of stress and worry about so many adult things. I now realized that our marriage had crippled me. It had kept me from learning about the hard stuff and having to do the work. When Jack died, I resembled a mental paraplegic needing to relearn how to function.

From struggle you find freedom. Learning to navigate your own waters makes you captain of the ship, and you quickly find out that any other rank is a waste of time.

The next morning, I came into the kitchen hoping to find Kessler in his usual morning attire—shirtless, with track pants on—and a ball cap hiding his bedhead. Nothing perked me up like seeing his upper body escape from clothes, especially if his skin was still sweaty from a recent workout. The mental image always made me smile.

Instead, black suitcases lined the length of the hallway leading into the foyer, and Kessler was showered and fully clothed.

"What is all of this? Are you going somewhere?" The words caught in my throat, and I wrung my hands together.

"Ahem." He cleared his throat, leaning his hands against the granite countertops and hanging his ears between his arms. He spoke to the floor. "Wade asked me to be the opening act for his first couple of shows, and the tour starts in a few days. I thought I'd get a head start, so me and the boys can go over some songs and work out a set list. It's been a while since we played together, and I don't want to sound rusty on stage."

"You're opening for Wade? Kessler Carlisle is the opening act for Wade Rutledge?"

"A year ago, no, I wouldn't have been the opening act for anyone. But, when you put your pride over everything else, it's usually the only thing you're left with." He spoke with pain in his eyes.

As he made his way to the front door, a limousine pulled into the driveway. The driver began his walk up the path.

"Now? You're leaving right now? What if I hadn't been up yet? Were you just going to leave? Is there a note for me, explaining why you're too chicken-shit to talk this out?"

"Goddammit, I'll never understand women! This is unbelievable!" he hollered.

The limo driver was standing awkwardly at the open door, right in the middle of our argument.

Kessler turned to the man and, pointing to his luggage, said, "All of these go."

As the driver bent down to grab the first two, I warned, "Don't touch those bags!" startling him and making him jump back.

He looked back and forth at us, eyes pleading for instructions so he didn't have to ask or make another mistake.

Finally, Kessler handed over a twenty out of his cash roll and said, "Go on out to the car, and I'll be there in a minute."

"Yes, Mr. Carlisle," the man answered gratefully.

Kessler looked up at the ceiling, hands intertwined on the top of his hat. He let out a purposeful sigh. I blocked the doorway, my own hands planted firmly on my hips. This was a tactic I'd seen Hope and Mama D use on a regular basis, and it usually resulted in an argument's victory. I couldn't think of an argument I would have rather won than the one I was in just then. I pushed out my chest, balled up my fists, and glared at Kessler, in hopes that he'd be quick to see his error.

"Don't think I don't know what you're doing," he said. "You look like Mama D, but about thirty years younger."

"Don't change the subject."

"You said you wanted space!" he yelled backed, slapping his hands on his legs. "I'm trying to give you what you asked for. With me gone, you can decide if you want your old life back, or if I'm enough for you. What I'm not going to do is sit around here and beg you to stay, because I should be enough. And, as far as I'm concerned, I've done everything right by you!"

I quickly realized that my front wasn't working, and he was calling my bluff. I should have known better, because Kessler didn't play games. With him, you got what you saw, but you got all of him, which was something I loved about him. I immediately softened.

Putting my hands on his cheeks, I felt his sharp inhale. He closed his eyes as I pressed my forehead against his chin. "Don't go, Kessler. Me and you, baby. Remember?"

"I *have to* go," he said as he picked up a suitcase with each hand.

I filled my fists with his shirt and begged, "Say it, Kessler. Say, *me and you*. Let me hear you say that to me."

"I can't say that right now, Annie. I gotta go."

As the limo pulled out of the cul-de-sac, I couldn't hold my tears back any longer.

Why is it that every time I try to do the right thing, I seem to screw it up?

22

JACK

T he dream was always the same, and each time my screams woke me before I detonated.

The pavement absorbed the scorching heat of the daylight hours, as though it were a gossip with the juiciest secret, but as darkness fell, the secret was cast out into the entire city. No matter where you went, the heat was inescapable. Even in the dry air of the desert, clothes became a second skin, bonded to the body by constant sweat. At nightfall (a time when you would expect relief) the anger from the feverous afternoon retched from the pores of the concrete, punishing those who wandered around in an attempt to ignore it.

I arrived early at the café, in hopes of securing a table big enough for five chairs. While waiting for the others, I gently placed my duffel on the far edge of the rectangular table, shifting and adjusting the heavily meshed side pocket until I was satisfied with its placement. I snapped a couple of test shots. The bag was arranged in the perfect position to capture all five of us together in the same picture. My instinct was to get proof of this meeting.

My commander, John Savage, went over the operation orders for our next assignment. I repeatedly pressed my remote clicker, snapping picture after picture of the confabulation. The assignment was awkward in its preparation and graceless in its specifics, the complete opposite of any other mission I'd ever prepped for. My hunch was that these orders weren't coming from the government, but from John Savage himself.

The four of us were now standing in the office of a suspected terrorist headquarters, located in an elementary school. Savage sent Gail Adams, Patrick Riley, and a handful of others to clear the remaining rooms. As soon as we were alone, he reached into a filing cabinet and pulled out a bulky satchel, holding it as if it were a newly purchased pet store fish. I stepped forward to examine the contents more closely, and I was blindsided by the appearance of a bag of diamonds against my face. The force of the bag, combined with the weight of the diamonds, felt like a punch from a fist. I toppled over a metal chair. He screamed repeatedly in a droning voice, "If you protect her, she'll protect you, Jack!" I steadied myself and attempted to stand. Trying to focus on Savage's mantra, I only heard ear-piercing beeping, in rhythm with the seconds ticking on a clock. Looking down, I noticed that I was standing on a detonator. The countdown continued, each high-pitched tone becoming louder with the heat of

imminent death, and as my body petrified for the brace of impact, my own
screaming woke me up.

The ring tone on my disposable cell phone precisely matched the
countdown toward my dream-status death. During the first moments of
conscious blinking, I hesitated, unmoving. My fists strangled handfuls of
hotel comforter, yet my body remained stiffer than rigor mortis. Still
grappling with reality, I reached for the phone.

"Yeah?" I breathed into the receiver, massaging my cramping hands.

"Two o'clock at the usual place?" she instructed. The background
noise of traffic threatened to drown out her voice.

"I'll be there."

***

Platte City, Missouri, located twenty-something miles north of downtown Kansas City, was the definition of unassuming. Ten years ago, after
the final member of our team was in place, we had agreed to set up base
in a bucolic community close to an international airport. It just so happened that Roy's Farm and Feed store was on the market for a price we
couldn't pass up.

As I pulled into the parking lot, my Buick smashed the over-grown
weeds permeating the decrepitated and sun-bleached concrete. A dreaded
but familiar sense of duty encircled me, along with the warmth from the
car heater. After pressing the remote, a single garage door rose, revealing
a concrete ramp reminiscent of a mini parking garage. With my messen-
ger bag slung over my shoulder, I stopped at the scanner required to acti-
vate the interior metal doors. As part of the first generation to purchase a
home computer, I knew I would never get used to lasers scanning my
eyeballs for identity verification.

Gail Adams and Jamie Whitman were the first to report to our secret
pow-wow, but Agent Riley was unusually tardy. Whereas Gail and I had
been in constant contact since my disappearing act a year ago, this was
my first time seeing Jamie since we were in St. Croix together. I had recently discovered that he'd explicitly ignored my orders not to contact
Annie, in addition to compromising our government roles. I had come to
this meeting more than ready to hand out retribution.

"Crew," I stated, unpacking the contents of my bag and placing them
on the counter. "Where's Riley? He's never late."

"Jack, Riley is dead, "Gail informed me as she blotted her eyes. "The reports say he drowned in some kind of freak fishing accident."

I braced myself against the metal desk, as snapshot memories of Patrick Riley reeled through my mind. "What happened? Riley was fishing?" I asked the question to myself more than anyone else, trying to picture the ridiculousness of him on a fishing boat.

"They said fishing, if you're jackass enough to believe that report," Gail said. "He's from Detroit, for God's sake."

"The only way Riley drowned is if someone held him under," Jamie whispered. "That report is a load of bullshit."

Even though the news of Riley's death was crushing, my colossal ego superseded any kind of news about anyone. I was consumed with fury that Jamie had stepped out of the group and disobeyed my orders.

"That's not the only pile of shit I'm hearing today," I goaded, taking off my watch and glaring at Jamie. "I know you went to see Annie. You threw me under the fucking bus! You ratted me out, asshole!" I jumped across the table and knocked him to the floor.

Only a few punches were actually thrown. I just wanted Jamie to know that I was aware he had gone to Nashville, after I specifically asked him not to go to Annie's home. His loyalty had always been to this team, but for a moment he'd lost faith in my leadership, and his conscience had gotten the better of him.

"Dammit, you two!" Gail screamed as we wrestled around on the floor. "Now stop!" she hollered, dumping an entire Thermos of Gatorade over us. "You're acting like children. God, I'm sick of men."

Covered in cold fruit punch, we separated and immediately began dumping ice cubes out of our clothes.

"Jamie, you shouldn't have stepped out of the group, and I think you already know that," Gail said. "You knew Jack would kick your ass for it. But you," she lectured as she hovered over me, "you are *not* one to talk about stepping out. We begged you not to get married, try for a family, or let Annie know you weren't really dead. You went ahead and did *all* of it anyway! And let's not forget, I could have had a real friend, Jack. I liked Annie, and you ruined any chance of that friendship ever happening. So get off your fucking high horse, and check your ego at the door."

"I know, and I'm sorry…"

Gail cut me off. "We're wasting time talking about this. It's done. Are we all in agreement that Riley's death is suspicious?" She was getting right back down to business.

Jamie and I both nodded our heads.

"Then get off the fucking floor, and let's figure out our next move."

ANNIE

I t was selfish of Jack to ask me to give our relationship another chance, yet I turned around and did the same thing to Kessler. And just as I had walked away from Jack, Kessler walked away from me. I had spent the last month consumed with myself, and in turn, I'd probably ruined my chance with the man—who said so himself—had done right by me. As much as I wanted to continue to play the victim in this triangle, I clearly was not.

I walked through the bedroom surveying Kessler's mess of personal items and collecting dirty clothes to throw into the laundry. He was a terribly untidy person, leaving clothes right where he stepped out of them and knickknacks strewn all over the dresser. I began tidying up, lost in the quiet of an empty house. But, a single piece of jewelry stopped me cold. Kessler had left his hook bracelet sitting on the antique dresser. Yes, he had been angry when he left that morning, but until now, I hadn't realized how deep his anger resonated. He'd left the bracelet out in the open so I would know he meant business.

The hook bracelet is a signature piece of jewelry made in the Virgin Islands. The history of the simply constructed bracelet dates back centuries. Numerous stories speculate about the specific construction of the first hook, but the meaning of the bracelet, and of those who wear it, has never wavered. It represents the primal reason humans walk the earth and the essential element in the search for happiness: love.

The fable began with a maiden betrothed to a seafaring gentleman. At a time when weddings were only exchanges of lovelorn promises, this particular maiden had the foresight to create a tangible symbol of marriage. As her husband braved the stormy waters of the Caribbean, for months at a time she was left alone with her chores and heartache. Inspiration struck her one day while she foraged through his leftover fishing gear, and she began the makings of a memento of her love. Diligently measuring, clipping, and smoldering scraps together, the woman constructed what is today called the hook bracelet: a solid piece of metal with a small loop at the end, wrapped around the wrist and "hooked" into the open end of a horseshoe. Your relationship status defines how you wear the bracelet. If the open end of the horseshoe points up—towards your heart—this is a clear indication you have already found the love of your life. Your search for happiness has been fulfilled. When the horseshoe is worn pointed out toward the world, it is an open invitation to all the loveless lovers, declaring that you are open and willing to receive luck and love.

Twirling the hammered silver between my fingers, I contemplated the open end of the horseshoe enclosure.

Which position would I wear my hook, and toward whom would it point?

An image of my grandmother filled my head. I could have used her unbiased advice. Throughout my teenage years, she'd had a knack for squashing any kind of trouble I thought about getting into. She was famous for her one-liners, which would stop me from doing something stupid and surely regrettable. My three favorite pearls of her wisdom meant something entirely different when spoken individually, but in this moment, I realized that when the words were combined, the sentence had the exact advice I needed.

Always give your best effort, but keep it simple, and cooler heads will prevail.

She was speaking to me. I could feel it.

The fact of the matter was that I had not put forth my best effort. I'd been swimming in limbo for the past month, not moving toward Jack but not giving him a definite no, either. Why? Was I scared to let him go?

I let the thought sit for a moment. No, I wasn't scared to end my relationship with Jack. Why hadn't I, then? What was stopping me? I felt close to an answer, yet I couldn't quite put my finger on it.

Keep it simple. Am I mad, scared, and hurt? Yes was the answer to all of those questions, but that wasn't the main reason I couldn't break free.

Keep it simple. Do I still love him? Could I imagine my life without him? No, I didn't truly love him anymore, and I was still suspicious of our partially accurate memories together. I had known our fate at the cemetery, but I'd let my emotions railroad my actions.

Keep it simple. I found that hopping up and down in place sometimes helped to shake the thoughts out of hiding, dropping them into my lap.

"Ugh! What's wrong with me? Why won't I end this? I just want to know what you're still hiding, Jack!" I yelled at the top of my lungs. I stopped jumping when the epiphany smacked me.

I don't love Jack. I just want the closure that I wasn't privileged to after that asshole faked his death.

My reflection emulated this manifestation in the dressing-room mirror.

Grabbing my laptop from the desk, I settled on my favorite side of the sofa and began to do some fact-checking on my not-dead, could-be husband. The first Google search turned up exactly what I had expected: multiple men and Twitter accounts with the name Jack Whitman. I scrolled through several pages before finding Jack's business, Whitman Capital Funds. A picture of an unfamiliar man was attached to the article. I had never seen this person at the office before, but considering whom Jack and Jamie actually worked for, the man was probably a complete random. Whitman Capital Funds didn't even have a website, just an address in the yellow pages.

On the next page of my Google search, Jack's obituary came up, along with the disgusting picture of his car buried under the massive wing-span of a charcoaled pine tree. When I clicked on the link to the article, which had run in the *Kansas City Star*, a picture of Jack replaced that of the ashen Range Rover. It was one of those stuffy suit-and-tie headshots that businessmen use alongside any accolades they might have earned at their company. Every person smiles with that pompous grin, and an arrogant stench seems to waft from each picture. Sure, those pictures are used to boast company appeal, but to me, they always looked like geriatric school photos.

Jack was looking directly into the camera, directly at me, and the only word running through my head was *asshole*. I didn't need to read the article. I knew the words by heart, having read it several times over the past year.

My thoughts drifted away from the article and back into the past, when I was Jack's devoted and naïve wife. Before I let myself head too far down memory lane, I snapped out of my ridiculous daydream and continued my search for an answer that would satisfy my hunger for closure.

Nothing interesting about Jack Whitman, only lies and assholeness. How about Jack Stallings?

Links to mug shots, Twitter and Facebook profiles, a story about a retired basketball coach, and a few lawyers' websites crowded the screen. Continuing to scroll down, I found a blurb about a seventeen-year-old orphan from Seattle who had escaped a warehouse fire.

29

Just like "Whitman," "Stallings" offered little information.

"Nothing," I said with a sigh. Hunger pains began distracting me, so I closed my computer and went into the kitchen to make lunch.

Sitting in silence wasn't a strange feeling, and until ten months ago, when Kessler had come into my life, I'd been accustomed to the still of quiet.

Kessler, I thought. I picked up my phone to send him a text.

"I love you. Please call," I wrote.

Next I sent a text to my sister-in-law, Liz.

"Hey, love. Heard back from the lawyer yet? Still moving forward with the divorce? Let me know if you need me."

Liz had filed for divorce a month ago, but she told me Jamie was refusing to meet with her lawyer or sign any papers. He was convinced their marriage could survive the last ten years of deceit. *Asshole.* Jack hadn't mentioned the legality of our marriage yet, but that conversation would be happening sooner rather than later.

Ping, my incoming text signal went off. I grabbed the phone hoping to see Kessler's name, but it was from Liz.

"Nothing from the lawyer. Jamie is begging me to go to a week-long marriage boot camp. Mountains in Montana. Thinking about it. The kids, you know?"

"I get it. I can keep the kids. Let me know."

I thought Liz was a fool to reconcile with Jamie, but I didn't have kids, and I knew they were both trying to do what was right for Max and Mia.

I put my plate in the sink and took a handful of grapes back to my makeshift office on the couch. Grapes reminded me of my grandmother, and I could have used her wisdom about now. I shoved all of them into my mouth at once, hoping that would make a difference. When I opened my laptop, the screen from earlier, which I had forgotten to close, popped up. The article read:

> *Explosion Levels Seattle's Oldest Orphanage*
>
> *May 14, 1989*
>
> *St. Michael's Home for Boys was devastated in an apparent gas explosion in the early Sunday morning hours. St. Michael's was home to fifteen boys ranging in age from three to seventeen years*

old, along with six full-time employees. It was the longest-running orphanage in the state, having opened its doors in 1898. Emergency personnel arrived on the scene within minutes, but the building was "already engulfed and too dangerous to send my men into," stated Chief Curry. He speculated that the explosion happened in the boiler room, which unfortunately sat directly below the sleeping quarters. At this time, there are no survivors.

What a depressing story.

I scrolled down to look through several pictures that a reporter had captured. In the first picture, the structure was barely recognizable through the flames. As the photographs progressed, a crowd began to grow behind the official yellow tape, and a look of shock was plastered on each pedestrian's face.

After the final photo was a link to the news footage from the morning of the fire. I clicked on it. The clip opened with an on-the-scene reporter describing the details of the explosion. The cameraman jockeyed between the reporter and the Gothic stone building, which shot fire through every blown-out door and window. The camera cut back to the reporter. "Let's talk to an eyewitness who was on the scene when the fire broke out," he said.

A haggard, checker toothed man started to recount his version of events, while the reporter kept a huge black microphone level with the man's face. He didn't get far into his story (which was fine, because I could barely understand him) when a woman cut him off, yelling, "That's not how it happened!" As the two continued their banter, the camera slowly began to pan the crowd, and that's when I saw him.

Rewind, play, pause. *No, pause is too blurry. The footage is old.* My stomach dropped, like a freefall skydive. Rewind, play, rewind and play, again and again. Yes, I was sure of it. Jack Whitman, Stallings, or whatever the hell his name was stood in the crowd, front row, third from the left. I recognized him because I'd seen a similar photo of Jack when I was packing up my house in Kansas City to make the permanent move to Nashville. I ran to the garage and tore through boxes to find the one containing photo albums. Only six large cardboard boxes had made the move with me, so it just took an hour of digging. Flipping through the photos took a little longer, but I finally found the picture. A teenage Jack, wearing a soot-covered T-shirt and dirty jeans, watched the building burn from across the street.

Jack never said he lived in Seattle. Why wouldn't he ever mention this fire? Watching something this traumatic would surely leave an impression on someone.

Getting back onto my computer, I searched articles pertaining to the explosion, trying to gather enough information so that when I confronted Jack, he wouldn't be able to lie his way through another story. Most of the articles were only short blurbs with the same information, but then I came across a cross-link that led me to something interesting.

Survivor Found!

May 15, 1989

Jack Stallings (17) walked into the downtown Seattle precinct this afternoon asking for help. His body was bruised and cut, but a mild concussion was the worst of his injuries. Officers were astounded when the teenager recounted the series of events that took place early Sunday morning. "I woke up to high-pitched screeching, and I thought it was an alarm going off at the apartment complex next door," Mr. Stallings stated. "Heading downstairs to open the door is the last thing I remember, and this morning, I woke up in an alley on the next block." When Chief Curry was contacted for comment, he cheered, "What wonderful news! I can't imagine someone surviving such a substantial impact. God is good!" Jack was recently accepted to the West Point Military Academy and he will begin his first semester this fall. Donations can be made to help this young man through the Seattle Safety Network.

The picture that accompanied the article showed a much cleaner and better-dressed Jack. I couldn't stop staring at him.

Jack was an orphan? From Seattle?

How could I have been so blind? I didn't know anything about the man I'd married. I waited for an escalation of anger to boil my blood and heat my skin. To my surprise, neither rage nor tears ever came.

People exaggerate about all aspects of life, and for the most part, I could understand why. Their number of sexual partners, the amount of money they made, the importance of their position at work: all are understandable inflations of the truth, usually told because of some degree of shame. As far as I was concerned, as soon as someone asked for a person's hand in marriage, any exaggerations, even on the smallest scale, became lies. I had discovered over the last year that lies were the only consistency in my marriage. I would have understood any truth Jack told me—even the ones he couldn't tell me. I would have understood them all.

The newspaper article couldn't have been accurate. Every person in this orphanage dies in an explosion, and the next day a boy waltzes into the police station with all his body parts still intact, claiming to be the lone survivor? No one followed up on his story? No one checked this kid out? It was either an actual miracle or shoddy police work. The pit in my stomach made me lean toward the latter. The only way to set my mind at ease was to call in a favor.

JACK

After exchanging apologies and handshakes for the ten-minute lapse of sanity, we gave Patrick Riley the moments of silence and respect he deserved. Riley had been a dutiful solider, who always stood behind the line and covered those who went in first. Most important, he was a brother and a son. He had played by the rules throughout his government career. Only recently and unjustly had his name become scathed by false accusations, and unfortunately, because of my intense persuasion, he had gone rogue. In fact, at this point, we were all considered blackguard.

"Jamie, as much as I value you as a part of this team, I'm letting you go," I informed him.

Gail shot me a wide-eyed look, and Jamie stared at me with a mixture of hope and confusion.

"I know you've wanted out for a long time, and as far as I'm concerned, you're exiting the position with the highest honors. Go be with your family, and finally give them the undivided attention they deserve. I'm sorry about the shiner on your eye, but please keep our scuffle to yourself. The only thing your wife needs to hear is that you're home for good." I spoke with a fleck of bitterness.

Jamie was taking Liz to a marriage retreat in Montana. He had convinced her to shelve the divorce papers long enough to try and reconnect on the trip; it was obvious that being with his wife and kids was all he thought about. I saw the far-off gaze that followed a quick look at the family photo shoved in his wallet, and the hardened, too-long stare at a family in a mini-van on the highway. It was time to cut him loose. I didn't feel right telling him about our last mission. If he were to be killed under my command, I would never forgive myself.

I'd screwed up so much of my life in the pursuit of perfection: a wife, an unborn child, numerous friendships, and overall normalcy. I categorized people and the lies I told them according to a moral expense account, arrogating my own needs or government policy before the human lives around me. I hadn't turned out this way by accident, and considering the brilliant scheme that had gotten me through the doors of West Point, I certainly wasn't an innocent lamb. But I had changed. My unfortunate upbringing, although disappointing from a child's eye, had molded me into a master of stratagem, now with a particular interest in the well-being of politicians—especially those with fraudulent pasts.

As a teenager, my hustling hadn't been all-encompassing. Coming up with a plan never presumed difficult, although my haste was a personality flaw that made me glaze over the important details of fabrication. It wasn't until after I had been brought into the CIA that I really learned to manhandle fiction. They taught me the art of deception on a worldwide stage, and I was a more-than-willing student, the best student.

Even though I had dedicated all facets of myself to the government machine, there is one aspect of a human that, even after being controlled, can escape confinement and break free. The CIA had no way to lock down my conscience. Maturity in a man brings unexpected growth, even in the parts of the mind previously considered dormant. Over the last twenty years, I had been the type of man the government needed on its side. Now I was the type of man it feared.

As the metal doors closed behind Jamie, I hoped it wouldn't be the last time we saw each other, but guarantees proved fruitless.

"I know what you're thinking," Gail whispered as the automatic dead-bolt spun with the slamming of the doors. "You can't do this alone, and besides, I've pretty much missed the opportunity to have a life. Those greeting cards that read 'Life begins at fifty' are written by twenty-five-year-olds who haven't experienced the joys of a turkey neck." She grabbed the loose skin under her chin and jostled it from side to side.

"Gross," I laughed. "I guess there won't be an argument as to who we eat first if we ever get stranded on an island."

"Don't worry, I'll volunteer," she offered while patting my back. "I know you're packed, so I won't even confirm the details with you. I've got my GO bag downstairs, and Washington, D.C. is a thousand miles from here. Are you driving, or am I?"

"I am, but we need to make one stop first," I said, neglecting to tell her about a three-hundred-mile detour to Nashville.

A smile stretched across my face, and excitement tingled in my finger-tips. I didn't know how Annie would receive my visit. I was asking a lot from our memory pool, but I prayed she would focus on the good ones.

I'd taken the longest road to finally make it home. Here was to hoping D.C. would be the final stop in the journey, although I didn't want to plan too far ahead. There was always the possibility that I could spend the rest of my life in the nation's capital—where our leader's congre-gate—digging up dirt on the powers that be. I didn't have that many shovels, or the strength to dig that many graves.

John Savage, the vice president of the United States, had never worked for the people of America, only for himself. I had to admit that Washing-ton had done an excellent job of confusing the American people with smoke and mirrors, the oldest trick in the book. The public didn't have a clue about the person behind the smiling endorsement, and they were intentionally kept distracted by the marketing of the electoral dog-and-pony show.

After twenty years in the CIA, I had seen behind the curtain. I knew who pulled the strings. Unfortunately for Mr. Savage, he had a front-row ticket to *my* show, and I had a plan to end his career—as well as his life.

KESSLER

My first concert back was everything I remembered and wanted it to be. As soon as I walked out on stage, the rupture of surprise from the crowd felt like the warmest hug. I heard the genuine joy in their voices, and I embraced the familiar ride of turning and twisting up the crowd. We all sang our hearts out in that arena. Indianapolis did me right.

Fans (especially super-fans) are a fickle breed of family. Musicians who take the time to get to know their fan clubs have the possibility of life-long loyalty from them. To understand your most devoted fan, you need to remember all the way back to when you were one. Music is a tool so powerful that it brings people from all different ends of the earth together in one place, at one time, everyone high on the same emotions. The right song heard at the right moment can shift someone's mood and change his or her outlook on the entire day.

Over the years, I'd heard numerous fan testimonials about what my music meant to their lives—either helping them through a low patch, or just by bringing them happiness when a certain song came on the radio. That was the part of touring I had always loved: the fans. The connection with the people who loved my music was so strong. When we were together, and I sang their favorite song, we connected, and the rest of the world faded away. For two hours, they didn't think about the house payment that was due, the boyfriend who cheated, or the boss they hated. When I was on stage, I gave them everything I had, all of my energy, until the lights came up and reality found us again.

As you're first coming up in the business, your focus is on the dollar signs. Most artists have been thirsty for so long that the first taste of water doesn't come close to curing the drought. But once you've released a couple of records and gained a steady fan base, you start to feel hydrated and able to relax. The part where fame gets tricky is when you get caught in a flood. When the overwhelming flow of attention and money isolates you, survival mode kicks in. You spend most of your daily energy trying to stay afloat and keep your life from capsizing.

The recipe to erase Annie from my thoughts was within reach. The ingredients were laid out in front of me, and all I had to do was throw them in a bowl and stir. Depending on how I looked at the situation, this wasn't a bad problem to have. I easily could have fallen back into my old ways of shutting people out to search for the next best thing. I was already familiar with the pattern, and a couple of one-nighters with a few groupies would help to lubricate the transition. But I had never let myself fall this far into a woman before, and I was too deeply in love with Annie to completely reincarnate my former self.

The special kind of sickness specifically associated with the turmoil of a breaking heart rose and fell like ocean waves in my stomach. I wanted Annie to myself, wanted her husband to stay dead, and wanted 100 percent certainty that if I fought for her, she would choose me. I'd been on this earth long enough to know that such desires were ridiculous to even entertain. That was the reason I still hadn't called or made any attempt to communication with her since leaving. I'd picked up the phone several times over the last week, but the possibility of her voice telling me it was over between us stopped me from making an actual call.

Light from the muted television screen kept me from lying in total darkness in my hotel suite, and the quiet kept me from sleeping. The part of touring I hated most: the night. Even when I'd managed to get myself sufficiently drunk enough to sleep with the next woman, I had never slept through those early morning hours. Dawn was an interesting time of day. Most of the nation was still asleep; the ones who were up were awake for a reason. Unless you had a newborn baby or flawless athletic determination, your eyes were open because of a spinning mind, which sleep wouldn't slow down.

I scrolled through Annie's texts. Although, she had written all the words that previously would have sent me running home, she still hadn't said what I needed to hear: *I only want you.*

Its five o'clock. Surely, she's up.

I pulled up my recent calls list and tapped on her name. On the fourth ring she answered.

"Hey, darlin'. Up with the chickens this morning?" Mama D asked, giggling into the phone.

"I don't think I've actually been to sleep yet. A lot on my mind, I guess."

"Oh, I see. This wouldn't have anything to do with a beautiful blonde who lives next door to me, would it?" She obviously knew the answer before asking the question.

"Yes, it would. I'm scared that she's going back to her ex, and that she's going to leave me."

"Leave *you?* Are you at home in Nashville?"

"No, I'm in Indianapolis, back on tour with Wade. I told you last week I was going."

"Oh, my mistake, dear. It seems like you're doin' a whole lot of worryin' for nothin', then. How is Annie gonna leave you when you've already left her?"

Ouch, that stung.

"She said she wanted space," I replied, "so I was trying to give her what she asked for. I didn't end the relationship, but we aren't in a good place right now."

"Oh, Kessler, women say a lot of things, and the real men know how to sift through the poppycock. Do you love her?"

"Yes. More than I'd like to admit."

"Then quit your squawkin' and get your hackles up, or you'll end up lettin' a fox in your henhouse," she warned. "'One day cock of the walk, the next day a feather duster,' my mama used to always say."

"Um, I don't even know what that means. Do you have any advice that doesn't pertain to chickens?" I asked, completely confused.

"Nope, not this mornin', baby. You're a big boy, Kessler, and you'll figure it out. I'll see ya when you get back," she added, as if that were my answer.

Mama D had the most random catch phrases, but her advice was always spot-on. If she ever got senile, no one would suspect it for years. As had been the case a thousand other times in my life, I thought, *D*amn, *that woman is always right.*

I lay back down in the darkness and consciously unlocked the images of Annie that I'd previously held hostage from my mind, in an attempt to guard my heart. It felt good to let myself openly think about her, instead of only allowing a flash of her face, before forcing the image into the place where unwanted memories collected.

I remembered every detail: her constant scent of laundered clothes, the way one eyebrow rose higher than the other when she laughed, the softness of her lips. The hardness of my smile slowly trickled down. My mind was suddenly back in St. Croix, and my hand was gently stroking my growing dick.

From the moment she walked into the Soggy Bottom on the first night we met, a constant breeze had run through the bar and across her dress, making her nipples pronounced through the thin cotton fabric. I pictured the way she turned and smiled at me that night when we had to say good-bye. I'd never forget that moment. It was the exact instant I discovered that I was capable of love. Flash to the first time we made love, when I was finally allowed to put my hands on those previously untouchable breasts. Our bodies molded perfectly together, each of her curves an exact match to mine. She moaned breathy, affectionate sounds when I did something right, unabashedly guiding my fingers around her body to show me the way.

The images kept in time with my hand. My thoughts escalated as I pictured her eyes finding mine, before the purple tip of my hard-on disappeared into the warmth of her smiling mouth. She climbed on top of me, completely uninhibited, her blonde hair swinging from side to side across her chest, and I spread her perfectly round ass to reach my maximum depth inside of her. She excited me like no woman ever before.

I'm inside of her
She's moaning, I'm trying to keep up
She's smiling with her eyes
Don't look away
Her skin, my God, her skin's so soft
Painful fingernails dig into my chest
The pain excites me more
Our feet are touching
Our fingers entwined
She's wet, everything is wet

I actually shouted out loud with the final image and the release of my anxiety. This was exactly what I needed to finally calm down. The same silly grin from our first sexscapade in St. Croix was now plastered on my face. I threw my clothes in a bag and jumped into the shower. I wanted her. I needed her. I had to see her, and I had to believe that she felt the same way about me.

ANNIE

"Hello?" I answered my buzzing phone.

"Annie, it's good to hear your voice," Officer Grady replied. "I'm sorry I've taken so long to get back to you, but I think I have the information you're looking for."

"I knew you'd come through for me, and I appreciate your effort, big guy."

"Of course, I'd do anything for you. Jack's accident was my first DRT, and you were the first wife I told her husband wasn't coming home. You taught me a lot about sympathy that day, and I'm a better officer because of you."

"I appreciate your kindness. Now, how good of an officer were you today?" I asked.

"I'll let you be the judge. Here's what I've got. I pulled up the records under Jack Whitman, and there was nothing unusual about those. He grew up in Kansas City, his parents are deceased, and he was the CEO of Whitman Capitol Funds until his death on June 3, 2012. All of this you already know. Next, I pulled up the documents on that Seattle fire you asked me about. Twenty people were listed as deceased: fourteen minors and six staff members. One minor, Jack Stallings, was the sole survivor of the explosion."

"Okay, so nothing new there either. Thanks for helping…"

Grady cut me off. "Wait, you didn't let me finish. You already know this stuff. You're the one who gave me the information. If this were all I had for you, then I would have told you earlier that I'd done a terrible job today. What you don't know is this. I checked Jack Stallings's records. He grew up in a Seattle orphanage, his parents are deceased, of course, but that's where his life stops. The newspaper article said he was to attend the West Point Military Academy in the fall of 1989, and there is a picture of Jack—your Jack—attached, but there are no records of his attendance."

"Unfortunately, this makes sense to me. I told you I couldn't give you all the details about why I'm making this inquiry of you, but from what you've told me, the story adds up."

"Annie, would you hold your damn horses a minute and let me finish?"

"I'm sorry, Grady. I just thought that *you* were now up to speed, and there couldn't possibly be more information."

"Well then, you thought wrong. There must be a good reason why you're tight-lipped about the details, and I don't need to know them. You have your reasons. We always do. But, I haven't even gotten to the good stuff yet." He spoke in a low voice. I pictured him hunkered down in his cubicle, shielding others from eavesdropping on our conversation.

"I'm all ears," I replied, perking up with the hope of new information.

"As I was saying, I was confused as to why Jack never made it to West Point, because several thousands of dollars were donated to the Seattle Safety Network to help get him back on his feet. I began wondering what happened to the money. Records clearly show that it was deposited to him in the form of a savings account. I decided to go back and sift through his past some more, just to see if I'd missed something, a clue maybe. When tracking a missing person, specifically a minor, the best place to start is always the public school system. And bingo, I found a high-school track club picture of Jack Stallings from Harding High School, along with an article about an upcoming track meet the school was hosting. I zoomed in on Jack's face. But it isn't Jack—your husband Jack. The picture is of his roommate from the orphanage. Jack Stallings may have become Jack Whitman later in life, but he sure as hell wasn't born Jack Stallings. The kid in the track picture is the real Jack Stallings, not your husband."

"Wait, what?" I was incredibly confused.

"The real Jack Stallings died in that fire. Your Jack took his place and picked up his life where the fire ended it. The Seattle Police Department's lack of fact-checking—when they believed there was a survivor of the fire—is embarrassing. But 1989 was one of the worst years in Seattle's crime history, and my guess is that they needed a feel-good story for the community to rally behind. Sometimes when devastating news is reported, people pray for miracles, and they'll grab ahold of anything that looks like one."

"You're sure? You are absolutely sure there are two different people with the same identity?" I asked the questions with slow words, so there was no possibility of a misunderstanding.

"I can't prove it beyond paper, but I'm positive, Annie. I have copies of the birth certificate and public school attendance records, along with all the yearbook photos. Jack Whitman has taken on a different identity more than once."

JACK

Spring was the best time for traveling east on Interstate 70. Missouri landscapes could become monotonous during a lengthy car ride, but the outside air was just beginning to turn warm, enticing the vegetation to sprout. Dogwood and redbud blooms dotted the blue skyline, like pink and white speckles of paint. Coming after a long and cold Missouri winter, spring was full of possibilities. It was another chance to start over.

"Our exit is coming up. You're going to take I-270 north to Chicago," Gail instructed.

As I pulled into the far right lane, Gail started yelling, "Get in the left lane. North goes to Chicago! You're going to miss the exit!"

"Calm down, we're just taking a short detour. There's nothing to worry about, just lie back and enjoy the scenery."

"A detour? The sign said south to Memphis. Why in the hell would we go to Memphis, Jack?"

"Would you relax already?" I asked.

Gail was one of the smartest women I knew, and it only took her seconds to figure me out.

"Don't you do it, Jack. Don't mess with that poor girl anymore. Haven't you done enough to her already? For God's sake, give her a chance at happiness!"

"I am! We were happy together once, and I know that if she'll just give me the chance, I can make her happy again."

Gail pulled back her sunglasses and gave me the coldest stare I had ever gotten from a woman. We didn't disagree on many issues, but her frosty silence spoke loud and clear on this one. She would realize that Annie and I were destined to be together when she saw how happy Annie would be to see me. She would understand the depth of our love when she saw us embrace.

We stopped to fill up about an hour outside of Nashville. Gail still hadn't said one word to me. As I turned the ignition off, she clutched my arm and let out a long sigh.

"I've known you for decades, Jack, and I've always been honest with you. I'm being honest with you now. The first day Annie came into my office, she was a mess. Her skin color was unnatural, and the thick purple circles underneath her eyes looked like they had been purposefully painted on. She shuffled her feet as she walked, clearly lacking the strength to even pick them up off the floor. I wanted to hold on to her deflated and sagging body, to tell her the truth, and make her better. But, I couldn't, because I was already part of your plan, and my loyalty will always lie with you. I've never forgiven myself for that, Jack, and I think that if you had seen her that day, if you had really seen her brokenness up close, you would have felt the same way. I can't stop you from what you're about to do, but I'm disappointed in you, Jack, so very disappointed. You're also missing the possibility that Annie isn't going to jump into your arms and take you back. She's not your wife anymore, even though you continue to call her that. You'd better prepare yourself for what heartbreak feels like—what Annie felt like when she thought you were dead—and I want you to know now, I'm not going to feel sorry for you."

I appreciated Gail's concern, and I understood her protectiveness over Annie's feelings. Gail had spent her entire adult life surrounded by men. As the doyenne of our misfit crew, she had physically and mentally held her own against any male encounter, but she was tired of having to do so. She had clicked with Annie and gained her trust, but because of me, she knew a solid friendship could never work. I felt a twinge of guilt about that, yet I continued to move forward. Disease breeds in stagnant ponds. Being good at my job required constant forward motion, or infection was inevitable. Only, during the last ten years of marriage, I had acquired an antidote, a cure for the requirements of my job. I prayed that Annie would see it the same way.

"Can you meet me?" I text her.

"I'm not getting on a plane for you, Jack," she quickly wrote back.

"Meet me in an hour at the Percolator on Fifth Street."

"You're in Franklin?"

"Yes. Please meet me. I need to see you."

"I'll be there, and I can't wait to see you!" she wrote, instantly calming my nerves.

I turned to the repulsed passenger in my car and relayed my enthusiasm as I read Annie's last text out loud, emphasizing the exclamation point at the end.

Gail shook her head and warned, "This is a bad idea, Jack. A bad idea for everyone."

***

Downtown Franklin was the epitome of what every Stepford wife in America dreamed about. Identical trees lined the stroller-friendly, extra-wide sidewalks, while every ten feet was an inviting, strategically placed park bench. Retail shop windows competed against one another with creative mannequin displays, like a Southern version of Barney's; restaurants did the same with the most original door decals. Easy-listening music piped through street lights, following pedestrians to every next block. Each face was a carbon copy of the next. The women were dressed with casual elegance, every strand of styled hair and every sparkly accessory decisively placed. The already-tan men wore expensive jeans and T-shirts. All tried hard to look like they'd thrown themselves together in the most flawless way.

Gail and I sat in our parallel-parked car, watching the people pass by—some with shopping bags, others walking dogs.

Without turning to look at me, in a slow voice of disbelief, Gail said, "Oh my God, this is Mayberry. We're in fucking Mayberry."

I snorted out agreement in the form of a chuckle.

"I mean, look right there." She pointed to an impeccably dressed elderly woman walking her golden retriever. "There's Aunt Bee."

This time I choked on a drink of water. I almost gave myself a hernia coughing the air back into my lungs. Gail began slapping me on the back, pure joy in every blow.

"The Percolator is three doors down. Can you hang back, so I can spend some time alone with Annie?" I asked after I got my voice back.

"Better yet, why don't you just forget I came with you? I'm too embarrassed to look her in the eye, and I would appreciate if you just didn't mention me at all." She stared down at the dirty floorboard mats. "I'll just walk around not fitting in, and you can send me a text when it's time to go. Stay safe, and don't be a fool." She always said those words to me before we parted ways.

46

"Okay, wish me luck," I said, smiling because she knew me so well.

"Your version of luck is a lot different than mine," she replied. We shut the car doors at the same time and headed in different directions.

KESSLER

The tour was headed to Louisville, but the next show was still two days away. From there, three more stops, and then we were bringing the music back home to Nashville, my final show. But I couldn't wait that long to see Annie again. My decision to jerk off before I left the hotel was probably the best one I'd made in a while. Otherwise I would have been driving for four painful hours across two states, with a constant hard-on to accompany the images of Annie. Her face haunted me in the most exhilarating way.

Following my last conversation with Mama D (a "talkin' to" is how we refer to a vocal lashing in the South), I'd come to understand that I shouldn't have left. I realized now that I had left the door wide open for Jack to walk through, and I'd given Annie a reason to let him in. I was going back to Nashville to prove to Annie that I was an idiot, and to say that I never should have left. Annie was not just chosen *by* me; she was chosen *for* me. I'd searched for an earthly explanation as to how the most perfectly flawed woman had effortlessly walked out onto that balcony and changed the entire direction of my life with a quiet golf clap, but there wasn't one. Never in my life had I bird-dogged a woman, and certainly not twice, but I didn't want to be the type of man who continued to walk away—especially from something as big as the rest of my life.

At a young age, my father had taught me the intricacies of becoming a man, but unfortunately, he died before I actually became one. Sitting on the front porch of our back forty was where most of those lessons occurred, and it was also where I'd strummed my first guitar. My daddy was self-taught. He could listen to a song only once and have the chords worked out in under an hour. My mama would stand in the kitchen making dinner from scratch, yelling at us for wasting time out there, but she always followed up her rant with a song request. Those were the fragile memories I tightly held onto.

Not counting gospel hymns, the first song he taught me was "'Please Come to Boston,'" by Dave Loggins. I connected with the song right away, and I practiced with aggressive perfection-seeking until the notes wove with my voice, like silk in sheets. Loggins also wrote the song "Augusta," a tribute to the Masters golf tournament, and that made us instant fans of golf, a faithful audience every April. In hindsight, I wished "Boston" hadn't been my first song. Music is similar to a woman: your first usually shapes you, without your even knowing it, until your senses are ingrained with the words and the memories.

After he passed, I was the only family my mama had left, so any relationship advice I got was made of her words. Bless her heart, she'd raised me the best way she knew how, but my father's death had devastated her. With my best interest in mind, she tried to prevent me from loving a woman with complete vulnerability. Looking back, I knew she was only trying to protect me, but through her vigilance, she'd taught me to run. And just like the man in the Dave Loggins song, I never once considered leaving the road for a woman. My successful façade of the impressive parade of women, and the years of running from a relationship was layered into my skin, one conquest on top of another, too thickly bonded for separation.

Though my selfish pride wouldn't change overnight, I knew I would never forgive myself if I didn't finally open my heart to the possibility of devastation.

The closer I got to home, the bigger my smile became. The thoughts of Annie's hands on my shirtless chest sunk through the pores of my skin, all the way to my bones.

Immediately, the realistic side of my brain chirped in my ear. *She could have her bags packed and one foot out the door. Drop the fairytale, Kess. Women leave just as often as men.*

I pushed those thoughts aside as my rental car slowly drove down the quarter-mile, red asphalt driveway. The garage doors were closed, and I'd forgotten to bring my opener. Using my key, I unlocked the heavy wooden front door. On the other side: silence. I strained to hear sounds, her sounds, the ones that made our house a home, the kinds I would recognize blindfolded and in the dark. Only dead air awaited me.

"Annie? Baby, you here?" I shouted. My words echoed against the dark hardwood floors and up the circular staircase.

I walked through the kitchen and opened the garage door to Annie's empty parking space. Heading back into the bedroom, I threw my suitcase in the closet and grabbed my hook bracelet off the worn dresser, sliding it around my wrist with the horseshoe toward my heart. I had left it to send her a message, the wrong message.

Another mistake.

I wracked my brain, thinking of where she could be or when she might be home. My best guess was next door.

"Hey, sugar! How's your mama and them?" Hope asked, answering the phone with her customary Southern greeting. "Wade behavin'?"

"He was fine when I left him, but you know that's never a guarantee. Actually, I drove home this morning, and I'm looking for Annie. Is she over there by chance? I'd like to talk to her."

"Sorry, honey, I haven't seen her since yesterday. She even dropped out of our morning run today, sayin' something about doing research. I asked her if she needed my help, but she said everything was all right, and she was gettin' along fine *by herself.*" Hope was emphasizing the fact that I'd walked out on Annie.

"Obviously *you've* talked to Mama D, and now all the women know my business."

"Looks that way, baby," she teased in her snottiest, high school, mean girl voice. "I know you wanna talk to her, and I'm glad you made the drive, Kess. It'll mean a lot to her. Sorry I don't know where she is, but Franklin's still a small town. She'll turn up. Call her phone if you haven't already."

"All right, thanks Hope. If you see her before I do, tell her I'm looking for her."

"Will do, darlin'. Take care."

I wanted to see her, not talk to her on the phone. Reluctantly, I tapped on her name for the first time in over a week. Nervousness trembled my fingers, as if this were my first call to her *ever.* I must have underestimated my jitters, because the ringing in my phone seemed to echo through the entire downstairs. I stood up and walked across to the kitchen, and saw her phone light up the veins in the granite countertop.

Damn, she left it here.

As I picked up her phone, my stomach internally buckled, as though I had been kicked with a steel-toed boot. The screen showed two missed calls: J and Kess. There were three major problems with this scenario. One, Annie had changed my contact name from baby to Kess. *Hated that!* Two, J was obviously Jack calling Annie. *Hated that more!* And three, when I slid the phone's locked screen over to the main screen, her last texts popped up.

The good news: I found out that Annie was on her way downtown, to a coffee house called the Percolator. The bad news, for me anyway: she was meeting Jack. She was obviously running late; Jack had texted to ask if she was still coming.

Jesus, I'm sick. I'm fucking sick!

The thought of his hands on her skin and his tongue in her mouth gave me sweats and cramping, as if I were about to projectile vomit across the kitchen. I chugged a bottle of water from the fridge to keep my mouth from over-salivating, and to keep me from choking on my disgusting thoughts.

His last text was sent three minutes ago. She's not there yet. I still have a chance. I grabbed my keys and ran out to the rental car.

True to my past, I was once again running. But, this time I was moving toward someone, toward *her*, and I drove like hell to get there.

It's time Jack and I had a proper face-to-face introduction and a come-to-Jesus realization. Annie is my girl. I know it, she knows it, and I'd bet a bag of diamonds he knows it, too.

JACK

Waiting for Annie in the virtually empty bistro was as close to civilian torture as I'd ever experienced. The paradoxical role reversals hadn't been entirely lost on me. Whether she hadn't realized it until recently, Annie had spent the last ten years waiting on me. I'd been free to come and go on a moment's notice, with little explanation. At the beginning of our marriage, Annie had asked specific questions about what my job entailed, the supposed clients who hired me, and the details of the cities I visited. I loved her for putting emphasis on the importance of my job and being interested and present in the details, but her diligence almost compromised a number of my missions. I learned early that when I elaborated and droned on about the boring elements of my work trips, Annie asked fewer questions. I could pinpoint the actual day I came home after being gone for a week, and she coined her new question, "How was it?"

"Fine," became my usual reply. Once this routine began, we were both happier. I didn't have to lie to Annie in specific detail, and she didn't have to act interested. The welcome home sex happened faster, as did the relaxing in bed together, which I liked almost as much as the sex. Almost. Life was good for me in those days, and as far as Annie knew it, things were good for her too.

Now that Annie knew I worked for the CIA, I knew we couldn't completely recapture our past. But, she also couldn't ignore the wonderful memories we'd made together. She couldn't deny that we still meant something to each other, or that we shared an arsenal of good moments.

I picked a small corner table in front of the picture window, so I could see her before she saw me. As I was gathering myself in the last seconds, running down my list of all the right things to say, one last time, I saw him. When he ran up to the window, shielding his eyes on the glass and searching inside for her, I knew exactly who he was.

Kessler Carlisle had become a major roadblock and all-around pain in my ass, concerning my new life with Annie. I must admit, the first time I saw them in St. Croix on the beach together was a sharp blow to my ego. I hated him for all the reasons Annie had fallen in love with him. He was certainly my competition, but I understood what drew her to him. Understanding the enemy was usually a successful strategic move, and I studied Kessler more than a potential assassin.

Surveying and eventually killing terrorists wasn't something that ever weighed on my conscience. Before the trigger was pulled, they were considered a threat, and after the discharge the problem was solved. I'd never seen a target as an actual person before, so the act of taking a human life had never packed me with emotional baggage. Unfortunately, my ability to mentally cut myself off from any state of affairs had trickled into my personal life, or at least into the shred of one I was still hanging onto.

My plight with Kessler was an entirely different beast than what I was accustomed to. This was a real man. He had a life with friends and family, a high-profile job that kept him in the media, and a woman (my wife) who was falling in love with him. My entertainment of these notions was my first inkling that I had outgrown my current government position, and the first sign that I might make a move toward defrauding my country.

Keeping tabs on Annie in St. Croix had been easily done, using a number of rental boats and the advanced military gear I'd collected over the last two decades. I had watched her walk the beaches or leisurely lie by the pool, and even though I kept myself hidden, I still believed I was a part of her life. I knew that once she'd booked a plane ticket to St. Croix, it was only a matter of time before she found the diamonds. But, disastrously for me, she found Kessler first.

Jamie had advised me that the owners of those diamonds had located them at St. Croix Banking. Even though it ripped me apart to watch Annie grow closer to Kessler, I had put her in St. Croix, in danger, and she was still my responsibility.

I wouldn't have given Kessler's life a second thought on the restaurant patio that morning, but the target needed to be taken out. And, I couldn't watch Annie fall apart again, with the loss of another man.

Stupid fucking conscience.

The urgency in his body mechanics and the panic in his eyes transmitted through the large glass window. I immediately stood at attention, bracing myself for our official introduction. I motioned for him to come inside.

Measuring a head shorter than me, Kessler had the stereotypical celebrity physique. He was a handsome man—and I wasn't too proud to admit that—but he looked like a gym rat, not prison-strong. It only took me two seconds to size him up. I was 100 percent sure I would secure the upper hand in a physical altercation, which I would try my hardest to avoid. Any hope of getting back together with Annie would be gone if I laid a hand on Kessler. I was 100 perfect sure of that as well.

Reaching out my hand in a cavalier gesture, I asked, "Kessler Carlisle, I presume? I'm Jack Whitman."

"I know who you are, and I'm not shaking your hand," he responded. "This isn't some reenactment of a gentlemen's duel, so if you think we're going to chat over coffee while you explain to me why I should bow out, you're fucking delirious."

"Fair enough. I thought for Annie's sake we could keep this civil."

"I'm not interested in anything you have to say, and quite frankly, I think you're a dick. I know you're here to spew some psychobabble bullshit about honor and duty and code of silence, in order to get what you want. You threw your life with Annie away, and she doesn't love you anymore."

"I acknowledge your passion for the subject, but in this case, you're wrong," I informed him, holding out the last text Annie had sent me.

Hurt flashed in his eyes as he read the worst sentence he could possibly have imagined: "I'll be there, and I can't wait to see you!"

"I understand exactly how you're feeling right now. Believe me, I do. I lost her once, to you. Annie has been through so much already, and I wouldn't blame you for standing your ground. But, if she were to walk in here and see us fighting, we'd both lose her. I don't want to put her through that."

"Well, how fucking noble of you, Jack. You're the expert on causing Annie pain, so I'd have to agree with you on this one. I love her, and she feels the same way about me. Otherwise this wouldn't be a hard decision for her."

"I appreciate your candor, but you're trying to compete with a decade of marriage and all the memories that accompany it. Going by what her last text said, she's going to walk in here and put her arms around me as I stroke her hair—it's one of those special things we do—then, she's going to kiss me. We'll sit down and talk, while she puts one hand on my cheek and we hold hands under the table. I'm sorry, Kessler, but we have over ten years of history together, which ten months with you won't erase."

He stood rigid, puffing his chest out and clenching his jaw. He wanted to fight. I played his emotions like a tuning fork on his spine. Kessler Carlisle was no match for me. He was beat, and whether he wanted to admit it now or not, when he eventually saw Annie and me together, the truth would find him. I would make sure that every claim I'd made became fact, and that events played out exactly how I had promised.

"If Annie is coming here," he replied, "I don't want to upset her, but I'm not just going to duck down and do nothing. She needs to make her own choice. If she chooses you, then I'll never bother her again, because I respect her—something I think you should know more about in your line of work. Speaking of that, Jack, what is Annie supposed to do while you're off saving the world? Is she going to move from city to city, living in hotels, waiting to see if you come home? That's not what she wants out of life. She's not looking for that kind of adventure. Annie wants the security of coming home to the same house, in the same city, and to the same man, who's earned the right to call her baby. Maybe you do have ten years with her, but I figured that out in only ten months. You're so blind, or you're unwilling to put Annie's needs above your own. I'm not sure which it is. You lost her because of your ego, something I'm familiar with. It will happen again. I promise you that."

Touché.

He loved her; that was obvious even to me. But, I wasn't used to losing, and I wasn't going to start now.

"What a lovely speech, but I'm done listening to you talk about my wife. And, I'm afraid that if you don't leave now, our little chat could become violent," I urged him.

"Yeah, you keep mentioning 'your wife,' but your current marital status is only in your head. As far as the law is concerned, you're dead, and Annie is a widow. I'll remember that the next time I'm making love to *your wife*," he smirked, disregarding my previous warning.

"Get out of here, Kessler, or you'll be sorry—because I'm going to make you fucking sorry. I know you're aware of what I do for a living, and as I recall, your life has already been spared by my hands. Don't push me to change that." I spoke in an almost-whisper. Over the years, I'd learned that shouting only caused defensive reactions. A low, stern voice always relayed the seriousness of a promise.

Our eyes were deadlocked and our feet firmly planted. Too many seconds had ticked by for an actual fist fight. I read Kessler like a manual, and he was too concerned about making the wrong choice and blowing it with Annie, and also getting his ass kicked on his own turf. That never sat well with any man.

"This isn't over," he calmly stated.

"Until next time, then," I replied as he turned and walked out the door.

I put my face to the glass and watched him turn the corner, hoping Annie didn't have the chance to see him.

As much as I wanted to disregard his insight into my wife, I couldn't, because he had made extremely valid points. I would use them to my advantage, as I always did.

ANNIE

Getting a text from Jack was unexpected, but I should have been used to him popping up whenever it suited his needs. When the letter J came across the phone's screen, I felt more annoyed than anything else. Kessler and I had both wasted enough time on him, and I was finally ready to move on.

I hadn't heard from Kess in over a week, and paranoia was beginning to set in. By even entertaining thoughts of Jack, I was making a huge but forgivable mistake. If Kess had just called me, I would have smoothed out this knotted tangle of emotions.

As I arrived downtown to meet Jack, I realized that my phone was still sitting on the kitchen counter at home. Backtracking through traffic, my patience diminished every second. If Kessler called, I didn't want my voicemail to pick up. I needed to hear his voice, and he needed to hear the desperation in mine. Jack had thrown me off guard. I'd let myself get frazzled thinking about how our conversation would play out.

I didn't remember to grab my wallet either, which wasn't an issue because I wouldn't be staying at the coffee house long enough to purchase anything. Getting back to Kessler—my head resting in the nook of his arm, my leg draped across his thigh, our feet touching at the bottom of the sheets—was all I cared about. Jack had made his own bed, and I would never lie in it again.

Parallel-parking was not my forte, but I found a rock star spot across the street from the most historical (and my favorite) building downtown. The Franklin Theater had opened its doors in 1937 and had been the entertainment heartbeat of this small town for the last seventy-six years. Compared to the blaring signage of big city skyscrapers, the Franklin's signature red letter marquee look minuscule, but nestled among fifteen blocks of mom-and-pop restaurants and boutiques, the theater was bigger than life. Any musician with any clout this side of the Mason-Dixon had walked through its original, frosted glass double-doors, either to play *to* an audience or to be entertained *from* the audience. The interiors were draped with multiple four-foot sconces and miles of heavy vintage curtains.

My first concert there had been two months ago, and the moment Kessler and I entered through those doors, I'd felt the energy of the past all around us. Afterward, I had encouraged Kessler to do a one-night-only show there. He'd made the mistake of thinking he couldn't have the two things he wanted most: a normal life and the chance to make music. It was blatantly obvious to me that he was grieving the loss of live performance.

So I'd mentioned to him that the Franklin Theater would be a great place to start getting back on stage. He nonchalantly said he'd think about the suggestion. Apparently he'd thought about getting back on stage a lot, considering that he had taken off on a whim to head across the Midwest with Wade.

I realized that several minutes had passed as I stood staring in a daze, remembering what had seemed at the time like insignificant moments between us, and knowing now that there are no such moments between two people in love. All of the tiny, everyday exchanges of kisses and conversations actually added up to become more important than the few big ones.

A body-bending sigh escaped my mouth—along with all the air in my body—so intentional that my turquoise Kate Spade purse slipped out of my hand and spilled onto the sidewalk. After lunch one day, Kessler and I had window-shopped on the way back to our car, and I'd seen the bag hanging on the arm of a well-dressed mannequin. I mentioned to him how expensive the Charles Street Reis collection from Kate Spade was, and how gorgeous the mannequin looked holding the tote. The very next day, he'd surprised me with a gift for no reason, and I'd been carrying the purse ever since.

This is stupid. I'm so fucking stupid! I never should have given Kessler a reason to leave. I've been over Jack since St. Croix, since the first night at the Soggy Bottom, when my heart began falling for Kess. I'm sorry it took my head so long to catch up.

The Percolator was one block over and one block down Fifth Street. The closer I got, the faster I walked. The music that accompanied the Wicked Witch of the West *in The Wizard of Oz* blared in my head. All the selfish bullshit things Jack had done over the last ten years were coming to a head right now, at that moment, and my mind was blazing red with fury. I approached the big picture window in front of the restaurant, and I saw Jack sitting at a table, looking casual—except for the smirk on his face—as though it were just another day in his life.

"Andrea!" he exclaimed, perking up as I walked through the door, like I was a lost puppy who had just found her way home.

I'd already forgotten that he called me by my full name. I don't like it.

"Hello, Jack. What are you doing here?" I asked as he wrapped his arms around me and lifted me up off the ground.

"Please, Andrea, hug me back," he whispered. He set me back down and began to stroke my hair, like he used to—back in the days when I didn't think he was a lying asshole.

I lightly put my arms around him in an attempt to pacify his ego, and the familiar smell of his cologne circled around us. He tugged at my hair until my head was poised in the perfect position for him to kiss me; I used that moment as a scale to measure the weight of my feelings. I let him lock his lips with mine, and I did my best to kiss him back, giving a valiant effort to our exchange. I did feel something for him, but it bordered on pity more than any other emotion.

"I'm really glad you're here," I said as a smile unfolded across my face.

"You don't know how happy it makes me to hear you say that. Not a day has gone by when I haven't thought of you, thought of us together again. I'm so glad you're willing to forgive me. You have something special, Annie, a way about you, and I've never stopped loving you." He was rambling, as though his words were fact and the past was now behind us.

His sharp blue eyes penetrated me. They were intensely alert, and only when he smiled did they soften, along with the creases around his cheek bones. I'd been lost in those eyes before. It was easy to lose your way when his focus was entirely on you. So much of Jack was exact and stringent. I had known by the end of our first date that he was a serious man, probably incapable of silliness. Karaoke and dance parties weren't in my future. But within that severity, he had the ability to entice me with a glimpse of velvety tenderness, and soon, his softness was all I saw.

I was dangerously close to wrapping myself back into his warmth; I'd made that mistake before. As potent as those feelings appeared to be, they were also drainable—truth rushed over me as I sat looking at the man I'd married, who went by several different names. Finally, I could tell Kessler what he had wanted so badly to hear. The thought relaxed me in the most blissful way.

Keep it simple and tell the truth. Cooler heads will prevail.

"Annie? Where did you go? You haven't said anything."

"I'm sorry, I got caught up thinking about the past," I admitted, noticing that he kept glancing out the window. "Actually, I've been thinking a lot about the past, but in this case my feelings are quite the opposite of yours." I cupped his cheek and tapped it lightly with my hand as I spoke.

He put his hand on mine, and our fingers entwined. A bewildered, or maybe cognitive, look flashed in his eyes.

"I'm confused. How so?" he asked.

"When you were reminiscing about me, did you ever once have to ask yourself, who *is* Annie Whitman? Did you ever get a sick feeling in your stomach or crawling skin when you pictured my face? How about when I left the house? Did you ever wonder if I was lying about where I was going, or who I was going to meet?"

"Well, no, but I understand what you're getting at. Listen..."

I cut him off. "You know, Jack, I never wondered about those things either, until I found the lockbox you left me in the basement. Jamie nailed it when he told me I never should have married you. I don't trust you, and concerning us, you lie like a parochial schoolboy: with steady hands and a smile on your face. I think you've convinced yourself that truth is only for the privileged, and the rest of us are suckers."

His new reality was rapidly setting in, covering him like a thick, woolen blanket.

"Just let me explain," he began again.

"Oh no, Jack. For ten years all you've done is talk, and today it's my turn." My smile grew impossibly big. "I came here wanting answers to questions you didn't even know I had the ability to ask. Seattle, for example: what was it like to be a teenager in Seattle? Feel like talking about that?"

Even though his eyes never wavered, my question registered in his jaw, and I saw his fist clench. I had learned some tricks of the trade, too. I didn't care if he answered, because I couldn't care less about hearing another story from him. So, I kept on talking.

"I was in a fit of rage only a block from here," I continued, "but now that we're sitting across from each other and I'm looking into your eyes, I feel sorry for you. I pity that what you thought we had together doesn't come close to what I feel for Kessler. Really, I should be thanking you, because if your self-consumption hadn't completely and totally shattered me, I never would have known how good piecing myself back together could be."

He sat quietly with his eyes lowered to the floor. I had broken him, as much as someone who wasn't fully capable of commitment could break.

"Annie," he began to say as he roughly rubbed his hands up and down his face. "I want to say all the right words, the ones that will make you change your mind and will keep you from loving him."

"You can't, because there aren't any, and that would only be in *your* best interest. You don't love me, Jack. Maybe you never have. I think you're in love with the idea of me: a warm body with a pretty face, who holds you close and turns you on when you are emotionally available. It's ironic that a man who was hand-picked for his intelligence can actually be so stupid."

"Yes, you're right. I certainly feel stupid right now, but you can help me. Teach me how to be a better husband. I know you're the perfect woman for me." He reached for my hand across the small bistro table.

"See, more about you. Don't you get it? I'm not interested in teaching someone how to love me, especially when I'm in love with a man who already knows how. You're forty-three-years-old, Jack. You chose a career instead of a life, which is a perfectly acceptable choice. But, it's not *my* choice. Your portrayal of perfection isn't me. It's the opposite of me. I've finally planted roots, and you need a woman who wants to grow wings."

"This is the end? Is it really over between us?" His voice caught in his throat, and those same captivating eyes burned into me.

Annoyed that he needed one more affirmation, that I hadn't already been crystal in my blatant finality, I said, "Yes. For, the second time in *my* life, there is no us."

KESSLER

S tomping back to my car, I was all kinds of pissed. No man wants to acknowledge that he's been defeated by another, but I gave a shit about Jack and his threats. I didn't leave because of him; I left because of her. If Annie were to see us together in the coffee house, the unbearable pressure of a choice would press down on her. Our love for the same woman would demand she make an immediate decision. If she chose me, there would always be a small voice of doubt in my mind saying that I had forced her preference, and that she had chosen me out of distress. I would always live with the fear of losing her, after losing myself *to* her.

That being said, I still wanted to see her. I wanted to watch her interact with Jack, to judge the honesty of her body language as they talked. I did an about-face away from my rental car, then walked back up the street and pressed the button for the stoplight. Jimmy Buffett sang through the speakers in the cross-walk, "I miss you so badly, girl I love you so madly, and feeling so sad since I've been gone."

Probably could have done without that song. Thanks, Jimmy.

A red Chevy truck gave me cover—I leaned against the extended bed and watched Annie walk inside. Holding my breath, I read into her every movement for the next few minutes. My first thought was about her appearance. She wasn't done up in hair and makeup, and her outfit wasn't put together for a show stopping entrance. She looked normal in jeans and a cardigan, which gave me a victorious feeling. She wasn't trying to impress Jack; her clothes had been an afterthought.

After those initial feelings of triumph came defeat in the most crushing way. Everything happened exactly as Jack had described. As he stroked her hair, she hugged him, put her arms around him, and let him kiss her, before she turned into him and returned the love. During the next gesture and then the next, I continued to sink farther into the burden of my feet; gravity was no match for heartbreak. While they sat together at the table, Jack continuing to look my way, I realized that I'd enough. I'd been beat, fair and square. She had chosen him. I expected a phone call to confirm that, along with a moving truck for her things.

Fuck. Well, that's that.

I still had a show to do in Louisville, then three more dates before Nashville. I was professionally committed by a contract and personally grateful to Wade, so holding up my end of our deal was nonnegotiable. I would finish out my shows on the tour, and then I would go back to hiding in St. Croix. My only problem was that I had fully opened my life up to Annie, and no matter where I might try to forget her, she was already everywhere I wanted be.

I need to consider selling my houses, so I don't picture her in every room.

Thank God my pity party to Kentucky was only a two-and-a-half-hour drive from Nashville. The thought of checking into my hotel room and taking a long shower provided the only inspiration I had to get me there. I was broken into parts of myself that I'd always considered unbreakable, and I was reminded of my mama's lessons. This was the exact reason she'd always told me, "Don't go falling in love." I'd let her down, let Annie down, and most important, I'd let myself down.

Wade was right: I am a pussy.

I checked into my hotel room under my signature alias, Ernest Hemingway. Five years prior, I had come across a quote from Hemingway: "The first draft of anything is shit." Because I'm a musician and songwriter, those words spoke to me, to the innermost core of my creative soul. They apply not only to music and writing, but to life in general. Ball-handling gets better with every game, parents seem to make better grandparents, and maybe that's also why the divorce rate is so high. If you mess up the first marriage, you have a better chance at getting it right the second time. I didn't know, but I would have taken advice from anyone just then, dead or alive.

Mr. Hemingway's quote had grabbed my attention, and naturally, I wanted to know what other life lessons he had written about. So, I loaded up on material. I felt like an idiot walking into the downtown Franklin bookstore, buying books written by such a revered author—not to mention a Pulitzer and Nobel Prize-winner. People stared as I ducked far beneath my ball cap, hauling around literature I'd certainly need a translator to understand.

The further I got into Hemingway (his novels and his life) the more I related to him on a personal level. The needs he spent his life chasing were the same needs that scared him the most, and eventually, they were the ones that caused his death. I was sure that if he were still alive, he would give two shits if some country music artist put him on a pedestal, but that notion only made me respect him more.

Instead of lying in bed and wallowing in bitterness, I used my emotions productively and channeled Hemingway. Three hours later, a monumental ballad was born. Writing a love song was like succumbing to a bottle of Xanax, followed by the high of crystal meth. For the song to work—make the ladies swoon and help the men get laid—you had to fall into the misery, let it overtake you, and speak directly from the heart. If the pain was palpable through the music, you'd written a winner. The upside of ripping yourself apart happened when the song was finished. That was when the crack high hit. Knowing you'd written a panty-dropper did wonders for the ego.

I knew Wade was next door, so I took my guitar and leather notebook over to ask him his thoughts. I didn't even get the chance to knock before he swung open the French doors, as if he were the one high on crack.

"Oh, buddy, this one is good! This one is real, real good!" he said excitedly, with wild eyes and outstretched arms.

"Why is it that every time we're in a sleeping environment, you never have on pants? For God's sake, please start wearing them. I'm a little bothered that you've been enjoying this song through the walls in nothing but tighty-whities." I was teasing him, but I was also seriously disgusted.

"Get over yourself, and come in here. I've been playing along on my side, but I think you need to change this"—he added to what I had already written—"and your voice should hit higher on the chorus after the bridge." He pulled on jeans as he spoke. We sat down and began to play in unison.

Wade and I spent the rest of the daylight hours working on the tune, sidestepping any real conversation about the pain that had written this song. I was grateful that he didn't mention Annie, but Wade would eventually ask the hard questions. That's who he was, and one of the reasons our friendship had spanned twenty-something years.

"Let's do this song tomorrow night, Kess," he squeaked in his excited voice.

"No way, we just finished it. I have to sleep on it for a week before I play it in front of anyone."

"Come on, just a test run. Me and you, acoustic on-stage. What do you say?"

"Me and you," he'd said. She's even places we haven't been together; she's everywhere.

64

"I already said no, dude! I didn't write the song because shit is totally awesome. It stings. She hurt me. I'm fucking hurting! You'll have to wait until I get okay with that first," I said, letting the pain bleed through me.

"All right, I get it. I'm sorry, buddy. I didn't need to ask, but I talked to Hope, and she said you went back to Nashville. When I didn't see Annie in the lobby with you, and all this sad shit was pouring into my room, I figured things hadn't worked out like you planned."

"No, they didn't, but she made her choice. It wasn't me. I don't want to talk about her anymore. I want to get drunk and leave this day at the bottom of the bottle." I perked up at the thought of complete alcoholic annihilation.

"You don't have to ask me twice," Wade said. A smile stretched his thick black mustache to the tips of his cheek bones. "Let's hit Plain Jane's!"

"Okay, just promise not to piss your pants," I teased, and Wade followed up my hilarity with a swift punch in my chest.

The thought of walking into a trendy steakhouse on the Saturday of Derby weekend—with drunkenness a high priority and alongside the ringleader of troublemaking—exhausted me. Considering my emotional state, I knew it was a terrible idea. I knew it, was absolutely positive of it, but I did it anyway.

The night escalated in only a matter of minutes. But, the morning hours were the ones that possibly ruined my life.

JACK

"Let's go," my text to Gail read.

Walking back to my car without Annie produced a mix of emotions. I let her words sink in. The logical thinker in me agreed wholeheartedly with just about everything she'd said, but the insanely competitive side of me could not accept her finality.

Hopefully Gail would go easy on me.

She was waiting in the car with a large grocery paper sack sitting in her lap. The ugliest porcelain rooster face I'd ever seen peeked out from the top.

"What the hell is that?" I asked, unsuccessfully trying to look away.

"It's a rooster," she answered.

"I can see it's a rooster, but why is it in here?"

"Every Southern woman knows you must have some kind of rooster décor in your kitchen, to bring you love and luck. I was in that antique store over there"—she waved to an elderly woman, who was standing in front of the store waving back to her—"and she gave me all kinds of advice pertaining to the ways of the South."

"But you aren't Southern," I said, confused as to how this rooster was going to help Gail in luck or love.

"Yes, I realize that, but unfortunately this is the only kind of cock I'm going to get right now. So, how did it go? I appreciate your not bringing Annie to the car and making me face her. I guess this rooster is lucky after all."

"No need to thank me. It wasn't a choice. You were right, she doesn't love me anymore, and she can't go back to the way things were before I left. I genuinely thought I still had a chance with her, but she pulverized my ego with her words. Now that I'm saying it out loud, I suspect I deserved it. I did, however, meet a Mr. Kessler Carlisle."

"No! He came to stop you and profess his love to Annie? How romantic." Gail put her fingers to her lips and held a far-off gaze out the windshield.

I couldn't help but laugh at Gail, the hardest woman I knew, having the softest spot for Harlequin romance.

"Not exactly the way I looked at it, but I did what I always do: I sabotaged their meeting. He left before Annie got there, and I never told her that Kessler had been there to see her. Plus, I made him believe he didn't stand a chance with her against me. Wishful thinking, I guess."

"You *are* an asshole, but that personality gem is what's made you so successful in business. There is a woman, a beautiful and crazy woman, somewhere in this world who will accept you for who you are, and the little you have to give will be enough for her."

"I don't have the time to try again," I said. Gail patted my hand where it rested on the leather console.

"That's okay. The best scenario is the one where you don't have to try. When are you going to admit that I'm right about pretty much everything concerning you, and give me the proper thanks I'm due?"

"Never. I'll never admit something so ridiculously wrong, and I'm not sure what you think you're due," I said playfully, both of us knowing how right she was.

"It doesn't have to be right now. You can thank me later. Now," she pulled out her accordion folder, "I have two plane tickets to Switzerland and plenty of information on our pal, John Savage. Let's go get that son of a bitch."

Even though spring had bloomed in the Midwest, the farther east we drove, the more outside temperatures dropped. Snow progressively dotted the landscape, until its white illuminating glow lit up the interstate as much as the passing headlights did.

Now that the relationship with Annie was officially over, I went into work mode. Throwing myself into my last mission was my only defense against the miserable life I had created. It was all I had left. This was it: my last job, last man, and last murder. After my face-to-face with John Savage, I would officially be dead. I had nothing else to live for anyway.

ANNIE

T he walk back to the car seemed to happen on an entirely different day from when I'd parked an hour ago. The sun shone through the clouds, warming the air—along with the rest of my life. Closure is like a fun-house-mirror trick of the mind. Your life may be exactly the same before you hear or say what weighs on your heart, but after a verbal purge, all things seem possible. Thinking is clearer, breathing is deeper, and vision is twenty-twenty. I had gone into my meeting with Jack in black and white, and I came out in Technicolor.

I was hungry to make up for lost time with Kessler; the images of us naked in bed together consumed me. When I pictured his hands rubbing my thighs or my legs pressing his torso against me, I became free of my past and any guilt that followed. I was completely free to love Kessler, and once again, I was making that choice on my own. He would never know the remarkable amount of respect I held for him and his decision to give me time, because I would never have the words to fully articulate my gratitude. His instinct for how to handle me over the last month surprised even me. It certainly was not what I'd asked for, but my closure today was proof of his abilities. I couldn't wait to wrap my arms around him.

He still hadn't returned my texts or phone calls. After talking to Hope (who had talked to Wade), I found out that he had a free night in Louisville before a show the next day. I knew he'd been upset and standoffish during the last month because of my stupidity, but I had a plan to surprise him and help change his mind.

"Hey!" I said when Hope answered the phone.

"You sound happy today. I take it you made a love connection this morning," she said confidently.

"Wait, what do you mean? With Jack?"

"Jack?" she yelled into the phone. "You saw Jack?"

"Yes, but now I have a feeling you were talking about Kessler," I said, piecing the morning together.

"Oh, no, Annie. Oh, no, girl," she sighed.

"What's going on?"

"Kessler was in town looking for you. He called me and wanted to know if I knew where you were. He loves you, Annie. He came back to fight for you. I told him how proud I was that he'd finally let himself be loved, and that he'd let himself truly love someone else, 'cause that someone is you. I didn't know you were meeting Jack. Jesus, I hope he doesn't know, either."

My heart sank at the thought of Kessler seeing Jack and me together.

"I'm going to Louisville. I have to see him and explain. I told Jack it's over, because it is. Kessler has always been the right man for me. He needs to know that."

"I love the element of surprise, but you need to get yourself dolled up first. You want tonight to be special, and you want Kessler to know how much you've anticipated being with him, if you know what I mean," she urged, hinting at something I didn't understand.

"Like a makeover?" I was clearly missing the point.

"Um, yes, of sorts. When Wade's been on tour and we haven't seen each other in a while, I always go to my girl Lucy down at the European Waxing Spa for a little deforestation. She'll fix you up right quick, and once Kessler sees you, he won't be able to contain his excitement."

"I've never been waxed down there," I confessed. "I don't think I can spread my crotch in your girl Lucy's face. I don't have that in me." I felt like a wuss saying it out loud.

"All right, suit yourself, but I'm guaranteeing a wow factor if you do. Let me know if you change your mind. Mama's yelling 'bout somethin' so I gotta go, but let me know what happens!"

Maybe Hope had a point. A wow factor never hurt anyone. Little did I know, the next twenty-four hours were going to hurt. A lot.

***

I walked into the CVS pharmacy, and headed straight for the beauty aisle. Taking Hope's advice—some of it anyway—I found myself standing in front of seven shelves full of at-home waxing products. I'd decided to take matters into my own hands, thinking at the time that a Brazilian wax would hurt less if I was in control of the exact moment the wax strip came off. Spreading my legs apart to a total stranger was completely out of my bounds. Waxing estheticians look at vaginas all day, but I didn't want mine to be another statistic.

Out of a complete lack of knowledge, I picked the kit with the most professional-looking cover and the largest strips enclosed. It was a lot like picking out wine at the grocery store—I figured the nicest label would have the best product inside.

***

After downing a glass of chardonnay to dull the pain, I carefully read the instructions three different times to make sure I knew exactly what to do. The process seemed simple enough. Separating each strip by the perforated edges, I pulled four cold and hard rectangles of wax out of the individual packages, two for the front and two for the back. Rubbing the rectangle vigorously between my fingers (as the directions instructed), the warmth of my skin melted the wax until it became gooey.

Looks good so far. I might be able to do this.

I carefully placed each strip—goo side down—directly on my bikini line and firmly pressed on the cloth, until I was satisfied that the wax had enough time to latch onto the hair. I swallowed the last swig of wine and began an internal countdown, then stretched the skin taut and swiftly ripped the cloth in an upward motion.

"Yikes!" I yelled, out of anticipation more than pain.

Not bad. Way less pain than I thought. On to the next.

The second strip was much like the first, and the hair came off easily. I reached into the box, pulled out the wax-remover cloths, and cleaned off the leftover stickiness. Admiring my landscaping in the mirror, I decided that this was a vast improvement over shaving. I should have gotten onboard with this grooming avenue back in my twenties.

Another glass of wine for the back, I thought. I already felt my belly warming from the previous glass of chardonnay.

Waxing my ass was a little trickier. I contemplated several different angles in the stand-up mirror, ultimately deciding that a sitting position was my best option for exact placement. I slid back onto the closed toilet lid and leaned against the wall, sliding a large hand mirror underneath my crotch. I pulled my legs up into a birthing position. My vagina was magnified a thousand times for my appalled viewing pleasure.

Who knew I had so much hair there? More important, how have I walked around like this for thirty-something years?

I was horrified, as images of all the men who had ever gone down on me flashed through my mind. I now understood the cliché "hair pie" on an entirely intimate level.

Oh my God! This is awful! Why do men want to see this? More chardonnay.

Following the same routine on my bikini line, I carefully placed the warm waxy strips on each side of my inner ass. Crouching down on the toilet lid, with my feet spread as far apart as my butt cheeks, I began the countdown, this time out loud.

On the count of three, I ripped the strip toward my back. The burning pain of fire shot from my ass. Without thinking, I instinctively stood up in a knee-jerk reaction, and that did lessen the pain. I looked at the cloth strip in my hand, praying it would be full of disgusting hair. Instead, there was no wax on it. Painfully confused, I tried to step down off the toilet lid, when I was hit with brazen clarity.

I had waxed my ass shut.

"No! Oh my God, no!" I screamed. "What the hell have I done?"

I again tried to step down, but the slightest movement felt as though bees were stinging the inside of my ass. Being held prisoner on my own toilet lid was not how I'd expected to spend the afternoon. I held my breath and braced myself on the towel rack, letting out a yelp as I jumped feet-first onto the bathroom rug. Sweat collected at my temples. I was close to a full-blown panic attack. I tried to grab the instruction booklet, but it sat just out of reach. Taking tiny hops over to the sink, the bee's stung me the entire way. Frantically, I searched through the booklet for guidance on troubleshooting waxing your butthole closed. What I did find, at the bottom of the last page in teeny tiny print, was this little nugget:

Not for use on perianal or genital areas.
Use only one strip at a time.
If irritation occurs, discontinue use.

"What the hell?" I hollered. "Shouldn't you fuckers put that on the front of the box, and not on the last damn page in minuscule print? A man *must* have written this."

Next I read:

> *If you experience stinging when waxing, remove the wax immediately with the wipes provided, and rinse with cold water.*

"Yes, the wipes!"

I had totally forgotten about the wipes. There was a glimmer of hope that I wouldn't be calling 911 over this. Dumping the box's contents out onto the counter, I searched desperately for the wax-removal wipes. But, there weren't any more. During the overload of vanity I'd experienced while admiring my flawless bikini line, I had used them all.

"No!" I screamed again. "Water! The instructions mentioned that water would take off the wax."

I hopped over to the enormous shower, turned on the water, and baby-stepped into the full-power stream. With every painfully small step, I felt each hair being pulled out one at a time. I was now on the verge of crying. The water ran between my legs for over twenty minutes, and yet absolutely nothing changed. Frustration at the day's events began wearing me down. I'd had enough. Channeling the same strength I always found on a long run—when my body hurt and my mind told me to give up—I made a decision. This was going to hurt, and hurt badly, but I wasn't going to allow my body to dictate directions to my mind.

Without the countdown, and in an aggressive state, I high-kicked my right leg into the air, landing in a lunge position. Following my act of bravery was a blood-curdling scream fit for the best horror movie.

I sprawled out on the river-rock tile, crying from the pain of the wax, and the relief of it over. I noticed a clear glob of jelly stuck to the shower floor. I had just given birth to those used-up strips of wax. I was certain of that.

KESSLER

On our way to Plain Jane's, we cut through the Art District, which was packed with locals and tourists capping off the most exciting three weeks in the state of Kentucky.

Every year during the first weekend of May, the famous Kentucky Derby is held, but people start partying days before the fastest two minutes in sports even begin. Churchill Downs (where the Derby is held) is arguably the pinnacle of capitalism, and the essence of the American Dream. A pipedream could become reality, or reality could become a pipedream, depending on how much money you're willing to risk on the speed of a horse.

At the Derby, the class system of the haves and the have-nots is nonchalantly flaunted, all the way from the parking lot. Ironically, the horses are at the top of the hierarchy. On Millionaires' Row, women are dressed to the nines in stilettos and outrageous hats, and men wear three-piece suits made of many varieties of linen. They sit in suites, drink mint juleps, discuss the originality of their headpieces, swap stock tips, and gamble beau coup money. The setting is like Jones town, with a different kind of Kool-Aid. These are the "haves" in the arena.

The second-class citizens descend on the infield by the thousands, and on Derby Day, they total more than the population of a small city. These are the general admission folks, who drink beer out of plastic cups, dress in outrageously ordinary clothes, and come to party. They probably can't even see the actual race from the infield, but I guarantee you, they couldn't care less. Depending on whom you ask, these are the "have-nots."

Still hanging tightly to my Louisiana roots meant I identified more with the infield crowd. Bayou farmland, situated on the dirt-road side of the county line, was a place where the term "fancy" wasn't necessarily a good thing. Just because I could have afford a suite didn't mean I wanted to sit in one.

Plain Jane's Steakhouse was the choice restaurant of Millionaires' Row.

The valet at the restaurant stiffly opened our cab door and went about his reservation inquiries—meaning we'd better have one—until recognition registered in his eyes. After that moment, he was cheesy smiles and fake respect as he personally walked us up the outer flight of stairs to the main entrance. I couldn't hate him too much, because he was doing his job.

But the owner, now there was a guy I could definitely hate.

Jerry Plain was a restaurateur with seven successfully run restaurants across the United States. He split his time (and his wife) between Louisville, Chicago, and Charleston, and he was the ultimate trust-fund wanker. The Plain family had made their fortune in the forties running horses. No Plain Jane had been a long shot Derby and Preakness winner, but he fell short of the Triple Crown by losing in the Belmont Stakes. Even with the loss, No Plain Jane sold for millions of dollars, and the Plain family invested their new fortune in restaurants. Jerry Plain was a fourth-generation multimillionaire, and a first-rate douchebag.

No doubt, Jerry met Wade and me, plus the band, at the front doors to welcome us into his humble twenty-thousand-square-foot monstrosity. I played nice with handshakes and pleasantries, while he walked us to a semiprivate dining room. At such short notice, he had moved some tables around so the ten of us could sit comfortably. Once he'd explained to the patrons previously renting out the Belmont dining space that Kessler Carlisle and Wade Rutledge were picking up the tab for the cost of the room, they were happy to have us as well.

A younger waitress came over all starry-eyed and took our drink orders. Being that I was full of a combustible concoction of hurt and anger, surrounded by Louisville social climbers with obnoxiously loud laughter and collagen lips, all I cared about was getting drunk in hopes of blacking out my feelings.

"And for you, Mr. Carlisle?" the waitress asked.

"I'll take that bottle of Michter's Celebration Sour Mash bourbon I saw when we walked in," I replied.

I was wrong to think that the highlight of our waitress's night was waiting on celebrities. When I ordered the limited-release, four-thousand-dollar bottle of Kentucky bourbon, specific to a Louisville distillery, the stars in her eyes changed to dollar signs.

Now Wade, on the other hand, his eyes were definitely stars.

"You sure about that?" he asked after the waitress had run off and before I'd had a chance to change my mind.

Without speaking, I stuck my hand in his face and began draining my water glass. Hydration was always the key to escaping a hangover.

"Well, well," Wade said to the table. "Look who's finally decided to join the party!"

Following ass-kissing protocol, Jerry Plain hand-delivered my bottle of bourbon. An overly excited waitress followed behind, carrying the rest of the drinks along with several shot glasses and a camera.

The twenty thousand square feet of wall space in Plain Jane's were either covered in wine bottles or celebrity photos—the photos were all with Jerry, of course. If you happened to be in the social spotlight and eating at Plain Jane's, you were required to take a customary photo with the owner so he could show it off to the regular people, impressing them with his network of stars and disguising his tiny dick.

Wade and I put on our best smiles for the camera, and then I got down to the business of drinking. After several shots of Sour Mash, I began to feel like my old self again. The lovesick puppy gradually changed back to the lock-jawed bulldog, although I had to force the change. I'd been a puppy with Annie for so long, and I was surprised by how hard it was to find the bulldog again.

Don't think about her, I reminded myself several times over the course of the night. Those reminders only made me think of her more.

As the house band fired up the music, and while waiting for our steaks to arrive, I stretched my legs around the restaurant. I waved to a few people and signed a couple of autographs, then took a seat at the end of the bar. The main bar in the dining room was the feature piece of Plain Jane's. The horseshoe-shaped marble countertop spanned almost the entire width of the room, and tonight, it held seven bartenders. Hand-blown glass chandeliers and sculptures hung from insanely high ceilings, offering more-than-adequate lighting.

Because I was at the end of the horseshoe, I had the ability to watch all of the bar's patrons enjoy their company and their drinks. I caught the eye of a pretty brunette staring me down.

Shit. Please don't come over here.

As soon as we made eye contact, she immediately got out of her seat and began walking my way. That told me she was a troll. When you're on the scene as long as I'd been, you understand the difference between women and trolls. Girls who've had a night out on the town with friends, and who ended up making out with famous musicians, just by chance, are regular women. Trolls are women who frequent expensive places specifically to meet rich men, in hopes of eventually landing in the lap of luxury. This woman was definitely a troll.

"Hey there," she said, with a big smile and a sweet voice.

"Hello," I replied.

"What's a handsome man like you doing sitting all alone at the bar?"

"I'm not alone, just waiting on my food. My friends are in the back."

"Oh, great. I've got some friends here, too. Maybe we'll come back and say hello."

"Um, okay then. I should probably get going." I waved the bartender over and paid for her next drink, but only to be nice.

"See you later, Kessler," she said.

The moment that woman called me by name, I should have left the restaurant, gotten in a cab, gone back to my hotel room, and pined away for Annie. Instead, I did the opposite.

Just as I sat down to a steak that covered my oversized plate, in walked four heavily armed trolls. The girls spread out around the table, introducing themselves to the band members. The woman from the bar expertly pulled over a chair (she had done this before) and sat down next to me.

"Hey there again, I wanted to properly thank you for my drink. My name is Carlie," she whispered into my ear. Her hand immediately found my thigh.

"Really, it's no problem. I was just trying to be nice, Carlie."

Wade sat on the other side of me, cracking up at my expense.

Just keep drinking. Maybe she'll go away.

Because Carlie was only interested in fucking a celebrity, I thought I could handle her, as well as the bourbon. In both cases, I was wrong.

Time rapidly sped up, and before I realized what I was doing, Carlie had found a comfortable seat in my lap. I kept telling myself *don't go any further with this girl*, but after another shot, and then another, I wasn't doing anything to stop her from having her hand up my shirt or kissing my neck.

The other girls had found alternative seating with a few of the band members, after Wade had shooed one of them off.

"See, honey," he'd said, trying to pull his wedding ring over his knuckle. "It just doesn't seem to come off."

She took the hint and focused her energy on Drew, my drummer.

Apparently the volume from our table hit an unfriendly level, and the man who'd graciously let us pay for his rented dining space had reached his tolerance level.

"Look," he said, pointing his finger at the loudest one among us, "y'all might be okay with acting like assholes and having hookers at your table, but we're trying to have a rehearsal dinner over here. Make this the only time I have to come over. If I have to ask y'all again, I'm not going to be so nice."

Picking leftover rib eye out of his teeth with a sharp steak knife, Wade calmly looked up at the angry gentleman and said, "I don't necessarily appreciate your tone. I'm only halfway through my meal, so I'm gonna finish eating the rest of my food first. But, if you feel like comin' back over here, then you better bring some friends with you, 'cause you're gonna need 'em."

He didn't need to go get his buddies, because they were already behind him. I don't know who threw the first punch, but I don't think it mattered. Within seconds, a honky-tonk bar brawl had broken out in Jerry Plain's multimillion-dollar restaurant. Unfortunately, the punch I took from both the guy and the bourbon knocked me out.

I came to as the cab pulled up to the service elevator entrance. Wade and Carlie were dragging me out by my arms. I guess Wade must have felt sorry for me and thought such a willing one-night stand was what I needed to start getting over Annie.

Before the elevator doors opened, a paparazzo jumped out of the box-wood hedges that lined the portico. He began snapping pictures of the three of us. Wade pushed my weight onto Carlie, and she struggled to hold me up, screaming obscenities about me messing up her hair for the pictures. Towering over the photographer, Wade yanked the camera off his neck, as the guy yelled something about his First Amendment rights and suing us. Wade carefully tossed the camera in the air and then drop-kicked it across the parking lot, cracking himself up all the while. The camera landed smack in the three-tiered water fountain.

"Goooal!" Wade ran in circles, yelling at the top of his lungs, his arms mimicking a goal post.

"You redneck shithead!" The photographer dove into the water, chasing some extremely costly photos.

"All right, then. Good talk, son. Send me the bill, pipsqueak!" Wade hollered back, laughing the whole time.

He slid his arm underneath my shoulder, once again holding my weight. "Damn, dude, you need to get out more, 'cause you suck at partying."

We finally got to my hotel door.

Don't let her in.

I did.

She immediately pulled off her shirt.

Don't kiss her.

I did that, too.

Every next move with this girl felt wrong. Even though Annie had chosen Jack over me, I still felt like I was cheating on her. I didn't want to be with this woman, and as she stood naked in front of me, my dick still wasn't hard for her.

"I'm sorry, Annie," was the last thing I remember saying before blacking out again.

JACK

For being the city inhabited by America's leaders, Washington, D.C. is a shithole. The public school system is one of the worst in the country, the crime rate rises every year, and gangs run rampant on the streets—the most powerful one through Capitol Hill.

Living on both sides of the law, I was privileged with a unique perspective on the underworld dealings of politicians. "Ignorance is bliss" was the most appropriate cliché to use when it came to dissecting our government's leaders. I gladly would have gone back to ignorance, if turning back time were possible. Unfortunately, I couldn't, and truth be told, I was just as bad as they were. Even if the general public missed that, God surely wouldn't. Murder was murder void of any reasoning in his eyes. I would just have to continue to live with that.

After checking into the hotel, Gail and I took some time to freshen up. Tonight would be an important step in taking the vice president out of office. It would also be confirmation for John Savage: exterminating him was my goal. In my line of work, you were either confirmed dead or walking dead; you didn't actually exist. Showing my face to him would be like showing my cards at the poker table. I held a full house, and he needed to fold.

I put on my suit and smoothed my shirt out in front of the full-length mirror. Double-knotting my tie made me think of Annie. I used to pretend that I was hopeless with a tie, just to entice her to dote on me. She would sigh and act annoyed that I still hadn't figured out this manly rite of passage, but as she began crossing and looping, she would smile. It was a moment that stopped time and connected us physically and mentally. Sometimes it led to the tie being taken *off*, along with the rest of our clothes. I always hoped for that scenario, and she knew it.

I couldn't let myself think about her. I had to let her go.

Gail softly knocked at the door. I checked the peep hole for confirmation. She was dressed in a mint green mini-skirt, with a white silk tank top that was basically see-through. Gold heels gave her extra inches, making her almost as tall as me.

"Wow!" I exclaimed as I opened the door. "You look amazing. Are you sure you can run in those heels if a situation arises?"

"Please, if Carrie Bradshaw can do it, so can I."

"Is that someone I should know?"

"God, Jack, you're hopeless," she said, rolling her eyes at my lack of knowledge.

I had always envisioned Gail as one of the guys, and I'd never seen her in an outfit like this one before. She was a knock-out. She read the thoughts right from my head as I vivaciously took in her image.

"We've known each other too long, Jack," she informed me, wagging her finger in my face. "Besides, we're too much alike."

"What? I was only thinking about how beautiful you look. Nothing more," I lied.

"Why don't you try thinking with your other head? Are you ready for this? We're taking things to a place we can't come back from. It's the last chance to turn around."

"I know, and I could say the same to you, but I think we both know this is the right choice to make. He's a murderer. Forget about the shady politics that helped him even become the vice president. The bottom line is that he's a murderer. If he isn't stopped, the American public will never know his crimes. They'll never know the kind of man they voted into office."

"We should run a check," Gail said, fiddling with her transmitter and earpiece to make sure the connection relayed clear.

I went into the bathroom, closed the door, and began whispering lewd comments into the microphone tucked under the lapel of my jacket. Any transmission of sound the microphone recorded would immediately be downloaded into a voice recorder app on my iPhone. My hope was that Savage would admit to spearheading Riley's murder, to stealing from terrorists, and causing retaliation at the expense of the general public's lives. But I wasn't counting on it.

***

The Lobby Room Lounge, located on the basement floor of the Ritz Carlton, was a frequent dwelling for Washington's elite. The red paint on the taproom walls was an exact match to the moral bloodshed required to compete in this iniquitous cartel of politicians. The patrons of the Lobby Room were ostensible good ole boys, who were fighting the signs of aging harder than Hollywood starlets; ass-kissing lobbyists pretending to care about the next bills they were leeching; and women who'd had to strap on prosthetic cocks and balls each morning to stay in the hunt for power and world domination. No matter the genus, for all of them, personal agendas always superseded the good of the American public.

The metro was stationed two blocks east of the Ritz. As the doors of the train opened, I started my stopwatch. With the seconds ticking, we walked as fast as possible without running—which would immediately call attention to ourselves—down a block and a half and around a corner, coming to a stop under the awning of a nearby restaurant.

"Six minutes, not bad," I said, stopping the timer to get an accurate count. "Finish putting your outfit together, and turn on your earpiece. I'll contact you when I get into position."

"Yep, I'm on it." Gail tapped the tote bag hanging from her shoulder.

At exactly seven o'clock, a lengthy and slender brunette, with starkly white clip-in veneers, fake-colored green eyes, and bright red lips, aloofly strolled into the Lobby Room Lounge, taking a vacant seat at the bar.

"Hi," I heard her voice through the earpiece. "I'll have a vodka tonic with a twist, please."

With a twist. He's there.

Gail and I had concocted many code words and phrases, most of which pertained to alcohol; those seemed to be the easiest to remember over the years. A straight vodka tonic would have told me to stand down, because he wasn't there yet. But tonight, I could almost picture him all dolled up in his Armani suit, surrounded by his cronies, wearing a smug look on that stupid face (which I thought resembled a can of smashed assholes).

"Give me three minutes," I told her. I pulled out my pencil drill and began unscrewing the metal mesh panel attached to the outside of the basement's bathroom window. "Okay, clear me."

I heard the clicking of her heels on the marble as she made her way down the corridor, followed by the opening of an old door. Because of recent temperature fluctuations, the door got stuck in its jamb. A heavy breath—accompanied by a womanly grunt—was followed by the chirping of ancient hinges and, finally, the sound of plastic scraping across the floor. This led me to believe that the "out of service" sign was now stationed at the front of the door.

"Clear," she repeated back to me.

With my Allen wrench, I expertly loosened the weep system, the tiny holes in older windows that let condensation pass through to the outside. I slid the flat side of my pencil drill between the window panes and moved from it right to left. The locked handle released easily and the egress window shuttered. I pulled the shades up from the outside and slipped in through the small rectangular window, dropping silently with both feet onto the subway-tiled floor. After replacing the blinds to their original position, I stuffed myself into the toiletries closet, behind a carton of basic-grade toilet paper.

"Positioned," I whispered into my lapel.

I heard more breathing, as Gail removed the sign from the bathroom door and made her way across the room to John Savage. She was meticulous with disguises, and an expert in profiling. Since we had worked for Savage for many years, she knew about his weakness for hookers. One in particular had visited him on and off for almost a decade. It was no surprise that tonight, Gail had turned herself into a replica of his favorite concubine.

"Moving," she whispered.

"Yes?" Though she spoke calmly, the transmitter in her earrings clearly caught her words.

"Oh, I'm sorry," he said. "I thought you were someone else."

"Well, whom do you want me to be?" she asked in a breathy and sultry voice.

In the stifling heat of the linen closet, my hand covered my mouth in an attempt to smother the laughter trying to force its way out. As serious as my current situation was, this was also a little bit fun. Finding humor in every scenario had kept me in the business all those years.

"You know, you look very similar to an old friend I used to have," Savage said to Gail. "And I don't mean that in a bad way."

"No, I didn't know that, but thank you, handsome. I could be your *new* friend. I'm always looking for new friends." She clicked her teeth together, causing an echo in my earpiece.

"That might be nice. I'm sorry, but I didn't get your name, sweetheart."

"It's Ginger, like the spice," she replied. I heard him chuckle.

Oh my God! It must make for a difficult time when your dick leads you around most of the day. What an idiot.

"Oh!" I heard Gail yell.

"Oh, no! My shirt got all wet, and Jesus, I spilled my drink on you too! That man bumped my arm, and now look at us. You can completely see through my blouse!" she whined with fake frustration.

"Goddammit. Dump that asshole on the street while I clean myself up," he instructed a crony within ear shot. "Excuse me, please," he added.

"He's moving," Gail whispered to me.

The high-pitched creek of the wooden door, accompanied by the rhythmic opening of each bathroom stall, surely meant the Secret Service were doing a check.

"Clear," a number of voices agreed with each other.

The angry, biting words of John Savage followed.

"Just stand outside the goddamn door. I can piss by myself!"

I waited until I'd heard the stall door close, and then I soundlessly slid out of hiding. Positioning myself along the back wall, leaning against my hand as though I were smooth-talking a freshman at her locker, I waited for him to come out.

With the flush of the toilet and the opening of the stall door, it was show time.

"Hello, John. It's been a long time."

Almost on cue, the color drained from his face.

"What the fuck do you want?" he asked, trying to act effortless in his mannerisms. "I thought you were dead, at least I'd hoped you were." The white in his face gave him away.

"Hope springs eternal, I always say. You're a busy guy, so I won't keep you. But, that package I've been holding onto all these years: it's gone. I thought you should know."

His white face immediately turned red, and he grumbled in a low voice, "I don't know what you're talking about."

"Of course not. But, your wife does."

"Don't you fucking talk about my wife. Jackie has nothing to do with you."

83

"Jackie?" I had a deliberately confused look on my face, but I continued in a sing-song, teasing voice. "Oh, you thought I meant your actual wife. Sorry, wrong choice of words." Changing my tone to nothing less than serious, I continued: "What I should have said is, the Turkish girl you knocked up and paid to keep quiet."

His hands started to shake and his nostrils flared like those of a Spanish bull. At the moment, I had the upper hand.

"I... I don't know what you're talking about."

"I'll bet you nearly shit yourself when she told you she was having twins. Probably didn't see that one coming. Speaking of being blindsided, I didn't see you at Riley's funeral, Mr. Vice President. I thought we'd get a chance to catch up on old times."

His demeanor changed from scared rabbit to Cheshire Cat. He began washing his hands.

"It's too bad about Riley. You've got to be careful on a fishing boat, you know. Water can be a dangerous place to fool around. So can Washington, Jack. You think about that," he sneered, a smartass tone in his voice. "Mountains can be dangerous, too. Planes get lost all the time in spring storms."

I didn't understand. *What plane? Is he talking about the past?*

"You'd better check on that partner of yours, Jack."

Gail? Is he talking about Gail?

"I've been to couple's counseling, too. The whores used to get me into trouble, but my loyal wife has chosen to look past my indiscretions for the good of the family. But you wouldn't catch me flying to Montana this time of year. No sir." He smiled as he talked.

The last conversation I'd had with Jamie came rushing back to me. Jamie and Liz were on their way to a couples' retreat in the mountains of Montana. Their faces, along with the heartbroken eyes of their children, burned into the backs of my eyelids.

"If you mess with me," Savage threatened, "I'll reveal your identity to everyone you've fucked over the past twenty years. I'll email it out like a Christmas card."

"You're dead!" I growled, our noses almost touching. "And if you even think about coming after me, just remember that special letter I have, signed by you and past presidents. I'm sure the American public would love to see an original letter of marque, exonerating me of every crime you've ever ordered me to commit. Why don't *you* think about *that?*"

I swung the door open, to the surprise of his Secret Service. They drew their guns, but Savage held his hand up as a way of telling them to stand down. The worst scenario for his reelection campaign would be if someone were to get blown away in the bathroom of a Ritz Carlton.

"You guys suck at your job," I leered, passing between them, each one hockey-checking me while I tried to get by.

Even amid the commanding noises of the outside traffic, I could still hear Gail crying through my earpiece.

ANNIE

My waxing mishap—and by mishap I meant ripping seven layers of skin off my anus and unintentionally enlarging my asshole—set me back quite a few hours. Thank God I hadn't succumbed to the humiliation of puckered cheeks in a paramedic's face. After several ice packs and many cotton balls soaked in baby oil (which was slippery in my underwear, and kept giving me the feeling that I'd peed myself), walking wasn't completely out of the question anymore.

Even though the thought of having sex with my lady parts roughed up made my butt pucker, the thought of my fingers sliding down the inside of Kessler's pants made me wet anyway. I disappeared into the anticipation of our skin pressed together, of gently wrapping my hands around the warmth of his shaft. His eyes rolled back into his head after I'd toyed with him long enough was my favorite Kessler Carlisle face.

We hadn't had made love in almost a month, and not by my choice. I wasn't counting the awkward sex the night before he left as love making. I'm not sure what that was, but I understood his position; he was clearly guarding his heart. I longed for his fingers to rub up and down my skin, for the quick breaths of euphoria he breathed into my mouth when actual words had been lost in his mind, and most of all, for the animal instincts that overwhelmed us while we devoured each other.

I hadn't even left my house yet—Louisville was three hours away—and I already needed to change my panties.

I giggled thinking of the onset of girlish butterflies that always followed when he called me baby. He would softly whisper it on my lips, around my neck, and in my ear. I shivered as the mental audio ran through my skin, until an unconscious smile stretched across my face. After placing my overnight bag in the trunk, I was off.

Time to go get my man.

Louisville was basically a straight shot up I-65 North. As the interstate curved a hard left around downtown Nashville, I admired the lights still shining long after a responsible adult's bedtime. Restaurants and honky-tonks lined lower Broadway, and with two colleges (Vanderbilt and Belmont) nearby, customers couldn't be hard to come by. Imagining the young couples walking or stumbling out of the bars, always with signature drunken famishes, finding a seat on the curb to eat a vendor hotdog or pretzel, reminded me of my own college experience, and of the girlfriends who helped to make it the best time of my life.

Call Leslie, and finalize the girl's trip.

Once the media got ahold of Kessler's short stint with Wade's tour, my phone started blowing up. All the girls wanted to come to his final show in Nashville. Leslie was the only one of us who'd seen him in a stadium performance. I desperately wanted to be in that audience. I wanted to melt with his voice into the thousands of people who only knew the outside of Kessler Carlisle, while shining with the brightest secret of knowing his insides. By default, our next girls' trip had been planned.

It was already one-thirty in the morning. I knew I wouldn't get to the hotel in Louisville until a little after four. Hope had told me where the boys were staying, and I'd promised to send her a text when I made it. Driving through the vacant darkness of Kentucky was lonely. I turned on Sirius to keep me company, and to keep me awake. As soon as I found the Highway station, I was greeted with one of Kessler's songs. I pressed my foot down harder on the gas.

Get to him. Just get to him, Annie.

I finally pulled under the valet parking pass-through at the Savoy Hotel, making good time at just after four in the morning. From what I could see in the still of the dawn darkness, the building looked to be about a thousand years old, but it had been beautifully renovated. Even though I knew I might be waking her, I quickly sent Hope a text to let her know I'd made it.

A young man greeted me at the car door. Tipping him while declining his offer to take my bag, I stepped into the expansive revolving door. Like Clark Kent turning into Superman, I exited the outside darkness and was spat into the inside of a French country mansion from the early nineteen hundreds. The floral carpet and colonial reception desks offered the only hint of the twenty-first century. The remaining space of the lobby was covered in dignified antiques, which I was sure very rich and very dead people used to own.

Octagonal coiffed ceiling patterns spanned down onto marble walls with forty-foot archways, hugging each floor-to-ceiling window. Massive gold beams with delicate carvings ran up every support column, giving the illusion that the entire room had been carved out of one piece of stone. Hundreds of multi-sized equestrian pictures hung throughout the lobby, a nod to the distinguished history of Louisville. Each was housed in an intricately impressive gold frame. Everywhere I looked was the craftsmanship of hand-chiseled art, connected with the mortar of a different time. Buildings were not constructed this way anymore. Respect for the past was not habitual in today's world, and money of this caliber was not dropped into historic buildings like this one, a two-hundred-year-old diary you could reach out and touch. Someone loved this hotel and had gone to great financial lengths to show her affection.

A tired but well-dressed receptionist asked if I needed help, alluding to the fact that single women don't usually check into seven-hundred-dollar-a-night hotels without an agenda. I was well aware of her skepticism, and it actually made me smile, because I was about to do the exact thing she was trying to prevent.

"Yes, checking in, but my boyfriend has already arrived. I drove all night to get here, and I must look frightening." I was a little embarrassed—I realized I hadn't even looked in a mirror.

"That's okay, ma'am. I think you're lovely, but if you'd like to freshen up, there's a downstairs ladies lounge around the corner. Name, please?"

"The room is booked under Ernest Hemingway," I said uncomfortably. "Sounds strange, I know, but that's usually the name he uses."

Clicking away on her keyboard, her once-tired eyes shone when she exclaimed, "Oh, the Muhammad Ali suite. You're going to love it. Only two suites occupy the entire floor. Protocol at this hour is a courtesy call to the guest already checked in, just to let *him* know you're here." She lifted the receiver off the glossy oak desk.

"Wait! Please don't call him." It was obvious we were now talking about the same person. "Mr. Rutledge knows I'm coming, and I'm here to surprise my boyfriend, Kessler Carlisle. Please don't ruin the surprise," I begged her. I was lying, unless Hope had told Wade, he had no idea.

She quietly studied me, and I suddenly felt like a peasant in that enormously rich room. Her positive judgment would be my only chance at getting on the elevator. I wished I had put on some makeup, or at least brushed my hair.

"Okay." She smiled as she handed me the room card. "Your room is on the sixteenth floor, and you'll see the suite sign as you come off the elevator. I'm not supposed to do this, so please don't get me into trouble."

"Of course not. Thank you!"

The tacky floral carpet led me to the elevator doors. I took a deep breath as the metal box shot up to the sixteenth floor. I was so close to undressing myself and climbing into bed with the man who had gathered up my little pieces, remedying my heart. I bit down on my finger as I pictured myself sliding under the covers and gently waking him, my newly waxed bikini line rubbing against his bare skin.

I would finally get to tell him what he wanted to hear: "Me and you, baby." And this time, I would absolutely mean it. He would call me baby a thousand times, the weight of the word pressing my thighs into his, desperation pulling us together, and then I would fall into him and lose myself in the familiar smell of his intoxicating embrace. The dream of our reunion was pushing perfection.

The metal doors opened, and I followed the arrow pointing me toward the suite at the back of the hotel. As I turned down the last corner of the labyrinth hallway, I was figuratively sucker-punched in the gut. My dream had walked me right into a nightmare.

KESSLER

The hammering in my head kept in time with the pounding from my stomach. The bourbon was knocking; it wanted out. Throwing the covers back, I felt like I was rushing to the bathroom, but it seemed to take forever to actually get there. The moment the cold tiles stung my waking feet, I projectile-vomited in the toilet, on the toilet, and around the toilet. The sheer force sent a spray of brown liquid mixed with yellow bile—and probably the first three layers of stomach lining—splashing against the walls like an art project. I usually wasn't a puker. My stomach instantly felt relief, and although the vomit was truly disgusting, the massive volumes that had come from my insides were downright impressive.

The marble shower replicated the masonry from downstairs. My "new money" status should have made me impressed by the cost, but instead, it bored me. I hated marble. People always seemed so pleased to point out the new marble in their kitchens or bathrooms, but I found Carrara to be cold and clinical. Waking in the morning only to have my feet, which had spent the last eight hours wrapped in the sandy beaches of my bedroom sheets, get shocked with the friggin' Arctic blast of marble floors was a shit way to start the day.

My house in St. Croix was covered in alabaster floors, because the reno guy had talked me out of hardwood. When I got back to Cotton Falls, I'd tear out those stupid fucking floors, and donate them to a school or somewhere they could be of use.

The cold marble was nothing compared to the ice water spray from the showerhead. My dick instantly shriveled, trying to climb back into my body and find a warm place to hide. The dunk tank—as I liked to call it—always cured a night of drinking. It shocked the alcohol right out of my skin and awoke the rest of my body parts, forcing proper function.

As I toweled off, my mind slowly cleared. My memory began wiping the cobwebs from the haze of last night.

Bourbon, yes. That I definitely remember.

Fist-fight, I suddenly recalled, turning around to finally face the mirror and my purple eye.

Bourbon and a brawl, not the worst problems to have.

A red disk scathing the outside of my neck caught my attention. At first glance, I chalked it up to another battle wound from the restaurant ruckus. But after closer inspection, stretching and fingering the mark, a clearing chunk of memory materialized. I realized that it was an entirely different kind of wound.

No! I slapped the red hickey suddenly realizing that I had come into the bathroom naked. The ticker tape of that woman, Carlie, began un-rolling unwanted images like a series of film stills.

No, please God, no! Don't let her be here. Please don't let me have fucked up this bad.

I slowly opened the bathroom door to the pitch-dark of the hotel suite, following the angle of light that quietly swept through the bed-room. My relief was matched by the brightness of each newly uncovered inch, but fear of the unknown still hid in the leftover darkness. Almost every part of the room was now bright. I thought I'd dodged a bul-let—no, a shotgun shell—until I saw her spray of brunette hair sprawled out across a pillow.

Oh, fuck! I silently screamed. *No, no!* I balled my fists and internalized a temper-tantrum shaming session.

Get her out of here, you fucking idiot, before someone sees her!

Thank God the alcohol hadn't turned off my mental alarm, and I'd gotten up before dawn.

Four o'clock AM. No one will ever have to know about her.

That last thought merged with the flash of a digital camera in a dark parking lot, right before Wade kicked it fifty feet and scored a fountain touchdown.

Possible pictures for every news station in the free world! Annie would see them. She would see me as a total mess with another woman, and she'd think I don't love her. Dammit, I don't think this could get any worse.

And then it did.

The pounding on the suite doors was as furious as the simultaneous incoming texts to my phone. I took a look as I hurried to the door. They were all from Wade. The cold shower no longer had a positive effect on me; I began sweating and tasting bourbon again.

"What?" I quietly hollered as I opened the door to a panicked Wade. He had intense bedhead and a fat lip.

"Don't you fuckin' *what* me, Kessler!" he screamed back as quietly as possible. "I'm here to save your ass. That's what!"

"I messed up last night, and I'm sorry about your lip, but I'm about to get her out of here," I said, running my fingers through my hair, still with no idea as to how I was going to accomplish that. "You pounding on my door is only making me freak out more. Just calm down."

"Annie is here, at this hotel, right now," he slowly stated, pronouncing every word as though my life depended on each one of them. Grabbing my shoulders and shaking fear into me, he repeated, "She's here!"

"What?"

"Hope just called me to get some early-morning phone action, and she told me Annie is here to surprise you. Get that girl out of your room!"

"What?" I kept saying. His words weren't registering, and my feet couldn't move.

"Stop fuckin' sayin' *what*, and get your ass in gear," he ordered, pushing his way into the room.

He ran over to the bed and began shaking the woman, whom I'd obviously had sex with the night before and then stupidly let spend the night. I spotted my jeans, which were perfectly folded on the peach chaise lounge, and frantically pulled them on, putting my equilibrium to the test and almost falling over. After turning on the desk lamp, I started throwing all of her shit—she had neatly lined everything up across the desk—into her bag.

Lipstick, wallet, make-up, phone. Why is her phone out? Black lace panties and red heels. Thank God her bag is big enough for all this crap.

"What's going on?" she moaned as she sat up, rubbing her eyes. "Why are y'all yelling, and what time is it?"

"It's time for you to go, sweetheart," Wade told her, practically yanking her out of the bed. "My buddy is in a bit of a jam, and we need you to get moving. Don't worry, the front desk will call you a cab."

I grabbed her dress, which was also neatly folded on the desk, and tossed it over to her. She shot me a *"fuck you"* look as she caught it in the air.

"Look, Carlie," I said, "you seem like a nice lady, and I'm real sorry about this, but I'm in love with someone—deeply in love with someone. You caught me in a very strange moment of weakness, but we don't really have time to talk about that right now." I held her purse out to her.

She slipped the dress over her head and marched toward to me, grabbing her bag out of my hands.

"'You seem like a nice lady?'" she exaggerated, repeating my words with perfect sarcasm. "You're a pig, Kessler Carlisle. You can go to hell!"

I felt bad about how this was going down, but of course, I mostly felt bad for myself. Getting Carlie off this floor without Annie seeing her was priority number one. Now, assuming I got away with this, I would be able to confess my sins to Annie in my own time and my own way. My conscience would eat me alive if I didn't tell her the truth. I could only hope she would understand that I'd thought I lost her forever. It was the only lifesaver that would keep me afloat.

Standing quietly behind the door, I barely opened it and checked the hall.

"Okay, coast is clear. Go," I whispered.

As I stepped out into the hallway, with Wade and Carlie following behind, the woman who had flipped the script of my life, changing my entire outlook on intimacy, turned the corner. She saw the man I never wanted to become. My heart fell to my feet.

JACK

During the four-hour flight from Washington, D.C. to Switzerland, I studied Gail. For the last twenty years, Gail had been my right arm, sounding board, and life mentor, but watching her fully relax in unguarded sleep was eye-opening. Somewhere in the last ten years, the unstoppable forces of gravity and aging had infiltrated her fine-tuned body and mind. With the breaking rays of the first light over Europe seeping in through the oblong windows of our chartered jet, Gail looked all of her fifty years. The settled lines fanning out toward her cheekbones rose and fell with her breath, masking the long-ago adolescence of a girl and solidifying her current state of maturity.

When I thought of every mission over the last two decades, it was astonishing to me that we were both still alive. Being stabbed, chased, shot at, run over, and wanted dead gave two people an unbreakable bond that exceeded friendship or partnership. We were undoubtedly family. Both literally and figuratively, she had saved my life as I had saved hers. Although it was weird and dysfunctional, our partnership had become seamless, both of us knowing when to step forward or fall back based on just a look. Gail was the one woman who had out-lasted all the others in my life. My love for her was bottomless; her life to me was priceless. For those reasons, it was time to let her go—not only for my sake, but for hers as well. She deserved a life better than this, and a partner more capable than me. It was time for both of us to move on.

Since I had spent over half of my life reporting to a boss, the thought of civilian life frightened and exhilarated me. Like the natural exchange of sun and moon or the obvious downhill flow of water, breaking free of this life would be an inverse, like swimming upstream. Completely disassembling my thought processes and daily routines would take adjustments. But, Annie had done it in less than a year, and so could I.

"Annie." I usually said her name under my breath, and always with a mindful sigh.

I had to stop thinking about her, but that was something I hadn't forced myself to do yet. Annie wasn't just a woman I loved; she was the only piece of normalcy I'd ever had. Flying home from an assignment to Kansas City, to Annie, helped me feel authentic and allowed me a piece of tranquil existence in the world. Besides Gail, she was the only family I ever remembered having. If I were to release her from my thoughts, I would once again be an orphan, with no place or person to call home. Even though she couldn't have possibly known at the time, she had given me the gift of humanity.

Gail stirred in her reclining leather seat, and a quiet sob escaped her sleep, jerking her awake.

"Are we there?" she asked, stretching her legs under the wool blanket and uncovering her feet.

"Almost. We'll be landing shortly."

"Have you gotten ahold of Jamie yet?" she asked hopefully, diverting her eyes from mine. We both knew the answer.

"No, but I'll try again when we land."

We sat in a long silence before she spoke.

"He's picking us off, one at a time. First Riley, now Jamie, and I'm pretty sure Savage is saving you for last. I'm next, Jack. He's going to kill me next."

"Don't you even think that, Gail. I'll never let that happen!" I turned to face her, so she could see the promise in my eyes. "Besides," I added, softening my voice, "I'm going to get him before he gets us."

Death was a part of the job. There were never guarantees, as in life, but dying was a concept you could not indulge in contemplating. Thoughts of mortality led to fear, and fear was a direct line to death. Distress caused mistakes. Early on in this game, I had switched my thought process to one of inevitable acceptance instead of perpetual phobia. I was quite sure that was the sole reason I was still alive. Death was never welcome, but for all of us, it was unpreventable.

I was shamefully excited to have an excuse to talk to Annie again, even if my call was going to be about death, but I had yet to decide what to say to her. Liz and Annie had grown close again, and another round of fatality was something Annie couldn't handle alone. As much as I hated to imagine it, I hoped Kessler would be there for her, to hold her together when she might fall apart. He was the better man for that job, and certainly for Annie, and I knew my ego might have screwed that up for her.

Upon departing the plane, I handed the pilot a small duffel bag full of cash. Nowhere in the world was the economy thriving, and for the right price, you could buy an untraceable flight to Switzerland. John Savage

95

was right: planes disappeared all the time, and sometimes without crashing.

The delicious northern air rolled off the snowcapped mountains like a luge into my lungs, clearing any physical and mental sweating. The mountain air was unmatchable in its purity. It seared every part of my anatomy in a primal way.

We hailed a cab to a modern and busy hotel. Crowds of people milled around the lobby, discussing each piece of abstract art in several different languages. Within the last fifteen years, Switzerland had become a hodge-podge of ethnicities, with expats from all over the world helping to make up its almost eight million residents. It wasn't uncommon to hear numerous languages throughout the major cities, the English being a frequent secondary diction. Although the mingled dialect was usually broken and rigidly formal, I understood enough of it to participate in an actual conversation.

Gail and I checked into our room under the premise that we were husband and wife on an anniversary trip. We separately showered, and then discussed our roles for the first meeting. Gail was a flawless opener, nurturing the witness and gaining her trust. I usually finalized the closing, whether by a hand shake or a bullet to the head. We each had our strengths.

Getting the birth certificate of John Savage's illegitimate son wasn't necessary. It was more of a bonus in my master plan. Every piece of damning evidence I could prove was another flame to amplify the fire. Politicians use slippery tongues that love to talk, and without actually answering the question, another one has already been asked. Surprisingly, the general public seems to forget sin quickly, a combination that makes for a quick getaway.

I did, however, need the identity of Savage's illicit daughter—my entire plan hung on that pivotal piece of documentation.

Two years ago, I'd uncovered his covert second family. In his defense, you couldn't call them a family, because he had never actually parented his children. His only influence in their lives was through a checkbook.

Jamie had been the technological hacker in our foursome, and his expertise led him to accidentally stumble upon Savage's offshore accounts in Switzerland, Panama, and everywhere in between. I always knew Savage was dirty, but I hadn't realized just how filthy he was until I'd pressed Jamie to dig deeper into his hidden accounts.

Among the millions of dollars stashed away in different countries, Jamie had uncovered a yearly transaction to the same Swiss bank, and to the same account.

Sena Demir had collected one hundred thousand dollars each year for the last eighteen years. Fifty thousand per child, for an almost two-million-dollar total—all paid for by the American people. I speculated that the child support would run out when the twins turned eighteen, and Sena would most likely be extinguished along with the money. Savage didn't play around. A background check on her family in Turkey made it clear that she wouldn't be able to waltz back home with half-breed Caucasian babies and a smile on her face. Turkey doesn't play, either.

I'd spent the last two years hiding my own money in preparation for my disappearing act. I hated leaving Annie and the life we had built together. But, it didn't matter whether I followed orders or went rogue; I knew too much about John Savage, and either way, he would have killed us both. I couldn't put Annie in danger because of my life choices. As much as it sickened me to think of her with someone else, she would be alive. And, she deserved to live.

The possibility of getting those diamonds back was the only reason Savage had kept me alive, and now, he knew that possibility was gone. I needed Gail to help me get the birth certificates, but after we had accomplished that, I was going forward alone.

Gail and I pulled up to a line of row houses, each one painted a brightly cheerful color.

"Seven forty-four," Gail said, pointing out a blue housing unit.

The wind swept off Lake Zurich with biting teeth, chomping at my skin through my pants. Sailboats moaned and sighed with each rocking wave, and I smiled, knowing how easily I could have stolen one.

Sometimes, just knowing I possess the talent is more satisfying than actually using it.

I slid my trusty pencil drill into the deadbolt lock. With a few clicks of the eraser, the drill popped the lock off, and the door swung open. We walked the few flights of stairs to the top floor and knocked on the door of apartment 3G.

A woman responded, questioning us in broken German. I heard the peephole cover swing back as our eyes met through the circular optic globe. Once I had her attention, I put a picture of John Savage directly in her view. The metal cover immediately scraped the wooden door, followed by the sounds of furniture sliding across a hardwood floor. Doors slammed, and muffled screams came from the interior of the apartment.

"She's running," Gail said, still staring straight ahead.

"Mrs. Demir!" I called out. "We're coming in!"

The wooden door cracked open with little force. Sena Demir was crouching in the corner of a square living room, a butcher knife level with her throat. She screamed something in German or Turkish, or maybe both, but I failed to understand. I certainly hadn't come all this way for her to cut her head off in front of me.

"Friend! Friend!" Gail and I both began repeating.

As a sign of good faith, I slowly lowered my duffel bag onto the heavily worn floors and gently pushed it towards her.

"*Bak, çanta,*" I said in Turkish, encouraging her to look in the bag.

Crying and mumbling, with the outstretched knife pointed toward us, she unzipped the black suitcase, and then froze.

"Do you speak English, Mrs. Demir?" Gail asked her calmly.

Without verbally proving it, she nodded her head.

"We aren't here to hurt you, Sena," Gail said. "We're here to save you, from John Savage and, apparently yourself. You need to put down the knife before you hurt someone. Okay?"

With the picture of Savage still in my hand, I slowly walked toward Sena's crumpled body cowering in the corner. I softly took the knife from her white-knuckled fist. Placing the blade against the picture, I slashed through John Savage's assface.

Sena seemed to understand, and furiously nodding her head, she finally said, "Yes!"

Over a cup of hot tea, I explained who we were and the situation the three of us were in. By the last swallow, two freezer-burned birth certificates occupied my hot little hands. My complete honesty about my future plans to kill her baby daddy didn't seem to bother Sena in the least. Her kids had already safely moved to Denmark, and she'd never expected an extended life at the hands of John Savage. She told me he used to come around every year or so, roughing her up in front of her kids. Once, he had stuck a pistol in her mouth and warned her to keep it shut about him.

"You never have to worry about him ever hurting you again, Sena," I told her, sliding my arm around her shoulder and pulling her tightly to my side. "The last thing John Savage will taste is a gun in *his* mouth. I promise you."

She walked us out and even tried to give back some of the money. Though I didn't know her personally, I empathized with the snapshot of her past. We were separated by half a world, yet we had both gone through life connected to a despicable man like John Savage.

ANNIE

I dropped my rolling suitcase mid-walk, and the plastic handle caught a small corner of the blue and white toile wallpaper that was coming unglued from the wall. As the weight of the suitcase pulled the handle toward the ground, I wasn't sure if the distinct ripping sound was coming from the paper or my heart.

My mouth filled with salivating spit, and my throat closed instantly. Swallowing was no longer a function my body performed.

Kessler shirtless was usually one of my favorite ways for him to be, but that night—correction, that morning, four fifteen in the morning to be exact—I was utterly repulsed by his lack of clothes. His jeans had been haphazardly pulled on, and the waistband barely covered his ass. I assumed that in the rush of exiting his whore, he'd forgotten to secure the button-fly. I could actually see the top of his penis bending back into his pants, like a deflated version of the St. Louis arch. Pubic hair sprouted out the top of his jeans in celebration of his recent soiree.

This was playing out in front of me, and the scene was quite obviously real, but denial kept my feet from moving. As much as I wanted to, I *could not* look away. Complete disbelief coupled with the insane ridiculousness of it all spun through my mind, attempting to dismiss the moment as absolutely hallucinogenic.

I'll wake up from this. Yes, this can't be real. Kessler wouldn't be naked with someone. Why would he need to be naked with someone?

My pitiful attempt at internal dialogue was more pathetic than mental patients playing a game of ping-pong. And the most fascinating part of the entire scenario was that for two whole minutes—maybe it was only ten seconds, but who fucking cared, because it felt like ten hours—nobody moved. With the potential of a volatile and explosive situation, everyone, including the skank, stood frozen.

I slapped my hand to my mouth, just in time to catch my scream. As if we had all been set on pause, and noise was the mechanism that would finally press play, real time started again. Only, now, things moved in fast-forward.

"What's happening here?" I asked, already knowing the answer to my question. "Who the hell is she?" I pointed my finger at the washed-up slutbag. My sickening feelings began turning to anger.

"Aw, shit," Wade mumbled, staring at the floor.

"You bastard! I never should have come here!" I yelled. I bent over and clutched my guts, in case they were to suddenly fall out of my stomach and spill onto the floor.

"Baby, please!" Kessler pleaded, stretching his hand out to me as if he were approaching a wild animal, careful not to make any sudden movements.

Taking a step backward, I growled, "Don't you dare call me baby." I made sure he heard every word, so he didn't misconstrue the meaning. I spoke in a slow and even tone. "You don't have the right to call me that anymore. In fact, don't call me at all."

"It's not what you think!" he lied.

Wade and the whore stood slack-jawed, still in their freeze-tag positions.

"Are *you* fucking her?" I asked a white-faced and paranoid Wade.

"No," he answered, throwing his best buddy under the bus. He said it almost as if he were sorry it wasn't true.

"Well then, yeah, I'm pretty sure it's exactly what I think. Jesus, Kessler, I can smell the alcohol on you from here. I hope it was worth it. Worth us."

"Annie, please don't say that. Just let me explain!" he continued begging. "I love you!" His voiced cracked with each word, and tears began to roll down the sides of his cheeks.

"Sorry, buddy," Wade said, turning to Kessler. "I'll let y'all talk." He headed toward his room.

"Hey," the slut shouted to Wade. "I thought you were going to walk me out?"

"You managed to find your way up here," I said, "so I'm sure you can find yourself out. You've done enough already." I jabbed my finger at her, just wanting her to start something with me.

"Okay, okay," she replied. "I'm going. Oh, and Kessler, I'll call you." She smiled and gave him a wink as she headed back down the hall.

"Hey, hats off, Kess, she's going to call you. You must have done a real number on her last night." I was trying to force a front of sarcasm as I gathered my bag to escape this shit-storm. "I can't believe I waxed my ass for you!" I randomly blurted out. "Do you have any idea how painful that was?"

"No, but it sounds bad. I don't really understand what that means," he understandably replied. It didn't make sense. None of this made a damn bit of sense.

What my gut told me to do and what I actually did were polar opposites. I'd never seen Kessler cry before, and his pain hurt me, physically hurt the inside of me. Even though he had royally screwed me over, I still wanted to hold onto him, to pull him close to me in hopes that a shared pain would lessen the burden for each of us.

I wanted a lot of things to be different in that moment. I wanted to believe that he loved me. I wanted that woman to have stayed home, or I at least wanted Kessler to have the common sense to know that what he did was wrong, instead of just being sorry he got caught. I wished I hadn't pushed him out the door in the first place. But, most of all, I wished Jack had stayed gone. If he had, Kessler and I would have been asleep together in our bed at home.

The fact of the matter was that no amount of wanting or wishing to change the past was going to change what had happened here tonight. Kessler slept with another woman, *he'd had sex with another woman*, and nothing was going to change that either. The rest of our exchange was a blur of meaningless words that I couldn't participate in. Even if I'd wanted to, the throbbing buzz of adrenaline rushing through my ears prevented my full attention.

"Annie!" he yelled, coming after me.

I turned and faced him, my hand held out in a stop-sign mimic.

"Don't follow me, Kessler. If you ever loved me, just let me go."

"If I ever loved you?" he asked in an unrecognizable voice that cracked and broke with each syllable. "Are you fucking kidding me? How can you say that to me?"

His voice turned toward anger now, but I was too consumed with my own shock to listen to a lecture at four o'clock in the morning, in a hotel hallway, from the man I loved, who had recently had his dick inside another woman. He gave me his spiel, which of course he was going to do if the chance arose, but I forced myself to tune him out. Any man in this

102

situation would say whatever he could for a chance at forgiveness. I waved his words away as though I were shooing a fly, and I pretended to cut my losses.

Kessler was familiar with seeing me in a mess of emotions, a state I'd been in a number of times throughout our relationship. I made the choice to show him a different side of myself.

"I'm sorry, Kessler, but we've been through too much. It's just all been too much."

As much as I wanted to fall into him, instead I turned around and walked away.

KESSLER

The four of us stood in the rounded corner on the top floor of the hotel. Nobody wanted to make the first move. Annie's transparent look of immediate suffering ripped through me, synchronized with the paper tearing away from the wall. My insides lacerated with permanent scaring.

In the panic of getting Carlie out of the room, I had become consumed with myself, my feelings, and what was going to happen to me; I had most definitely become my former selfish self. Now that I had a first-hand account of how my actions were affecting the person I loved, shame replaced every emotion.

She just stood there, staring at me, waiting for someone to tell her this wasn't happening, Carlie wasn't real, and I hadn't completely screwed up our lives.

Why did you do this? I screamed at myself. *Look at her. Look at her face! You blew it, dumbass. You ruined everything!*

I wanted her to say something, start the yelling, tell me everything I already knew about myself, because her silence was painfully overpowering. As if she had read my narcissistic thoughts, she let out a high-pitched gasp, like the first desperate breath of someone who nearly drowned.

This was not the same woman who had stood on our porch a week ago, begging me not to leave her, pleading with me to say the words that would somehow magically keep us together. This woman here tonight was not a woman of desperation. This woman was mad.

"Baby, please!" I said, begging her to hear me out.

I cautiously moved toward her, because her eyes kept switching from sadness to anger, and I couldn't decide if she was going to fall into my arms or claw my eyes out. Obviously I hoped for a moment of weakness. I knew if she would let me wrap her in my arms, I could at least get her to listen to me.

It didn't turn out that way.

After Annie tore into Wade, who had tried to help me several times over the course of the night, it quickly became apparent that I'd lost her.

Of course I had. Why wouldn't she go? I had been with another woman. Even though the only memory I had of my time with Carlie was a sloppy kiss, I did remember picturing Annie's face, and wishing it were hers.

Grasping at anything to make her stay, I called out, "I love you!" But even I could hardly take myself seriously, while covered in the stench of leftover bourbon and stale puke.

Carlie was intentionally making my situation worse, jilted with the loss of her humility and the knowledge that her ship was not, in fact, coming in. I could give a shit about her. She had gotten what she came for, even if I couldn't remember giving it to her.

As Annie yelled at me, all I could think about was how disappointed my mama would have been if she'd seen me in this situation: being beat down with words by the woman I loved, who'd caught me in a hotel room with a gross woman I wouldn't have given the time of day to, had I not had a bottle of bourbon in me.

I'm disgusting.

I was finally in a relationship with a woman I was desperate to hold onto, and the second things got rough, I'd run. I should have stayed, fought for her, and never backed down from Jack, even if it meant getting my ass kicked. I never should have let my guard down with a woman like Carlie.

Even though I wasn't a sobbing mess, the tears were unstoppable. I quit trying to wipe them away. She was leaving, gathering her things and leaving me for good.

Stop her! Stop her, idiot! Don't just let her walk away!

"If you ever loved me, just let me go," she sobbed.

"Wait. What? If I ever loved you? Are you fucking kidding me? How can you say that to me?" My anger exploded at her. "Yes, I'm an asshole. Yes, this is a miserable situation and if I could take it back, I would! Please don't forget, I changed my whole life for you, Annie. I've never been the guy with transparent feelings, because I wasn't brought up that way. But, not once have I ever held back from completely losing myself in you. I kept coming back to you because I fell in love with you, so don't you ever question the honesty of my feelings!"

I forced her hand into mine, even though she pulled to get away. I yanked her arm down to my hip, leveling our eyes so she would have to look at me.

With our foreheads almost touching, and in a deliberately grave tone, I pleaded with every fiber of my being. "You are all I know. You're my home!" My tears were now freely flowing. "I thought I'd lost you, and I allowed myself to get lost in that misery. This kind of love terrifies me as much as it excites me, and sometimes I think it might swallow me whole. I shed my skin and handed you my heart, in a way that prevents me from ever giving it to someone else. Do you understand what that means? My love is permanent!"

The tension between us released. Her forehead rested against mine; her skin touching my skin felt as important as the air in my lungs. She wrapped her fingers in mine, and I breathed in the quiet sounds of anguish.

She spread her hand across my cheek, and our eyes connected again. "I'm sorry, Kessler, but we've been through too much. It's just all been too much."

She grabbed the handle of her suitcase and walked out of my life.

JACK

As the sun rose over Switzerland, streaks of white light swayed through the hotel windows, vibrating the reflection of the snow-capped mountains. Gail's bag sat on the kitchenette, stuffed full of the only possessions she considered worthy of taking to her next life. Every trace of her existence on this earth was already extinguished, leaving only her physical body.

We had gone in together on the Allen Enterprise Building on the Plaza in Kansas City, and before I "died," I had gifted her my half, knowing the profits would last her for the rest of her life. I'd repeated for Gail what I had done for Annie, because we knew this would be our last mission together. I would sleep soundly knowing that she could forever stay hidden, as long as the money never ran out. After today, Gail Adams would no longer exist, and within the next twenty-four hours, she would once again—same as me—become a different person. Only this time, Gail would get to be the person she had always wanted to be; we both would.

"Take care, you," Gail said, coughing out the words from inside my bear hug. "Stay safe, and don't be a fool. When you're finished with him, let yourself be loved, Jack. She's out there, waiting to rescue you."

"Rescue me?" I asked.

"Yes, you, Jack, more than anyone else I know."

"I still have plenty of work to do before the deal is done, and I don't plan on waving a white flag just yet," I told her. "Take care, you. I'll find you in the future."

"Not if I find you first."

She smiled, stroking my shoulder, and then began the walk to her new life. Her disappearance through the elevator doors was synchronous with the disappearance of my past. Even though the sense of loss stung, I took in a deep breath and smiled, because today, I could be whoever I wanted to be. I was certainly going to make the most of my new life.

***

Walking through the University of Zurich campus, my eyes fixated on every woman who crossed my path. My list of necessities was absolute, and I had to find the perfect match. I felt like a total creep checking out women possibly young enough to be my daughters. Luckily, the age range of the students was vast.

The distinguished campus was saturated in history, and the landscape captured the essence of a bright and cheery Transylvania. Contemporary buildings curved around floor-to-ceiling glass, diverging obtrusively from the perennial castles built long ago. But, just like the mixture of students and faculty, the architecture meshed, too.

Annie would love this place.

I spent an hour acclimatizing to my surroundings, and I bought a sack lunch to eat while waiting.

Walking into a converted château, I found the directory pin board. I was surprised to see that each office listing was translated into several different languages.

They're not even going to make this game hard for me.

Financial Aid was located on the fourth floor, and the waiting room spilled out into the narrow corridor. I glimpsed inside the office. Once I was satisfied that no one fit my description, I took an empty seat in the hallway. Pulling out my reading materials, I prepared myself for hours or even days of waiting.

Women of all ages and ethnic backgrounds fluctuated in and out through the office door as morning progressed into afternoon. Today was not looking like my day—until, that is, a dark-eyed Italian woman, with caramel skin, a medium build, and average height, sat down across from me.

Bingo!

Her physical appearance was almost spot-on, and her hair could easily be darkened. She was a perfect match. She fidgeted in her seat, crossing and then re-crossing her slim, petite legs and checking her watch, as if she were late for an impending appointment.

When her number was called like a cake pick-up in a bakery, she bounded out of her chair, the soft features in her face hardening, and her immaculately groomed eyebrows turning downward. She looked pissed. Through the glass double doors, I filed in behind her. I took a vacant seat next to her cubicle. Apparently the same iron-clad privacy afforded to anyone opening a Swiss bank account wasn't extended to university financial aid recipients, because I could understand everyone who spoke English. The office was set up like a DMV. Each open-air cubicle had a seat for the counselor and one for the student. It seemed to suggest the same scenario as in the States: the university had the money, the student needed the money, the begging ensued.

My delicious beauty took a seat in her cubicle and proceeded to pummel the financial aid counselor for dropping her classes. At one point during her tirade, she stood up, one fist pounding his desk and one finger jabbing in his face. Her fiery insanity immediately began to turn me on, and the fact that her debt to the university was quickly growing with every late payment made me salivate. She swiped her folder across his desk and onto the floor, cursing at him in broken English. This womanly hurricane rained down a storm of words and emotions on the unsuspecting employee, and as quickly as she'd come, she blew back out of the office, banging the glass door on the concrete wall.

This is the girl.

I followed her out of the building (expertly lagging behind), tailing her across campus and into downtown. For a compact woman, she carried a mighty stride, and this was not a leisurely walk. Her long caramel hair, which matched her skin, fluttered violently behind her, like a superhero's cape in flight. At one point, she answered her ringing phone. I couldn't hear her conversation, but her free hand gestured wildly in the air as she threw her head back and stomped her feet. I found myself smiling, trying to keep up with this explosive woman, whom I was quite sure had found herself another target on the other end of her phone.

Her tirade ended at the front door of a small diner, on the basement floor of a six-story building. I gave myself the customary five minutes before walking in behind her.

Stepping into the diner, I was struck with hilarity to find that the décor was blazingly American. Who knew that submersing myself in an entirely different country would bring me right back to the United States? Clichéd black and white checkered tile ran the length of the restaurant, which had turquoise booths and the staple retro counter. Silver swiveling stools stood in line underneath the bar, and the smell of greasy breakfast smacked me in the face. Elvis had the joint in full swing: "'Hound Dog'" was piping through the speakers.

The cashier spoke to me in German, gesturing to an empty seat at the counter with his extended and massively hairy arm. I nodded at the invitation, and as I sat down, Carmela (I'd decided to nickname her) came out of the kitchen in a standard yellow and brown uniform. She immediately began refilling coffee cups, barking orders at the kitchen guys, and smooth-talking the customers at the bar, calling each of the men by name.

Carmela was popular here, and she obviously had herself a fan club. The middle-aged and elderly men never missed an opportunity to check out her voluptuous breasts as she leaned across the counter, or to drool at the sight of her stacked backside when she bent over. Except for the combination of different languages, I could have been sitting in a diner in the middle of Iowa. The resemblance of décor and human nature was uncanny.

Slamming a coffee cup right-side up in front of me, she began filling it without asking me if I wanted any. She studied my face, her hand on her hip and a pen loosely hanging between two glistening, full lips.

"American?" she asked with a sexy accent and raised eyebrows.

I nodded, as her intensely dark eyes lasered through me. I couldn't decide if she was going to yell at me or climb over the counter and make out with me. Carmela was extremely hard to read; I loved that.

I ordered a sub-par "American" breakfast, even though it was late afternoon, and I ate through the rush of customers until I was the lone patron at the bar. Observation was usually the best method of discovery, and it beat the hell out of talking. Carmela's real name was Francesca. She was constantly checking her phone in between waiting on customers, although her boss sneered with each unattended moment, calling her out more than the other employees. Because of the status of her financial aid bills and her tendency to eat left-overs off customers' plates, I speculated that her monetary situation was *non bene*.

Francesca took an interest in me, or at the very least a curiosity. We kept catching each other's stares.

After spending a couple of hours at the restaurant, my outlook on Francesca and this job had changed. I'd come to Switzerland for me, under the premise of justice for the American people, but now that I'd invested myself in Francesca, I had to make my plan work. She had to say yes.

I asked for my tab and paid with cash, leaving her a three-hundred-dollar tip on the equivalent of a twenty-dollar meal.

That ought to get her attention.

I went outside and sat on a park bench, waiting for Francesca to come out.

As the sun set behind the Alps, the afternoon spring temperatures dropped exceedingly quickly. I wasn't dressed for winter weather. Losing track of Francesca didn't concern me; the university had her information (an easy hack), and I knew where she worked. Plus, I was quite good at finding people, so I pulled my shirt collar up around my neck to ward off the chill, and turned to walk back to the hotel.

"Ciao!" a woman's voice yelled. "Hey, you!" she hollered again, running up behind me.

I stopped to watch her approach. The egoistical male inside of me expected a grateful thank you from Francesca, but instead I fell victim to her wrath.

"What is this?" she demanded, shaking the tip I'd left her in my face. "You think because of this," she said, leaning over and filling both of her hands with her breasts, squeezing her already ample cleavage together, "and this," she continued, turning around and erotically rubbing her attractive tush, "I'm some kind of hooker? *Prostituta?*" she fired off in Italian.

"Of course not," I stated calmly, smiling because I couldn't look at her without feeling boyish, and the eyeful of breasts was top-notch. "I thought you did a great job, and you deserved a nice tip."

"Yes, because *everyone* leaves a three-hundred-dollar tip to a waitress in a diner, for no reason at all," she yelled, clearly apprehensive about my motives.

"I'm not like everyone. I have plenty of money, you wait tables to earn a living, and like I said before, I thought you did a great job."

My answer caught her off guard. She quietly studied me with a confused look on her face.

"What's wrong with you? Are you *mentalmente?*" she asked, circling her finger around her right temple, and wondering if I was a lunatic.

"Not that I know of."

"You have to be crazy to leave this, but don't expect me give it back." Now she was clutching the money to her chest. Parts of the bills were getting stuck in the grip of her tits.

"I didn't ask for the money back. Have a nice night, Francesca." I turned around and began my walk back to the hotel.

I got about a block down the street, when the same sexy voice called out for me to wait. Francesca came running up, her heels click, click, clicking on the pavement.

"I'm sorry," she huffed, running her fingers through her silky hair while catching her breath. "I don't know why I yelled at you. *Stressato*, I guess. When you left me that tip, I didn't know what to think. And thank you! Thank you for the tip. I really do need the money right now. I'm Francesca Mancini." She stretched out her hand.

"A pleasure to meet you, Francesca. I'm Jack," I replied, taking her hand in mine.

"Do you have a last name, Jack?"

"For now, it's just Jack. Would you like to get a drink with me?"

"Are you sure you're not *lunatico*?" she asked again, still wondering if I had a mental impairment.

"Maybe just a little bit."

"I'm Italian, so I can relate. We all get a little crazy sometimes. Okay, just Jack, I know a little place on the corner. I'll buy." The clicking of her heels led the way.

ANNIE

Three hours, two Starbucks, and a pack of Camels later, I pulled into my Tennessee driveway. Sitting slumped over the steering wheel, trying to come to terms with my past, present, and future, I had no idea what to do with myself. As I looked through the windshield at the beautifully renovated Tudor home, I suddenly felt like a guest. That wasn't my home anymore. The quarter-mile driveway, the land it ran through, and the house it paralleled had never actually been mine; they just felt that way.

The truth of the matter was that I could be pulling into any driveway of any residence just then, but if Kessler wasn't there, it would never be my home.

I was too tired to plan out the rest of my life in the car, and I'd been awake too long. I wanted to curl up in a ball and to wrap myself in denial. I knew firsthand that sleeping was the only way to accomplish this, and the best way to momentarily escape my life.

I walked over to Hope's house, since I also had firsthand knowledge that Wade was in a hotel room in Louisville sweating bullets for his friend, who had just fucked up his life over a dime-store Barbie. Passing the arbor, which was full of morning glories starting their climb over the arch of the trellis, I stopped to admire the craftsmanship of Kessler's woodwork.

I ran my hands along the sanded and stained beams, and was brought back to St. Croix and the morning after our first kiss. I had been skeptical of his kindness and humbled by his awkward actions when our eyes locked together; my body had wanted him before my mind caught up.

His dimple was an ever-present scale by which I measured a number of things. But, mostly it measured his happiness, and since I'd known him, rarely had it taken a break. I didn't have a word for it at the time, but standing underneath this beautiful arbor with the ability to look back, I knew the word was *home*. That's how I'd always felt around him.

"Oh, sugar!" Mama D crooned, stretching out her arms and then promptly smashing me against her ample but motherly breasts. "Get in here, honey. Are you hungry? I can whip you up some breakfast faster than you can swing a cat."

Rubbing my hooded and weary eyes, I said, "No thanks, Mama D. I'm full of lattes and cigarettes. I can't even think about eating."

"You do look on the dog end of things. I heard what happened, and you can guarantee I'm gonna have a talk with that boy. I certainly taught him to be more of a man than he's acting."

Of course she had already heard. That woman knew the end results of things before you even thought about doing them. Even through my total exhaustion, Mama D still made me smile. Only a small number of the people you meet in life possess the capacity for total honesty. Mama D couldn't lie to anyone, even if she'd tried; dishonesty wasn't in her genetic makeup. Her face gave you an answer before her words had the chance, and without even trying, her physical being was an open book. She gave you an honest answer, whether you wanted to hear the truth or not. I already loved her like a mother, and I understood why Kessler had chosen to become a part of the Rutledge family. They were just really good people.

"Hey, Annie," Hope said with a familiar sad voice.

It was a voice I knew all too well. After Jack died—*I still need a better word. Escaped, yes, the word is escaped*—after Jack escaped our marriage, people began treating me like a child, and I soon discovered what I lovingly called the "sad phases." Plenty of pitiful eyes enveloped me as if my pet had run away, always accompanied by a delicate touch of my surely breakable glass bones and by never-ending rah-rah assurances that *we* would get through his death together. My favorite nuggets were the whispers about my inevitable psychosis, spoken when those closest to me assumed I was too feeble to hear. The melancholy snowball of pretense grew bigger as the months pressed on.

"Jesus, girl, you stink to high heaven!" Hope exclaimed, pulling away in an exaggerated motion.

"I smoked," I confessed. I knew she would be disappointed by my lapse of willpower, but I was truly grateful to have bypassed the other sad phases.

"Whatever gets you through. How ya holding up, honey?"

"I'm tired, but I've been through worse, so I'll manage. I need to pack my things and find a place to live. For the first time maybe ever, I have no idea where to go." Tears began to pile in my eyes, but shear will kept them from falling.

"One thing at a time, honey. You stay here as long as you want, so that settles your living situation. We're happy to have you."

"You know," Mama D piped in, "If you think you're lost, the best thing to do is stay put. Otherwise you might go walkin' around in circles. Take a shower, rest a bit, and I'll wake you for lunch."

"Thank you, girls. I don't know what I'd do without y'all."

"The fact that you just said y'all means I'm successfully converting you into a Southerner, and there is no better thanks than that," Mama D cackled. "We're takin' over the world!" She sashayed back into the kitchen and began to pull out pots and pans.

"Thank you," I whispered to Hope.

"Lord, don't thank me. Just look at her in there, twirling and singing like a washed up Rockette. I swear, she's happiest when she thinks people need to eat, which is most of the time, but sad people are her favorite. She loves to stuff miserable faces with home cooking. Wait 'til she gets ahold of Kessler." She was whispering like a satisfied younger sibling, pleased with the knowledge of impending punishment. "He's gonna get the whompin' of his life!"

I covered myself with the chilly sheets of the Rutledge guest bed, and immediately found the illusion of sleep.

***

The smell of fried chicken dragged me out of my fantasy, in which life had been pleasant instead of a pendulum. I'd dreamed of Kessler on the balcony of Cotton Falls. Neither one of us spoke, but I sat in his lap with my knees pulled up to my neck, as his arms wrapped around my legs. His strong chest steeled against my back, our heads gently resting together. The Caribbean breeze aproned us, aiding the back and forth movement of the rocking chair. I wanted to stay in that chair with him forever.

As I sat on the edge of the bed waking and gathering myself, I heard Hope and Mama D doing a terrible job of whispering. Their strong southern roots prevented them from using a low murmur, even when they were trying.

"I don't know why," Hope whispered.

"Turn that thing off. She's gonna be up any minute," Mama D instructed.

"She's gonna see it, Mama. We can't hide this from her."

"She needs to eat first. Food will help."

"You always think food will help. People don't like to eat as much as you think they do."

"Oh, you don't know shit from Shinola. You're so skinny you'd have to stand up twice just to cast a shadow, so I'd hardly expect you to be an expert on the subject. Now turn it off!" she demanded.

"Turn what off?" I asked, walking into the kitchen and busting up their secret pow-wow.

They both began babbling in short, ridiculous, broken sentences, trying to get their unpracticed story straight.

"What's going on?" I asked, looking directly at the worst liar. Mama D instantly looked away, like a dog getting busted eating out of the garbage. "Well?"

"Sweetheart, you need some chicken first," Mama D replied, sliding over a glass of water.

"Sit," Hope instructed. She pulled out a barstool at the kitchen island. "I'm not gonna sugarcoat this, Annie. It's bad, real bad."

I gasped in a violent breath. "Kessler? Is he okay?"

"I doubt it. He's not dead or anything, but I bet right about now he wished he was. Hold your breath, honey."

Hope took the remote off the island and clicked the small kitchen TV on, but left the sound muted. The black screen disappeared; the channel they had been watching flicked on. "Breaking News" flashed in scarlet letters at the top corner of the screen. The ticker running across the bottom, detailing the story, was too small for me to read.

"What? What am I looking at? I don't understand," I said.

"Wait for it," Hope replied.

An enlarged photograph replaced the news anchor and constantly moving ticker words. I dropped my cup, shattering the glass against the tile floor. The picture was of Kessler and the whore.

A series of sexually graphic pictures flashed across the screen, each with the blackout bar across *his* eyes and *her* used up rotten crotch. I couldn't believe what I saw. There were so many pictures. This wasn't just revenge; this was humiliation on a national level. My first instinct was to call him. Setting last night aside, I wouldn't have wished this on my worst enemy. He didn't deserve a twenty-four-hour news channel continuously flashing the biggest mistake of his life, over and over again.

That being said, Kessler Carlisle was having one hell of a deservingly bad day.

They both stared at me, waiting for me to flip my shit, but instead I said, "I need to go for a run."

KESSLER

A hint of afternoon light sneaked in through the blackout curtains and woke me like a cruel joke. With no desire to participate in life that day, and with the scathing early hours of the morning still fresh, my near-happiness seemed like a lifetime ago. The depth of my shame made me physically uncomfortable.

Annie had come to Louisville for me. We were so close to putting the troubles of the last month behind us. It was absurd, and almost laughable, how close to the dream we had actually been. Only a matter of hours ago, I could have reached out and physically touched her, and if I closed my eyes, I could still feel the warmth of her forehead against mine. Closing my eyes helped me to feel a lot of Annie; at this point, imagining her was as close to her as I was going to get.

The weight of massive emptiness sat in my soul, advancing like an aggressive disease through my body. I'd lost my home and the heart that occupied it. I was sick with loneliness, shrinking into the loss of her love.

After folding my pillow in half and punching it several times, I propped it back under my neck. I lay in stillness, trying to reason with my conscience, but restlessness tortured me like worms crawling throughout my insides. I kicked my legs and beat the mattress with my fists. My mind was hemorrhaging with thoughts of Annie.

She came here to tell me she loved me. How could I have been with another woman? I'm so fucking stupid!

The spiteful part of heartbreak is that life keeps moving forward. No matter how much I'd managed to mess up my personal life, the show was still going on that night as scheduled. Promoters, venue owners, ticket holders, and fans had paid for a concert, and every part of my body would have to be broken for me to cancel; money doesn't care about the heart.

I switched on the television and began flipping through channels, looking for a news station. I wanted to celebrate the misery of someone else. Instead, I came across a slide show of amateur and grainy pictures of my continued demise.

"Oh, shit," I whispered. The blackout bar covered my eyes, but my name scrolled across the screen in big red letters.

"That bitch!" I yelled, seeing the pieces of last night come together. When Carlie had aggressively pursued me at the restaurant, I'd doubted she was a rookie seductress, but I had no idea how professional her intentions were. The pictures were ridiculously posed, with my arms and legs unnaturally positioned. I was so obviously passed out for all of them. It was like a murder scene without blood. Carlie had taken shot after shot of her best selfies, pursing her duck lips and sucking in her stomach.

I thought through my earlier puke session. I had walked into the bathroom naked, but my dick was as limp as a one-legged man. If I'd had sex the night before, my morning piss would have sprayed all over the toilet. Ask any man; it's another disgusting and barbaric trait of the male anatomy. The only thing my dick was full of was bourbon. I couldn't possibility have gotten hard enough to perform, even if I'd wanted to. Plus, my only memory of being with Carlie in the hotel room was wishing for Annie's naked skin firmly pressed into mine, her lips on my stomach, and my fingers in her hair.

I didn't have sex with Carlie. I was positive of that fact. Lacking proof to any of my claims was only a cliché of he said, she said. I didn't care what the general public thought of me. At this point, my only driving forces were the thought of my arms around Annie, and her faith in the knowledge that I was absolutely the man for her.

Carlie had constructed a payday for herself and publicly humiliated me on a worldwide scale. I should have been irate, and I should have called into the news station to defend myself. I should have backtracked through the details of last night, slung the dirt back into her face, gotten my lawyers involved, and sued the shit out of her. But, love makes a man act in crazy and unexpected ways.

I lay back down on the arsenal of fluffy and oversized hotel pillows, relaxing with the new shred of hope that I hadn't fucked up my life, that a new last chance with Annie was possible. I knew I hadn't had sex with Carlie, and the proof was right there in the pictures she took. Fate was an illusion like the most delusive magic trick, suddenly turning the imaginary into the possible. The misery of only minutes prior had now given me a fighting chance.

Carlie had sat down at a table well beyond her betting limits, and unknowingly, she'd showed her hand. But if I personally contacted her, she would only try to blackmail me, adding to her TMZ payday.

THE ACHILLES HEART   KARYN RAE

I needed to enlist the help of a professional, someone skilled at conning and terrifying unsuspecting victims, and then totally wrecking their lives.

He wasn't completely at fault for the situation I was in today, but he damn sure had his hand in the pot. I figured he owed me, and I knew he had the skills to scare the hell out of Carlie, blatantly proving her farce with the porno pictures. Luckily, I'd had the foresight to put his number in my phone as a security measure, in case he couldn't let go of Annie. This was almost comical: a few days ago, he had been my only competition, my roadblock to a life with the one woman who brought me to my knees. Now he was my only ally. As much as I hated to swallow my pride and ask him for help, Jack was my best hope to get Annie back.

JACK

C andlelight illuminated her flawless skin, aiding in her already visionary glow. Her carnal lips opened to reveal unusually square teeth, which flashed with every smile. Francesca was unlike any woman I'd met before. From her compact stature and less-than-compressed accessories, to her flagrant apathy for internal dialogue, she surprised me on every level. I reminded myself to focus on my immediate objective, but the reminder quickly faded whenever Italian words escaped from her salaciously full mouth.

"Why are you here in Zurich, Jack?"

Remembering the freshly sewn laceration of my previous life, I decided to resurrect a dormant skill that I planned on perfecting in the future. I told her the truth—the beginning of the truth anyway—baby-stepping my way to freedom from my innate natural tendency to constantly lie.

"I'm here for my job," I replied.

"And what is it you do?"

"I work in securities, protecting clients from others as well as themselves," I answered, proud that my reply wasn't a complete fabrication. "I'm actually headhunting for a temporary position. The job pays cash, and it will only take a few days to complete. Do you know of anyone who might be right for the role?"

She leaned back in her chair, crossing her arms against her heavy chest and staring directly into my eyes. Without even so much as a blink, she asked, "Is that what this is all about?" She circled a pointed finger over the wine bottle and then around our dinner plates.

"What do you mean?" I asked, taken aback.

"Please, do not take me for a fool, just Jack. Is this why you asked me to dinner, left me the expensive tip, and followed me from campus? To ask me to be hired for this temporary job?" She spoke in perfectly broken English, raising her eyebrows in satisfaction at her investigative work.

I shook my head and smiled, floored at her perception.

"Yes, it is."

And with three little words, I enlightened myself about how ethereal the truth felt. With that simple statement, I was conceding to the possibility of rejection, but in the same breath, I allowed a contingency of hope. Even if she kicked me under the table and called me a bastard, this was a moment I would forever look fondly upon. This was the new beginning I had been looking for.

"You Americans, with your perfect hair and white teeth," she began. "You travel to other countries wearing expensive designer clothes—which, by the way are five years behind everyone else's—throwing your American dollars around and speaking with a charming accent, so sure women will fall all around you. *Phfft.*" She made a sound like a hissing cat, while rolling her big brown eyes behind her long black lashes.

"Does this mean you aren't interested in the job?" I asked, trying to confirm her disgust in me.

"I didn't say that. How much does it pay?" She immediately changed her demeanor by straightening her spine, propping both of her elbows on the table, and entwining her fingers.

"Don't you want to know the details of the job first?"

"No, money first. If I don't like the money, then the details don't matter."

Blown away by her brass tactics, I couldn't keep myself from laughing out loud. This Italian cherry bomb, who was only as tall as my chest, had no idea what I was going to ask her to do, yet she'd opened the floor to negotiations on a job she might not even be qualified for. Her eyes shined with confidence like Fourth of July sparklers, as she spewed insults at me faster than the pyrotechnics of Roman candles.

I informed her, "The job pays five thousand dollars for two days of work."

She tried to pass as unimpressed, but her eyelids fluttered, her jaw clenched, and she slightly jerked her right foot. These were obvious signs of engrossment, and I immediately knew she wasn't going to pass up my offer.

"Seven thousand," she haggled.

"The price is five, but if you flawlessly execute the job, a bonus awaits you at the end."

She opened her red lips to retaliate against me, but I held my finger up before any aggressively sexy Italian words could fly out of her mouth.

"The bonus amount is strictly paid according to my discretion, and it is decided upon based on job performance."

Sitting back in her chair again and swirling the wine in her glass so that its legs reached almost to the rim, she smiled a satisfied smirk. "Okay, what do you want me to do?"

"First, I need you to dye your hair a dark brown. The color doesn't need to be starkly black, but you need to get rid of the blond highlights. Next, you need to dress exactly like you're dressed tonight: makeup, clothes, the whole package. Do you have any complaints so far?"

"No, we are good," she said intently.

"Meet me back here tomorrow afternoon at one o'clock. I'll need to take some pictures of you."

Her eyes immediately widened when she heard the word *pictures*, and I realized that my request sounded pornographic. I instantly corrected myself.

"No, not those kinds of pictures!" I insisted. "I'm taking the pictures to make an ID."

She tilted her to the side, and the skin furrowed between her polished eyebrows.

"Identification cards," I clarified. "You're going to need a few of them, and they need to be perfect. Are we still good?"

"Yes, we are good. I will get the brown hair and wear the makeup," she said, fondling the shiny strands around her fingers and lightly touching her mouth. She smoothed the hair across her lips like a brush, as if she had just painted them red. "If I do a good job, will you tell me your last name?"

Surprised by her interest, I replied, "Only if you do a good job."

"Okay, just Jack, I'll see you tomorrow afternoon." Her hand found my arm across the intimate corner table. She stood, and with only a wink and a smile, her heels carried her away.

ANNIE

O ver the last few months, my running shoes had seen little action. Choosing to spend the morning hours tucked in bed with Kessler, and staying up late together talking, as new couples do, I hadn't made running an immediate priority.

When you lose sight of a passion or alter your previous devotion, the sacrifice might go unnoticed, but eventually, the lack of active participation becomes as obvious as a phantom limb.

To me, running was so much more than burning calories, staying fit or living healthily. It was a way of life. Just like meditation or prayer for some, running was my religion. My sports bra was comparable to church clothes, and my shoes were like rosary beads.

The first mile totally sucked, however, and today, all the miles could have given me an aneurism.

I started in a slow walk, enjoying the feeling of my church clothes and taking the deep breaths that we only seem to remember to inhale when breathing the outside air into us. Despite the overall crappiness of the last few days, the tightness in my shoulders relaxed as I tipped my face to the sky and enjoyed the warmth of the sun.

The mental aspect of beginning a run is like that of an employer walking into the office's morning chaos. Within minutes, everything that weighed on my mind was jumping at the chance to get resolved. ADHD was usually a crippling personality trait of mine, but it came in handy when the overload of employees rushed my brain. Everyone got a few seconds of attention before I picked a problem to actually fix.

My lungs burned in regret because of all the cigarettes I'd chain-smoked on my early-morning drive back to Franklin. I hadn't smoked in months, but my first stop after I'd left the hotel was for gas and Camels.

No more smoking. Back to quitting.

The decision was easily made in the midst of my self-torture, two miles from home. I wasn't worried about futile willpower; my body was in too much pain to argue with my mind.

Next order of business was my predicament with Kessler. I loved him. *God, did I love him*, but picturing him with that tramp infuriated me. I didn't know how to move past the footage continuously running through my head.

Faith instructs everything happens for a reason, and I believed that wholeheartedly. When trudging across a river of shit, it's easy to get lost in the stench of self-pity, but who's to say there isn't something so much better waiting on the other side? Sometimes you need to be broken, so the light can shine through.

I couldn't stop my mind from picturing those photos, but something seemed off about them. I knew Kessler's mannerisms during a drunken blackout, which was obviously his state in the photographs. It didn't take a genius IQ to figure out why she had posted those pictures, all of which were *so* obviously handpicked by her to try and diminish her nasty slag status. But slut-shaming her wouldn't change my situation.

One photograph in particular, I couldn't get past.

Even though I wanted to sprint the last mile home, my side stitch kicked in, and I had to settle for a fast walk. I needed to see those pictures again.

KESSLER

I f they've just had their junk displayed on national television, most people might want to crawl into a hole and die. I, however, had a continuous stream of happiness running through my veins. Making this phone call made my palms sweat, but so did the thought of getting the better of Carlie. I was admittedly overly excited to stick it to her. I reminded myself that her misery wasn't the ultimate prize.

I couldn't just call Annie up and tell her, "Don't worry about the pictures, babe. The scene at the hotel was no big deal. How's your day and such?" She would have punched me through the phone. I needed to get my end of things straight before I could drop to my knees and ask for forgiveness.

As I dialed Jack's number, I felt like a student forced to call a teacher at home, after school hours. Even though I was most certainly a man, I suddenly felt like a child.

Short bursts of static replaced the ringing, but no voice spoke on the other end of the line.

"Hello? Jack, are you there?"

Breathing now replaced the static, and I knew he was listening.

"This is Kessler Carlisle, Jack. I'm guessing I'm the last person you want to talk to right now. Believe me, I'd rather be nearing the third day of food poisoning than be asking for your help, but I need it—your help that is."

"Is Annie okay? Is she hurt?" he finally said, breaking his silence with concern for the woman we both loved.

"Yes, she's okay, but she's also hurt. I've got to get ready for a show tonight, so I don't have much time to talk. You'll understand my problem if you just Google my name. I'm all over the news, and not for anything admirable. I know it's a stretch for me to be asking you for a favor, but the way I see things, you owe me."

"Ha!" He laughed into the phone. "I don't owe you shit, asswipe. You're the one who swooped in on *my* wife."

"We've already had that conversation, and nothing will change by having it again. Maybe you don't specifically owe me, but you certainly owe Annie, Jack. You knew she loved me, and you did everything in your power to stay in the game, giving your best effort to tear us apart. I understand that second place hurts, only because I've been there. But if you hadn't come back to re-fuck up her life, Annie wouldn't be so miserable right now. Neither one of us would."

The stillness on his end of the line gave me hope that he was listening and, maybe, digesting the facts I had clearly laid out.

"I'll kill you if you've hurt her," he said in a matter-of-fact manner.

"I would never intentionally do anything to hurt Annie, but unfortunately, I let my guard down, and I messed up. If you can put your hatred of me aside long enough to help her, I would be the one owing you. I never go back on my word, Jack."

"Shit," I heard him mutter under his breath. "I'll think about it and Google you, but if I'm not interested in my findings, I'm not doing a damn thing for you. I won't promise you anything—except a gruesome beat down—unless you lose this fucking number! Erase it from your phone, and don't even think about calling me again."

Suddenly panicked, I asked, "How am I supposed to get ahold of you?"

"You don't. If I feel like saving your ass *again*," he stated with cocky emphasis, "I'll get ahold of you."

His words were replaced with a dial tone.

I felt hopeful about the prospect of his help. I knew he loved Annie. Even though she hadn't chosen him over me, when you truly love someone, you want them to be happy no matter the cost. That was the exact reason I'd just made a phone call to a man I loathed, basically begging him to help me. I would risk anything for Annie, especially something as meaningless as my pride.

JACK

Though making Francesca a part of my plan was risky, I took all kinds of risks these days. A rigid structure used to dominate my every move; it was also the sole reason I'd stayed ten steps ahead of the game. It didn't take psychoanalysis for me to know I was losing my edge. However, a devil's advocate might have told me that my edge hadn't been lost. It was more like replaced. I was conscientiously making decisions I never would have entertained in the past, and strangely, I felt empowered by my choices.

Looking beyond myself—something I was still perfecting—it was clear that my so-called mistakes were coming full circle. How I chose to perceive those errors would most certainly lead me down one of two different courses of action. I was tired of legitimizing my decisions with empty justifications, and with the small truths of the night before, I was already hooked on the extreme euphoria that only authenticity could provide.

The ringing of my prepaid cell phone interrupted my inwardly religious moment. A shot of terror needled my heart. Only two people knew this number, and neither one of them had ever called it. Only desperation would force Gail to contact me; I immediately began praying that she wasn't on the other end of the line. I had also given the number to Annie, but only out of childish pride. Going into our last encounter, I had known my chances of winning her back into my life were close to nil. I was right—she had cut me loose. I would have cut me loose, too, and I held no resentment toward her. I didn't have that right.

I answered the incoming call with silence, prolonging the chaos. If I considered myself still on the fence about losing my edge, the voice on the other end forcefully pushed me off.

"This is Kessler Carlisle, Jack," he confidently stated.

Who the hell does this guy think he is?

He began a spiel about needing my expertise. It took some colossal balls for him to call me up out of the blue, after my wife had chosen to love him instead of me.

"Is Annie okay? Is she hurt?" I asked in a panic.

He began rambling instructions for me, *he was instructing me*, whining about how he'd blown his chance with Annie and why I should help him get her back.

"I know it's a stretch for me to be asking you for a favor, but the way I see things, you owe me," he added, as though he were asking to borrow my lawn mower, instead of twisting an already-abysmal knife.

"Ha!" I laughed into the phone. "I don't owe you shit, asswipe. You're the one who swooped in on *my* wife!"

"We've already had that conversation, and nothing will change by having it again," he said, wrenching the knife while using logic against me.

I need to stop calling her my wife. I walked away from her and gave up the privilege of that title. She's not my wife anymore.

It wasn't just that what he said was true. It was the fact that I cared. My heart felt as though I were in dealings with a terrorist. Allowing his depressing logic to settle was defining. For ten years, I had taken from Annie. She'd never wanted for anything tangible, and she was free to come and go as she pleased. What I had taken from her couldn't be measured on a scale. She had given me her life, trustingly put it in my hands as her protector, and I took it from her, giving none of myself in return.

"Shit," I muttered under my breath. "I'll think about it and Google you, but if I'm not interested in my findings, I'm not doing a damn thing for you."

Kessler had easily gotten my number and found me, which meant that anyone else could do the same. Starting a new life wouldn't even be a consideration if I continued to be so careless in this one.

"How am I supposed to get ahold of you?" he asked.

"You don't. If I feel like saving your ass *again*," I snarked, "I'll get ahold of you."

I hung up the phone conflicted, knowing I should help him because he could make Annie happy. But no one likes to eat shit, and bringing Annie and Kessler together would taste like a plate full. And anyway, I had a timeline of my own events, and I had to get to work.

***

Waiting outside the café, my body was relaxed, but my mind wrestled. The warmth of the sun negated the wind, and afternoon temperatures were on the rise. I'd set up a mock photo booth in my hotel room, and I had purchased a studio photography kit from a local camera shop down the block. I hadn't given Francesca my hotel information; I thought it best if we met on neutral ground. I wasn't totally careless—not yet, anyway.

At the thought of her name, she gradually appeared, her small figure coming into focus the closer she walked toward me.

"My God," I said aloud. I only meant to say it to myself.

"You like?" she asked, holding the bottom of her skirt and doing a twirl.

"Yes, very much," I stuttered, as though this were my first introduction to boobs.

Her raw umber hair color now matched the chocolate in her eyes, but it stood background to her center-stage red lips. Confidence seeped from her smile, yet her demeanor seemed different. Yesterday, she had been struggling financially, wearing cheap-looking orangish streaks in her hair, along with a chip on her shoulder. This morning, she looked polished and sophisticated, and even though she stood straighter and walked taller, she publicized a more relaxed woman. Her dress hugged her curves, *there were so many curves*, and her heels gave the illusion of extra-long legs. I realized I had my hand over my chest, as if that would keep my heart from exploding out of my body.

"You look beautiful," I said.

Blushing with sudden redness, she replied, "Thank you, just Jack. I feel like a million dollars."

"Let's see if we can make that a reality. Are you comfortable with going up to my hotel room? I know the question sounds shady, but you have my word: this is strictly business."

She crossed her legs and shifted her weight back and forth, clearly torn between what she wanted to do and what she had to do to get paid. We stood through an awkward moment. I knew there wasn't much I could say to prove I wasn't a psychopath.

Learning from the lessons of my past, I decided to give her something—a gesture of some sorts—to help ease her worry.

"I'll tell you what. I understand why you're uncomfortable. This isn't a common situation for either of us, and since you're doing something for me, I'm going to do something for you."

Her eyes rose toward mine, and her previously concave shoulders evened out.

"Last night, I said that if you completed the job, I would tell you my last name. This may seem insignificant to you, but it's quite the opposite for me. Telling you who I am could cost me my life. The last person to call me by my real name was my mother, when I was six years old," I confessed. "Do you still want to know?"

"Yes," she said, hanging on my every word.

"My first name is Jack, Jackson actually, and my last name is Allen. You're the first person I've said that to in thirty-eight years."

Her square teeth debuted behind her smile, and she said, "Okay, Jack Allen, I'll go with you."

I'd been more honest in the last twenty-four hours than in the last four decades. No matter where you go in life or what adversity trumps you, your name is something that usually sees you through everything. Your birth name is an identity that becomes woven into the fabric of your DNA. First you become the name, and after a short time in life, the name becomes you. No one could ever feel complete without a name; it signifies who you are. Having given up my moniker to serve the United States government, I hadn't realized that a name is a part of a whole. I should have known, because I was an expert on the subject. Hearing her call me by the name my mother had chosen specifically for me connected me to Francesca in a way I would never be able to fully express to her. I wanted to hear it again.

We strolled the four blocks back to my hotel, and she seemed to purposefully take her time. I was willing to go at her pace. I took the opportunity to get to know her better.

"How long have you lived in Zurich?" I asked.

"Ten years. Before that, I bounced around Italy from place to place, never being very good at staying in one spot. I came here to make a fresh start on my life, and ended up staying. How about you, Jack Allen? What's your story?"

"It's too long to tell, but in a way, it's similar to yours."

I opened the glass doors to the hotel lobby, and we both hurried to the waiting elevator. When I opened the door to my hotel room, I noticed that her face relaxed. My setup wasn't pornographic in the least, but rather was streamlined and professional.

"Here?" she asked, pointing to a desk chair under a photographer's umbrella reflector.

"Please," I replied, extending my hand.

I turned on the studio bulb and situated the white muslin backdrop, making sure Francesca was directly centered. Long ago, I had learned the basics of perfecting fake identification cards, having made hundreds for myself. Once you learned the exact paper quality details, researched the correct lettering font, downloaded the state or country seal, and used the appropriate lamination thickness, making a passport or ID was a piece of cake. The first few I made were terrible. That was before 9/11, and also before the securities industry became a billion-dollar business. Having perfected my craft over the years, Francesca's would be done by nightfall.

The more pictures I took, the more she relaxed, and I began to envision her as Rana, the illegitimate daughter of John Savage and Sena Demir. Francesca was definitely older than Rana, but only by a handful years, and except for that and her ethnicity, she was an exact match. A fake passport is easily constructed, but when dealing with triple-locked Swiss bank accounts, it's always best to have the real certificates to accompany the fake ones.

"Okay, Francesca, I think we've got it. I'll work on these this afternoon, and I should have them ready tomorrow morning."

"What time will I meet you?"

"I need to finish these first, but could you meet me later tonight?" I was hoping I didn't have to pass another scam artist test.

She tilted her head again, in the same fashion as she had last night—her look of processing a potential misunderstanding. Though I felt a little violating by profiling her, I found myself wondering if she had any other ticks, gestures, or signature moves.

"This is the part where you earn your money, Francesca. This is serious business, and you're walking into a lion's den. I need to make sure we are both confident that you know what you're doing."

"What *am* I doing?" she asked.

"Tomorrow morning, you're walking into Benziger Bauer Bank with your new IDs, and you're starting the process of draining a multi-million-dollar bank account."

ANNIE

Rounding the corner into the cul-de-sac, I got a glimpse of the life Kessler had been running from. He had gone to St. Croix, literally into hiding, to try and live his own life. Media vans and reporters littered the pavement along the street. The reporters were strategically placed far enough away from each other to steer clear of other stations shots, but they were close enough to the front gate to pounce on him if he ever thought about coming home.

As soon as I saw a female reporter pointing at me, I forgot all about my running pains. I sprinted to the Rutledge house and jumped the fence into the backyard. Hope was standing at the wall of windows that made up the back of her house, and she immediately pushed the disappearing sliding glass doors into each other, inviting me in.

"Good God!" I exclaimed as I ran inside the kitchen.

"Um-hmm," she mumbled, shaking her head. "Looks like you finally got to meet the press. How'd ya like 'em?"

"I've never seen anything like that before. They're like vultures, swooping in to pick at your body. Only, you don't know you're dead until you see them."

"Exactly, my dear," she agreed, stretching out each syllable of every word.

"Did she make it back?" Mama D hollered from the other room.

"I got her, Mama!"

Mama D came hurrying into the kitchen, her round behind moving faster than her little legs could carry her. "Y'all want some food?"

"Lord, woman," Hope said, smacking her forehead with the palm of her hand.

"I was just asking is all!" Mama D shot back.

"Actually, I'd love something to eat," I said. "Thank you for thinking of us," I pulled her into me, inhaling the faint scent of fried chicken en-grained in her clothing.

"I'm going to take a shower, and then I'll come out and help. Make sure you leave me something to do. I'm not freeloading over here."

"Better close the blinds before you get in the shower!" Hope yelled as I disappeared into the bedroom. "Otherwise they'll have the makings of a family album!"

The warmth of the water gave me goose bumps, and an unconscious smile spread across my lips. I thought of Kessler.

Damn them for making me feel sorry for him.

I was torn, feeling like my arms were being pulled in two different directions. Half of me—the half I had experienced today—understood why Kessler was a mess. My other half, the one that had been in a hotel hallway watching my boyfriend sneak a woman out of his room, wanted to punch him in the balls. But people don't stay together for fifty years because relationships are easy. They take work; you both do.

I dried off and checked my phone. The scenario was similar to what it had been like after everyone thought Jack died. I scrolled through the list of missed calls. Most, were from my friends. Some, however, were from the gossiping ladies of the Southside of Kansas City. I didn't need to listen to those voice mails, because I knew they had been made under the guise of sympathy. Not one of those women had called me since I left Kansas City. I was sure the rumor mill had started going at full speed once the pictures of Kessler hit the news. I knew every one of those fakers would have loved to get the firsthand scoop from Kessler's jilted girlfriend, but I wasn't giving interviews today.

I pulled up the recent call list and tapped my best friend's name. Leslie Abbot answered on the first ring.

"Annie. Are you okay?" she asked, using the pity voice of the sad phases.

"It's not as bad as you think."

"How? I saw the news, Annie. How is it not bad? Because right now, even Carl wants to kick his ass."

I couldn't help but laugh. The image of Leslie's husband trying to beat down Kessler in a street fight gave me the giggles.

"Tell Carl to settle down. I'd hate for him to rip his khaki pants or lose a button off his freshly pressed shirt."

Leslie's mental image obviously connected with mine, and we both couldn't stop the laughter.

"Should we still come to Nashville?"

"Yes, of course! I'm desperate to see you girls, and everyone has already bought her plane ticket. I can explain the details later, but I know Kessler didn't have sex with that woman. He certainly shat where he ate, but I can prove he's passed out in those pictures."

"Okay... I don't want to upset you, but what if they did it before he passed out?" she cautiously asked.

"As Mama D would say, the devils in the details. Don't worry about me. Can you call the other girls and make sure no one is backing out? I have a great weekend planned for us, and I can't wait to introduce you to Hope. You're going to love her!"

"I'm excited to meet her. I'll call everyone else. Love you!" she said, hanging up.

With the island countertop already filled of food, Mama D was in full mama mode. She was so predictable, and I loved that about her.

"Let's eat!" She crooned with the biggest smile.

Hope was right: that woman loved nothing more than making people miserably full. We gathered at the kitchen table and continued the life-long ritual of bitching about men.

"If I hadn't waxed myself raw, I would have gotten to the hotel before Kessler even thought about going out with Wade," I said while stuffing my face with a heavily buttered biscuit.

"Don't you even think about blaming yourself, because that's a bunch of bullshit," Hope lectured. "Kessler made this mess and dragged you into it with him. Just because he got his feelings hurt when he thought you and Jack were back together doesn't give him an excuse to run off and bang the next skank that saunters by. I've been out on the road, Annie, and there are a hundred in every city, not thinking about the wife or the family at home. All they want is fifteen minutes of celebrity dick."

"Language!" Mama D said, slapping Hope on the shoulder. "Y'all have a lot to learn about men. They can't help their feelings when they see a pretty woman, much less control themselves when one initiates interest in them."

"Puh-lease!" Hope retaliated, turning to challenge her mother's accusation.

"It's true," Mama D responded. "Annie, a man's penis is located on the outside of his body—"

Hope cut her off. "Gross, please let this be the last thing you have to say about a penis."

"We're all adults here, and I think Annie is in need of an anatomy lesson," Mama D continued.

"You were married to the same man for thirty years. What makes you an expert on any other man besides daddy?"

"You may think I've been old the entire time you've known me, but before I met your father, I had plenty of Southern suitors. Unless you're gonna add value to the conversation, pipe down so I can talk. As I was saying, men think about sex externally, because the penis is attached on the outside of the body. I'm not even sure if it's actually connected to the brain. Their sex drive is like that of wild animals—they're always hungry, and always in search of food. Once they find a food source, they stuff their faces until satisfied; only after feeling the effects of fullness do they think to look up. Men are full of more corn than Tennessee whiskey, and their capacity for emotional insight is underwhelming. Women are the opposite. They think of sex as an all-encompassing journey from the body to the mind. We internalize sex, because the vagina is on the inside of the body. It all makes perfect sense." She spoke proudly, while ripping a piece of chicken from the bone. "To a man, the only internal part of sex is the orgasm, and even that finds its own way out." She was now shaking the bone at both of us.

"Dear God, help us all," Hope prayed, steadying her hands on the table. "I love you, Annie, but hearing my mama use the word *orgasm* is something I can never un-hear. I can't turn time on that one."

She got up and started putting food away, but Mama D wasn't finished schooling me yet.

"All I was sayin', is, men are creatures of habit, and I believe it's harder for them to change their ways. It doesn't make it right, it just makes it so."

"If what you're saying is true," I replied, "then Kessler shouldn't have strayed, because I was the first woman he loved since being married to his ex-wife. He told me he'd never felt our kind of love before, and I believed him. I could see it in the way he looked at me."

"Honey, that just proves my point. You don't drown by fallin' into water. You drown 'cause you don't know how to swim. Kessler *will* learn how to swim with you, but right now, he's still tryin' to figure out how to tread water."

I sat there, letting the ridiculousness of her absolute logic set in.

"I'm scared we've been through too much already. This isn't a normal relationship."

"Sometimes you have to tear it down before you can build it back up," she said, grabbing my hand and changing the tone of her voice. "Look what scares you in the face, and try to understand it."

"Thank you, Mama D. You're a very insightful woman, even if it takes me a while to catch on."

"Get in line, baby. Sometimes I'm too smart for my own good. Now, let's go have some fun," she said with a wicked smile.

We looked out the front window to see law-breaking reporters standing on the lawn. One was trying to climb up a large oak tree to capture the perfect picture.

"Come on, y'all. In here," Hope said, motioning for us to follow her into the garage. She took the metal cover off a large red button set way back into the wall. "Okay, can y'all see 'em out there?"

Mama D and I went to the window.

"Fire!" Mama D yelled.

And swear to God, when Hope pressed that red button, it was like a Taser gun had shot the man out of that tree. He fell to the ground, landing on his back and grabbing his legs, and at the same time, trying to stand up and run away. He swerved and stumbled like a drunken sailor as he tried to get back to the safety of a public road. Mama D laughed so hard that drool ran down the side of her mouth.

"Oh! What just happened?" I asked, totally confused. "Is he okay? He fell out of there like he had been struck by lightening!"

"He did!" Hope responded. "Well, somethin' like that anyway. Wade has electricity hooked up to the trees around our house for that exact reason. The voltage plugs into the sprinkler system, like psychotic Christmas lights. Paparazzi think they're smart, and they climb up on the branches, hopin' to get a picture of us to sell. They haven't gotten any since we've had this red button." She was still giggling about her disturbing victory over the press.

"Y'all are sick, and a little crazy," I said, unable to keep from smiling.

"There's that word again. We're bringing her over!" Mama D hollered, throwing her head back and putting her arm around my waist. "Honey, in the South, we sit crazy on the front porch and hand it a cocktail. Who wants more food?"

KESSLER

I was nervous about how the crowd would react tonight, wondering if they would accept me as the musician they'd grown to love, or reject my new gigolo status.

People didn't spend hundreds of dollars on tickets, drinks, and a night out to a concert without expecting something in return. I had a partnership with my fans, and even though the partnership fluttered in and out between album releases and concerts, we both had an obligation to our relationship. I kept them in mind when writing songs, walking a fine line between reinventing the sound of each new album, and never losing my signature voice. In return, they bought and promoted my music with the best marketing that money can't buy: word of mouth.

When performing live, I brought all of my energy to the stage, and I kept my staple songs in the rotation. Every musician knows—even though we're dying to get new stuff out into the world—no one goes to a concert wanting to hear 70 percent new music. The partnership with my fans was a delicate equation, another balancing act, and if I tipped the scales too much one way or another, we both walked away disappointed.

When I was twenty years old and playing a honky-tonk outside of Amarillo, Texas, my band and I got our first taste of this equation. As the Panhandle summer evening went into full swing, the cowboys demanded to hear some country music. When I say *cowboys*, I don't mean suit-and-tie nine-to-fivers, who wear boots on a Friday night. I mean the kind of men who drive tractors more than trucks, sweating their balls off in oil fields or standing in shit while loading cattle.

The band set up behind a chain-link fence, and as soon as I walked out on stage, my heart became a lump in my throat. We played cover songs—even though I was only twenty, I wasn't stupid—but throughout the entire set, those men threw anything that would shatter into the fence. After our set, I was beat down and broken, smelling like warmed-over Lone Star beer and tending to the bloody cuts on my skin from the bottle pieces that had flown across the stage. I felt so sorry for myself, because I thought they'd hated us. It was my first realization that I might not have the guts to make it on the road.

As soon as the next band went on stage, something wonderful happened. The crowd treated them the exact same way. The crowd didn't hate us; they loved us, and broken beer bottles thrown at our faces were how they showed their affection. That night in Amarillo, I learned the importance of understanding my fans, and how serious my job to entertain them was. I had to take them away from the bullshit of the previous week, and make sure the show was good enough to last them through the next. Looking back, it was the most important lesson I ever learned on the road.

As the lights went down and the crowd rose up, I centered myself. Trying not to think about anything else, I focused on those people out there, who had chosen to spend their night with me. They had paid for a three-hour vacation, and I was going to give them one.

I was humbled by two standing ovations and homemade signs reading, "We're with you, Kessler!" and "Drop that ho, and do another show!" That one was my favorite. The fans did much more for me that night than I could ever do for them.

When Wade entered the stage, we high-fived and got to work on the crowd. The end of our second song was my cue to exit. I let Wade have the fans to himself.

I sat backstage and watched Wade work his magic. The women loved him. I mean they *loved* Wade. At forty-seven years old and with seventeen albums in his repertoire, he was in the best shape of his life. He had a damn near perfect family, and he had never been unfaithful to his wife. Not ever. It was amazing to me that a man who acted like a child when he got some alcohol into him could have his life perfected to the smallest millimeter, shitting gold on a daily basis. That's not to say that he hadn't taken the long road—which also happened to be the same road I was traveling on—to reach that point. The scars on his knuckles matched the scuffs on his buckle, and Wade had earned his position in life by fighting tooth and nail to get there.

I went back to my dressing room and pulled out my phone.

Nothing from Jack.

Maybe I was insane for believing he would step up and help me prove to Annie that Carlie had fabricated those pictures. But, for some reason, I did. I felt it. Even though he would never know it, I followed his directions and erased his number. I was showing a sign of good faith, if only to myself. I wanted to move forward with my life, to continue to make responsible choices.

I pulled up Annie's name in my contact list and stared at the letters glowing back at me. I wanted to call her so badly, but hearing her voice would only pacify me in that moment. As soon as we hung up, I would miss her even more.

After the concert, I headed back to my hotel (alone) and got ready to travel to the next show. The band was going out on the town again, but there was no way in hell I was leaving my room until daybreak. With the doors locked and the TV off, I fell asleep to the memories of St. Croix, and to the hope that Annie and I would soon be together again.

JACK

J ust as I'd planned, all the identification materials Francesca needed to close John Savage's bank accounts had been perfectly compiled. It was only nine o'clock, and we still had time for dinner and a practice round of role-playing. She had to be perfect—more perfect than she already was.

I sent her a text to meet me at the same restaurant, but she responded with the name of a different one. Going out on another ledge, I said I'd be there soon.

Francesca sat at a booth along the back wall of the Italian restaurant. I smiled in spite of myself, wholeheartedly accepting the nonverbal gesture she had extended me.

"Hello, Jack Allen," she said with a smile.

I love the way she says my whole name. My real name.

"Hello, Francesca. You look lovely tonight."

She continued smiling shyly, unable to take a full drink of her red wine because her smile got in the way.

"You can call me Frannie. Everyone else does."

"You mentioned that before, but if it's all right with you, I'll stick with Francesca. I like the way your name rolls off my tongue."

"We have that settled then. Shall we order first, before the business?"

"That sounds fine. What's good here?"

"Everything!" she exclaimed. "This is the most authentic food in the city, from my part of Italy."

"And where exactly is your part of Italy?" I was intrigued by even small tidbits about her.

"Reggio di Calabria," she answered in perfect Italian. "Reggio is a large city on the southern shore of the peninsula, across the Strait of Messina from Sicily. It's known as the toe of the boot."

"Did you like growing up there?"

"Not really. The coastline is beautifully pebbled, but for me, the area has an ugly past." She stared into her empty wine glass and twirled a straw. The waiter approached for a refill.

"Is that why you moved around so much?"

She smiled, instead of closing herself off from my probing questions.

"You were listening," she said with surprise. "I usually have to yell or make big gestures to convince people to listen to me. It's all boobs and ass with most men. I'd given up hope of anything else. Thank you, Jack Allen, for giving me hope."

"I'll listen to you for as long as you would like to talk, Francesca. You know, you don't have to call me by my full name. You can just call me Jack."

"I know, but it seems to me that you have missed out on so many years of hearing your own name. I should help you make up for lost time."

"You already have." I held my wine glass across the table toward her and waited for her to clink her goblet against mine.

She pulled a fresh straw out of her purse—the same as last night—and dropped the long end into her glass.

"I have to ask. What's with the straws?"

She nonchalantly shrugged her shoulders and said, "My grandmother used to give them to me, to bribe me to stay quiet while she worked. It was the only nice gesture she ever made toward me, so I've always used them. Straws are useful for a number of things. You'd be surprised."

"I'll take your word for it," I replied, reveling at her quirkiness.

She ordered my meal in the most spectacularly fluid conversation with the waiter, and then, as we waited for our food, she told me about her life. Apparently her parents had died when she was still a child, same as mine, and she had been passed around her family, until they stopped noticing she was there. Once she moved to northern Italy, she was officially disowned—there was very bad blood between the two sides of the country.

Mezzogiorno. It was considered painfully uncivil, she told me, when northerners used that word to describe their southern countrymen.

Northern Italians welcomed travelers (and money) from all countries, even going so far as to translate into several different languages on signage and in speech, to help visitors enjoy their stay. Capitalism was in

143

full swing, with tours and wine tastings, while the smaller towns made money from hostels and restaurants.

The jagged cliff line of southern Italy was less populated with tourists than the sprawling hills of the north. The intensely lived way of life was adored by those on holiday, but most visitors only traveled a short distance, and didn't actually move beyond the southern side of Rome. In the south, Italian pride and the traditions of the Old World ran as deep as the ocean resting on the rocks. The homes that teetered along the cliffs looked as though they had been cut from the same rock they sat on, leaving little, if any, transition between earth-made stone and manmade architecture.

I enjoyed the meal she had chosen for me, but I liked her company more. After the second bottle of wine, I lost hope of rehearsing her bank appearance, but John Savage could wait another day. I'd waited for this day for years, and I wanted it to be flawless. I could wait, too.

Francesca's eyes shined when she discussed the prospect of traveling the world. In my small amount of profiling that night, I got the idea that she was ready to begin again, in another town, at any moment.

For my benefit, she spoke mostly in English. But my blood pressure spiked when she threw in the occasional Italian word, rolling her tongue along the back of her upper teeth and pursing her lips together, speaking in slow motion.

"Say something to me in Italian," I asked her.

She sat back in the booth, and without so much as a moment's hesitation, she said, *"Non ho intenzione di fanculo, Giacomo."*

The words flowed more softly than a freshwater creek, and my mind swam with the possible meanings.

"Will you translate that to English?"

She nodded her head and leaned across the table. My dick instantly became alive as her plump lips closed in on me. She seemed to relish my obvious enjoyment of her closeness, and she dragged our moment out as long as possible.

Finally, she translated: "I'm not going to fuck you, Jack."

Damn, what the hell just happened?

144

I'd let her play me, and she had executed the insult flawlessly. Suddenly, I wasn't worried about her bank performance. She would be Oscar-worthy.

ANNIE

S neaking through the arbor back to my side of the yard, I followed the dirt path through the lawn, which was so worn down that it no longer had the ability to grow grass. As I walked along the trail, I thought of Kessler. His feet were the reason behind the dirt. He'd gone back and forth across this stretch of clearing for either: a party, advice, or food. And, each time he came back home, I suspected he was full of all three.

I was suspicious of loitering reporters, and my eyes darted back and forth through the trees while my ears stayed vigilant. Until that day, I hadn't realized how deep violations could feel when your personal space is attacked and your character defiled. How could anyone become accustomed to this lifestyle? That was a question that needed serious consideration.

I busied myself with housecleaning while I waited for my friends to arrive. What a different scenario this girls' trip would be compared to our trip to St. Croix. Last fall, my life had been flipped upside down when my marriage ended in the worst possible way. Then, after I'd found the lockbox in my basement, I had become obsessed with the next clue and then the next, unable to focus on anything but Jack. Until I met Kessler.

At the time, I had been comfortable in misery, but unbeknownst to me, I still had room for joy. Fate intervened in the form of a man waiting for me in St. Croix, who would show me just how easily I could tap into that joy. He loved me—I knew he did—but like anyone who takes another chance at love, I also chanced the possibility of heartbreak.

Don't let that be us. We deserve to be happy.

The gate buzzer rang like a doorbell. I prayed it wasn't a reporter. I pressed the speaker, and a carful of frantic women hysterically screamed at me from the other side.

"Open the gate and let us in!" Tori yelled, while the others filled in the background noise with their voices.

I'd completely forgotten that the girls would have to drive through the mess of vultures. They had been forced to stop at the gate until I buzzed them in.

"I'm so sorry! Is the gate opening?" I unnecessarily yelled back.

Turning the camera on—I always forgot to turn the camera on—I saw reporters swarming around their town car, shoving cameras and microphones up against the windows of the Lincoln. I watched closely as the car pulled through and, making sure one of those leeches didn't slide through the black iron fence, I turned the alarm back on and ran to the front door.

The car's back doors opened simultaneously, and my best friends poured out.

These girls were my heart. We had been through so much—marriage, babies, divorce, and death—and we'd done it all together. How was anyone expected to flourish amid life's victories or defeats without friends? The notion seemed impossible, not to mention a depressing way to live. They'd picked me up from the bottom and, together, lifted me to the top—they were my encouragers, sounding boards, teachers, and companions. My life wasn't as full without them.

"Hey!" we all yelled at the same time, dancing around and hugging each other.

Even though they had driven from the airport in the same car, it was only now that we were finally all together.

"My God," Tori said in disbelief.

"How long have they been out there?" Claire chimed in.

"I don't really know. I guess since the story broke," I said. They all looked at me with the sad eyes. "I've been spending the night with Hope. I did get to see one of them electrocuted, though. That was nice."

"Jesus, Annie, you live here?" Jenna said, changing the subject while surveying the expansive landscape and enormous brick Tudor home.

"Yep, but I've been going back and forth on that for the last few days."

"Kessler Carlisle lives here. I'm staying in Kessler Carlisle's house for the weekend!" Leslie exclaimed, her voice escalating at the reality of her celebrity moment. "I'm sorry, Annie, I know you're mad at him, but you need to give me just a minute with this. As soon as the tour is over, I'll go back to being mad at him, too."

"I don't even know if I'm mad anymore. I'm something, but I don't think mad is the right word. I'll explain once y'all get settled."

All four pairs of eyes looked at me, and I knew exactly what they were thinking.

"I'm not sure why I keep saying that word. It's the third time I've said *y'all* in the last two days. I blame Hope and Mama D, who I can't wait to introduce you to. Spend thirty minutes with them, and they'll have you scratching your heads, trying to figure out what the hell they're talking about. Come on, let's go inside!"

"Everyone can have her own room," I continued, "unless someone wants to bunk up. Whatever you want to do is fine with me."

We painstakingly went over every inch of the house, while Leslie took about two hundred selfies. Because we were stopping at every photograph on the wall to oooh and ahhh at all the different people in them, it took us over an hour. We spent at least thirty minutes in Kessler's downstairs studio alone, and we had to stop a second time when passing the same pictures.

"If you were staying the weekend in Tom Petty's house, you'd take your sweet time, too!" Leslie barked. "This is it for me. These are my people. I've grown up listening to all the songs the people in these photographs sang. I can die a happy woman. Now, let's drink."

"I have wine for the fancy girls, and for us," I pointed my finger at Tori, "I have vodka and Crystal Light. Let's hang here tonight, and tomorrow we can go over to Hope's house. We'll only stay a little while, and then maybe we can take a swim. We can go wherever you want tomorrow night. Saturday is Kessler's concert. Is everyone okay with staying in tonight and catching up?"

The question was asked out of courtesy, because I already knew the answer. The first night of our girls' trips was strictly reserved for talking. Every year, we each brought our photographs from college. (Back then, you had to take your film into the store to be developed, and three days later you walked out with pictures you actually held in your hands.) We each contributed our own large envelope filled of random pictures from Willie's or the Fieldhouse, Quinton's or Tonic, the house on Rollins Street, the softball games at Cosmo Park, Halloween's and several dance parties. This was by far my favorite night of our get-togethers. The whole weekend was still ahead of us, and the rest of the world ceased to exist.

"Are we allowed to talk about Kessler yet?" Claire asked, more frankly than her sweet demeanor usually allowed.

"No, not yet. Not until I'm on my third drink. Whip out the pictures," I instructed.

We laughed at our horrible outfits, namely the ones with the handkerchief tops that only had material on the front and two strings holding the back together. All of our cheeks still had baby fat, and not a wrinkle appeared on any of our faces, even though we were always smiling. There seems to be a reaction for every action; if wrinkles were a consequence of years of laughter, then I was happy to take my punishment.

"Thank God that clothing phase is over," I said. "Babies, we were just babies in these pictures." I sat back in my chair and thought about how naïve I was in those days.

I had learned so much since then, some good lessons and some bad. But, all of those lessons had brought me to this point, and I wasn't sorry about any of them.

Well, almost any of them. There was one bodily function that I felt was my right as a woman, and when the conversation turned to kids, my one regret in life surfaced. It always did.

I got everyone another round of drinks, and I listened to the girls talk about their husbands and kids. They hammered out sleeping, eating, and back-talking issues. Leslie had the most advice to give, since her daughters were the oldest and she'd already been through most of the difficult toddler times. I was happy they had each other to turn to when problems arose, but I also knew there were plenty of mass texts and emails throughout the years that I'd had no reason to be a part of.

"Okay, no more kid talk," Jenna directed. "We're on vacation. You're on your third drink," she said to me. "Can we talk about him now?"

All eyes narrowed and ears perked up.

"Yes," I sighed. "What do you want to know?"

Everyone started in at once with chatter and opinions, questioning every detail of the last few days and leaving no room for any answers.

"Whoa, whoa!" I yelled, waving my arms like an air traffic controller. "I'll just tell you what happened."

I started with the waxing portion of the program, and true to her nature, Leslie cracked herself up. I knew she would be the one to laugh at my painful procedure, but whenever she started laughing, her giggles had a way of permeating any serious situation. I told them about the Savoy Hotel, and I laid out every detail of who stood where and who said what, just so we wouldn't have to rehash it later. Then we all discussed every-one's reaction to turning on the news and seeing Crotch Rocket with my boyfriend, naked in bed. After a full round of slander, bitchiness, and idle threats, which only your best friends would make, we were finally all up to speed.

"How could you think he's innocent in that situation, Annie?" Leslie asked, worried that I might suddenly care about him being a celebrity, and that I might be willing to sweep his indiscretions under the rug.

"I didn't say he was innocent. Taking a woman to his hotel room—and everything that led to that point—is asshole. What I said was that I could prove he didn't have sex with her. From what Wade told Hope, Kessler finished an insane amount of whiskey before he ever left the restaurant. That girl was at his table and all over him, but Wade said Kessler didn't encourage anything. He wasn't making out with her, although he didn't send her away, either. His participation was with his drink, not his com-pany. Kessler had seen Jack kiss me in a restaurant downtown, and I sus-pect his ego was the reason he tried to give it a go with the whore."

"What!" They all started in again, and if I hadn't loved them so much, I would have gone to bed right then, just to mess with them. Instead, I laughed and poured myself another drink.

"Are we all comfortable?" I asked. They hunkered down for part two of the story. "Yes, Jack came to see me, and he did kiss me, but I told him it was over. I told him I loved Kessler, and he needed to let me go. When Kessler saw us kissing, he thought I was gone for good—at least that's what Wade said. So, I don't really blame him for getting hammered and letting some skank fall all over him. Is everyone following so far?" I asked to a quietly nodding group of heads. "The reason I know he was set up is because his blackout-drunk face was clearly captured in those pictures. And ladies, I hate to burst your celebrity bubble, but Kessler couldn't have gotten it up for the Virgin Mary, even if the command were from God himself. Look at this." I walked to the kitchen TV and cued up the footage I'd recorded, pausing at an enlarged picture.

"See all this stuff?" I pointed to a dress, a pair of jeans, a shirt, and some women's makeup, all left on the desk in the background of the pic-ture. "All of the clothes are perfectly folded, and the makeup is sorted out in a line. Either the maid tidied up while they were fucking, or this girl has OCD, and she made things perfect because she couldn't help herself. I've lived with Kessler for ten months, and not once have I seen him fold any clothes. He's usually digging through the pockets of dirty pants on the floor, looking for his car keys."

I certainly had their attention now, and I thought I had their agreement.

"Well, what do you know about that," Claire replied, still staring at the picture on the TV. "So, you think she took those pictures to get paid."

"I do, and she obviously did."

Everyone started in again. This time the slut-shaming was high-voltage.

KESSLER

Turning on the television, I was pleasantly surprised to that find more pressing news than my sex scandal was being covered. My porno pictures still made an appearance, but apparently I wasn't considered a top story that day, which was fine by me. I couldn't help thinking about Carlie, and wondering if she'd done this out of desperation or complete arrogance. Did she like the miniscule amount of fame, or was she following the teachings of a mentor? A definite answer didn't matter, because the deed had been done. Any way you sliced it, she was a wrecking ball who had demolished me.

My ringing phone pulled me out of my thoughts.

"Private Caller" flashed across the screen.

It's Jack!

"Yes!" I yelled into the phone, overly excited that I had been right about Jack.

"You're an idiot," he said.

"I know, and that's why I called you."

"You have three minutes before a trace happens, and I hang up. I suggest you keep your mouth shut and maximize your time."

I wasn't sure if I should waste time by saying *yes, I understand* or if I should just keep quiet. I was reduced to a child again by the authority of his voice. So, I kept my mouth shut.

"Good," he said, seemingly happy not to hear my voice. "First, you're a colossal jackass. Why you would mess with that trashy woman is beyond me, but I'll admit I had a part in pushing you toward her. You were right about Annie—all of it. Everything you said to me in the bistro was almost her words verbatim, and ultimately, I tricked you into fucking up."

I thought he might help me, but I had no idea he was calling with a confession of sins. With only three minutes of his time, my gloating was out of the question. It was also completely unnecessary. This was not the Jack I'd heard about. He was going against the grain of his personality, and his offering up of this type of information was almost unsettling. Now I was on guard for another trick.

"Second, I'm guessing you've been wallowing in self-pity, because if I know Annie as well as I think I do, she's mad as hell. However, she's also an extremely forgiving person. Take our relationship, for example. I was supposed to be dead, and when she found out I was alive, she didn't kill me herself. She's a saint in my book. She'll forgive you, not because you deserve forgiveness, but because she believes in happy endings. And, for some ungodly reason, she wants her fairytale forever to be with you."

I smiled at the mental picture of Annie confirming her love for me to Jack. I'd known from the first moment I saw her that she was *my* forever, and hearing Jack seal our fate together made my heart instantly swell to a medically abnormal size.

"Now, don't start thinking you can ever screw up again, because even though she loves you, she'll also drop you hard on your ass. I should know. Your situation with Carlie Sexton—yes, for the love of God, her last name is actually Sexton—you never saw coming."

"What do you mean?" I asked before I could stop the words from escaping my mouth.

"Do you want me to answer questions, or do you want information? You have forty-five seconds left."

"Sorry," I whispered.

"You aren't the first man who's slipped through the sexually transmitted diseased hands of Carlie Sexton. I checked her out through Intel, a government website I have access to, and she's scammed a number of men who thought it would be easier to pay her to go away, rather than lose their families. You, however, are her first attempt at fame. She probably saw you as her biggest payday yet, and instead of blackmailing you, she went over your head and collected her check from the media. If I weren't going to get involved, I'd tell you to get a lawyer, but since I'm saving your ass *again*," a point he continued to make, "the only thing you need to worry about is your dick swelling up with a particularly special brand of trailer park STD. Since there are only ten seconds left, I'll just tell you: I'm handling it, and she won't be a problem for anyone again."

And then the line went dead.

Oh my God. Is he going to kill her? Jesus, I didn't want her dead!

With no number to call back, I filled with panic. What if Jack wiped this woman off the face of the earth? I knew he certainly had the skills to back up a promise like the one he'd just made, but I'd never meant for him to physically harm her.

My only hope was for him to call me back, but at the moment, I had to pack the rest of my clothes and head to the bus. The next city awaited; it always did.

JACK

After dinner with Francesca, I strolled back to my hotel room on a high that only two hours of quality conversation with a woman could give. She was a mixture of all things opposite, and even though I couldn't conceive of how all those different personality traits were housed in one woman, the results fascinated me. Francesca was sweet and salty, introverted and then suddenly an explicit extrovert, and strangely quirky with her extensive supply of straws.

The one constant through all of her personalities was her smile.

Ahhh, I thought, picturing it. *You've gone and lost it, Jack.*

Although I hadn't felt this way about someone since my first date with Annie, the feeling was unmistakable, and it wasn't something you could ever forget. I was swooning over a woman.

A cold shower eased my swoon and turned my thoughts to a side matter that obviously needed to be handled. After drying off, I opened my laptop and Googled my once-archrival's name. I had researched Kessler Carlisle several times over the previous months, but I'd never gotten these kinds of results.

Jesus Almighty. No wonder he called me. I'm all he's got.

As I scrolled through page after page of the worst pornographic iPhone photos, the competitor in me had to laugh. Only a complete numbskull would leave an opportunity like this wide open. But, the side of me that would always feel protective of Annie knew I needed to help this jackass out of the mess he'd created.

Going onto the Intel website could have been dicey, but I'd stolen plenty of login-in names and passwords before exiting the program. Some of them would be obsolete by now. The dinosaurs who knew as much as third graders about technology would be the easiest targets.

Quickly and expertly, I logged onto Intel and ran a check on this woman.

What was amazing to me was that the media had plastered naked pictures of two people in bed together, with only one of their names running across the screen. The woman who'd sold these photos of herself with another man was the person with a right to privacy. And it wasn't like the American people noticed or even cared. These low-grade morals were why the media could make money on you when you we're on the way up, and then again when they knocked you off your pedestal—only to make another round of cash on your "out of the ashes" rise to the top.

I'll never understand why people feed this machine, I thought as I noticed how many hits each picture had accumulated on Google.

"Ah-ha!" I said aloud. "I got her!"

Carlie Sexton, *Jesus, the irony*, was a forty-two-year-old divorcée with two grown children, both of whom had spent time in jail for petty crimes. In fact, all three members of the Sexton family had brushed up against the law. Her rap sheet was nonviolent, but plenty long. Yet, charges never seemed to get filed on her; there had been a handful of arrests, but never any convictions.

Looking through the specifics of each arrest, I saw that they all bordered on blackmail, and they all involved men. Carlie had made a profession out of Sexton. She blatantly stole either money or property from married men, and she took enough of their integrity to get paid before giving it back. My guess was that a couple thousand dollars wasn't worth losing their families over.

I did find several parole violations, and if the Louisville Police Department got wind of her latest scam, she would most definitely earn herself a new mug shot. When the camera was turned on Carlie, the pictures didn't turn out so well—some of her mug shots were beyond hideous. Without a nice dress and plenty of makeup, Carlie Sexton looked like life, and several men had ridden her hard. I might give her a little leeway for the fluorescent jailhouse lighting, but Christ Almighty, I could almost see the tire tracks running across her face.

Quickly jotting down her last known addresses—both of which were in Louisville—and her recent phone numbers, I knew I had the goods on ole Carlie. I'm not a lowly looking man, and she might be happy to see me at first. But, she would only need to spend a small amount of time with me before changing her mind.

I felt that I was going way over and beyond my responsibilities as exhusband (or something like that) by helping Kessler nail this bitch. As I saw things, Kessler and the rest of the men in Kentucky would thank me if they knew what I was going to do.

They say a million dollars is a million problems—only the people who don't have that kind of money say that—and John Savage would soon have sixty fewer problems in his life.

Maybe I should introduce him to Carlie.

ANNIE

Awake before anyone else, I began wiping down the kitchen counters and filling the trashcan with empty wine bottles. The smell of red wine took me back to St. Croix, and to the last time I had gorged myself on pinot noir. Every now and again I'd have a glass, but after over-consuming fermented alcohol, I couldn't find the joy in even small doses.

With the entire day ahead of us, my excitement brimmed over. Mama D was catering a huge spread of food for the girls, and I guessed that she was already flying around her kitchen. The smell of something fried would soon be wafting across the yard, stronger than the sound of a dinner bell, letting us know that lunch was ready.

As the girls trickled downstairs, one at a time, I pulled out coffee mugs to help us start the day.

"How did you sleep in Kessler Carlisle's house?" I asked Leslie, adding a wink to my question.

"Fantastic, but the stars in my eyes have already lost some of their glow. When you see someone play your favorite songs live on stage, you tend to forget they're regular people. He doesn't seem like that big of a deal to me anymore," she said.

"Well, I'm glad to hear you say that, because he's not. But, at the same time, to me, he's so much more."

"I take it you're back to swooning?" Jenna asked, picking at a pastry I'd gotten from my favorite bakery that morning.

"Yes," I agreed with an impossible smile. "I think I am."

"Thank God," Tori said. "You deserve to get properly laid and just coast for a while. Any more of these ups and downs and you're likely to get car sick. I don't know how you aren't locked up in a padded room yet."

"Are those reporters still out front?" Claire asked.

"The cul-de-sac was empty when I went out for muffins early this morning," I said, "but I'm sure there will be some stragglers hanging around today." I made a quick check of the front gate camera. "The coast is still clear. After breakfast, let's clean up and walk around downtown. Franklin has the cutest boutiques, with a mish-mash of all things different. Since you guys are staying in the heart of county music this weekend, and since we're going to Kessler's concert tomorrow night, someone has to buy a pair of cowboy boots! It would be a shame if no one left with a staple item."

"I don't need any more boots. What's another Tennessee staple?" Tori asked.

"I don't know. Moonshine, maybe?"

"I guess I know what souvenir I'm taking home." Tori laughed out her words.

***

We spent a few hours strolling in and out of niche boutiques. The girls kept commenting on the quaintness of downtown. Claire thought it looked like it was straight out of *Southern Living* magazine. She was right—every season framed the Tennessee oak trees like a living picture. After she had gone into the last vintage home store—under the premise of doing research for her antique store in South Carolina—we headed back to the car for an early supper with the Rutledge girls.

Mama D had her signature spread of Southern food laid out all over the kitchen. Her face beamed with pride, not only because of the food perfection, but also because she was important enough to be introduced to my friends. I saw her happiness exposed in her smile as she greeted each one of my best friends. It was like watching a groom wait at the end of the aisle for his bride.

We took our plates out to the patio, and I sat back and listened, consumed with warmth, as the closest people to family I might ever have chitchatted back and forth. It was as though they'd known each other for years.

Since Jenna was a chef at a family-style restaurant in Denver, she and Mama D hit it off instantly. She immediately began asking questions about Mama D's breading process and which herbs she'd used in the sugar snap peas. Even though Jenna was trained in the culinary arts, she always ingested edible information into her brain, and Mama D had a lifetime of experience with a skillet. I knew a mutual respect would easily form between those two.

The conversation on the other side of me was less than shocking as well. Leslie pumped Hope harder than the flattest bicycle tire, enamored with any detail Hope gave of Wade's childish shenanigans. I shot Hope a pleading, *I'm sorry look*, but true to her impeccable Southern charm, she smiled and winked, letting me know that Leslie was more than welcome to ask her anything.

Once the small talk began to dwindle, the conversation—and all eyes—turned to me.

"Is Kessler coming home before the show tomorrow night?" Mama D asked, silencing the henhouse.

"I don't know. My feelings have been too mixed up for me to call him. One minute I'm lost in thought with my arms around his neck, inhaling the scent of Old Spice, and the next I'm picturing his name running across the television screen in red letters. My heart wants to rip his clothes off, but my brain steps in and tells me to reach down and choke his nuts. If I call him and hear his voice, I'll be lost in him."

"Sounds like you already are," Tori unexpectedly offered.

"You know, if I didn't know better, I'd think you're rooting for me and Kessler," I said, turning my full attention to her. "Which shocks me, because I thought you'd be the last person to stick up for him, given the fact that your husband somewhat publicly cheated on you."

Tori laughed, clearly over her ex and the pain he'd caused her. "I agree, Annie. I'll be honest. After I saw the news, I was ready to pack your shit for you, even if you didn't want to leave him. Now that I'm here and I see you, I don't know, something's different about you. You have a life here totally opposite from what you had in Kansas City, and I don't mean the money. With Jack you seemed guarded—like most of you was available to the outside world, but only he had access to the rest of you. Your home was beautiful, but in a clinical way. The furniture seemed staged to trick a guest into thinking someone lived there. I always questioned the level of warmth. When we first walked through your house yesterday, I felt your presence inside. Even though you've only lived there a short time, I saw you in every room. The colorful bed linens, the furniture arrangement, caftans thrown over all the comfy chairs, and the random, unprofessional pictures that hang on the walls of every room: I felt like I was walking through *your* home.

"I see your face when you say his name," she continued, "and it's one I haven't ever seen before. Yes, I was burned by marriage too, and maybe that's why I've kept such a close eye on you. I'd hate for you to make the same mistake I did. But I just don't see that. Not here in Tennessee, and not with Kessler. It seems like you belong here, and always have."

By the end of her speech, every woman on the patio was blotting her eyes and draining her drink. Mama D got out of her chair and went directly over to Tori, mashing Tori's petite body into her ample, loving arms.

"My, God," Hope whispered, "You should get a job with Hallmark, on love's behalf. Well said, Tori. We should definitely drink to that!"

The chatter ramped up again, and Hope and I got everyone another round of cocktails. As I mixed a new batch of Crystal Light, she stopped filling the glasses with vodka, and I felt her eyes bore a new hole in my head.

"You might as well put your two cents in," I encouraged her. "I know you're just dying to, so go on and get it over with."

"Usually I keep my nose out of other people's personal business, but not when it concerns Kessler. He's my family, Annie. I know what he did to you was forgivably awful, but I was the one who took his phone call. I heard his voice, and I felt his excitement over the line. He was running to you, even though his entire life has been about running away. That's why he was with that girl. I bet he was so shocked at the pain of heartbreak, he didn't know what was happening to him."

"I understand what you're saying, but after we first met and he left St. Croix, he came back because he missed me. Even if I understand *why* he did what he did, you're not going to sugarcoat this for him."

"Believe me, darlin', there is no sugar left in this situation. Just remember, he came back to you in St. Croix because he had the option. That's why he was sluttin' it up with that girl, He thought he was out of options."

"Hope, I'm going to forgive him. In fact, I already have. The truth of the matter is that I'm scared he's already changed his mind about me."

"What? No way. Kessler loves you!" she gloated.

"Look at me, Hope. Since the first moment I met Kessler, my life—and most of the rest of it—has been a mess. Who would want that burden around him all the time? He's basically a simple man, and I barged in and messed all that up for him, complicating the way he lives his life."

She took my chin in her hand and smiled, gently shaking it from side to side. "Silly girl, Kessler wasn't living *until* you barged in. Whatever you decide, just remember that fact. Now, I've got a big surprise for y'all tomorrow!" she said, changing the subject and clapping her hands together.

"Please, no more surprises. Don't you think we've had enough of those?" I asked.

"It's a good surprise, and Leslie is gonna love it! The show starts at seven, so we need to leave here by six. Traffic will be a beast heading into Nashville, especially around Bridgestone Arena. That means y'all need to be showered by two. My surprise will be at your gate around that time. Buzz them in."

KESSLER

Tonight's show was a replica of the last one. My fans still loved me. I stuffed Jack and Carlie into a small corner of my mind and focused entirely on the crowd. That part was easy to do, because when the lights went down and the crowd got to their feet, the ride began. Time happened slowly at first, but the next song and then the next sped up the minutes like the fastest rollercoaster.

Once Wade took over, I went back to rest in my dressing room until I was needed for the encore. Cracking open a beer, I sat back and studied the large but vacant space. A year ago, I would have cursed the stale concrete walls, thinking my career should have demanded a more luxurious room than this one. Now, in a completely different state of mind, I was singing in a sold-out-stadium—on a whim—and who the fuck cared what my dressing room looked like?

Before Annie, my life had been too perfect, so I'd had to create things to bitch about. Too many fans, too much money, and too many people depending on me: those were the issues I thought I had. But now that I had loved and lost a woman, I could see that those supposed problems only paled in comparison to my loss.

Annie had changed me—completely for the better. For years, I had serial-dated much younger women, thinking at the time that I knew all the reasons why. Sure, the physical aspects of a twenty-five-year-old were hard to ignore; the tits alone were worth their salt. But I hadn't necessarily worked at those relationships, and when they were over I never shed a tear, or really even cared. (Even so, I loved to play my "I just don't understand" card when Hope or Mama D tried to figure out what went wrong with every next girl.)

Losing Annie had made that part of my life crystal clear. I had chosen the twenty-five-year-olds to make sure they didn't last. I'd specifically picked women who would tire of my absence, realize we had little in common, and, eventually, hit the bricks.

"Huh," I said aloud as I matured twenty intellectual years in only thirty minutes.

I wasn't pissed off at myself, and I didn't consider my life to be wasted time, because all of those choices had brought me to Annie. Even though I had no idea what I would say to her, I still prayed to God she would show up to our concert the next night.

Hope never missed it when Wade performed within a fifty-mile radius, and my faith in her coaxing abilities ran deep. I knew she would use every possible manipulation tactic to get Annie to the arena—not just because I wanted her to, but because Hope was a sucker for any love story. And besides her own, Annie and I had the next best one.

After the buzz of the concert faded, Wade and I decompressed in the vacant hotel lobby with a couple of drinks.

"Big day for you tomorrow, huh?" Wade asked while chewing the whiskey-soaked ice cubes from his rocks glass.

"Do you mean the final show?"

"Aw hell, Kessler, cut the crap. Have I ever showed concern for your performance before?"

"Well, that was a loaded question. I didn't know what you were asking about."

"Bullshit. You knew exactly what I meant. You're scared shitless that she won't show up, and you'll have to go back to your old life. Only, it won't be your old life, because now you know how good love feels. You'll have to start a new life, a shittier life, where the images and memories of the woman who once made you feel invincible will plague your every waking moment. And even when the freshness of the pain fades, you'll find that it never actually goes away. By then, the chip on your shoulder will have grown bigger, and the circle of people you love will have gotten smaller. Forget about the twenty-something girls, 'cause one day you'll wake up and realize you're too old to date *anyone*. And the real bitch of your situation is, you won't care. By that point, you'll be a lonely old man with an unjustified and self-righteous perception of what love means, and you'll live out the rest of your days unfulfilled and unadmittedly sad. When you're on your deathbed, you'll look back, able to pinpoint the one moment when you should have fallen on your knees, ground them into the dirt, and said every right word that would have made her stay. But instead, you let your pride and stupidity get in the way. You ended up wasting the rest of your life." As he finished, he held his glass in a cheers gesture, a smile on his face.

164

"What the fuck, man?" I asked, completely blown away by Wade's descriptive foresight into the next fifty years of my lonely and bitter existence. "What the hell are you doing to me?"

"Being honest. But, don't worry—whether you blow it tomorrow or manage to save your own life, I'll be your friend no matter what."

"Well, I gotta tell ya, friend, that was the worst mental picture you could have possibly painted for me. So, thanks for nothing."

"If you'd been listening, you would be thanking me, because it's the exact road you're on. If you want to enjoy the rest of your life, you'd better realize that it begins and ends with Annie. I'm not saying you won't find someone else. I'm sure you will, but she'll never feel like Annie. You best believe that, brother."

"Jesus, Wade. Don't you think I know all of this? Don't you think I want her back? I don't know what gesture to make to get her to forgive me!"

"Kess, a gesture is making coffee in the mornin', or puttin' your wet towels in the dirty clothes instead of leavin' them on the floor. Women don't want gestures. They want a display. Even if she won't say so, Annie wants you to slice open your insides like a gutted fish, and bleed out all the right words."

"If I knew the right words, I already would have said them!" I stood up, the force of my quickness knocking the chair out from under me. I was pissed at his advice, which was easier said than done.

"There he is," Wade calmly said, tapping his finger on my chest. "This is the guy who knows the right words." He placed his empty glass on the table and walked away without further comment.

Picking the chair up off the floor, I sat back down in it and rested my head on my hands.

This is going to be a long night.

JACK

The knock on my door surprised me. Francesca was early. I looked through the peephole to make sure she was the person standing on the other side, but I also took the moment to soak her up without her knowledge. She stood in a tight black dress, wearing red stilettos that matched her lips and holding to-go coffees in each hand. My day was already made.

Her smile grew as the door swung open. She handed me a coffee and walked in, without waiting for an invitation. I loved her confidence.

She looked me up and down and asked, "Were you expecting someone?"

I was confused at first, but quickly realized that she was talking about the way I was dressed.

"No, not at all. I'm sorry for my rude attire, but I just got out of the shower," I replied, still towel-drying my hair. "Please come in and make yourself comfortable. So, how did it go at the bank this morning? Did you get the secondary account set up? "

"A slice of cake," she proudly said, butchering the cliché. "I walked in and opened the account with the money you gave me. Carmela Mancini is a proud patron of Benziger Bauer Bank. I did everything you told me to do, with no mistakes. At first I was nervous, but it's amazing how powerful money can make you feel."

"Many people feel the same way, Francesca, but believe me, the power of money is an all-or-nothing game. The majority of the players end up giving all and getting nothing in return—the money always wins."

She tilted her head in silent thought, staring at me. I swore she was checking me out. From the moment I met her, she had been nothing but mixed signals. Well, except for the part when she explicitly told me she wasn't going to fuck me. That part I heard loud and clear.

She reached into her bag, pulled out the paperwork from the bank, and handed it over for me to look through.

"Let me get dressed first," I said, grabbing a T-shirt off the back of the chair she was sitting in. "Excellent, this is perfect. You've done a great job so far, Francesca," I said while thumbing through the account folder. "Would you like to have breakfast with me?"

"Again with the food," she mumbled. "I don't understand you, Jack Allen. Twice I have eaten with you, and twice I have been in your hotel room. In my country, these are the actions of a serious suitor. You are certainly serious, but maybe not about suiting me. Most of the men I've spent time with are taking their clothes off, not putting them on. If you are not interested in me, you are being extremely rude by not saying so."

Once again, Francesca had sucker-punched me in the gut with her bold and unexpected dialogue.

"I'm sorry if I've offended you," I replied, "but that's the opposite of what my actions meant. I told you before, I'm not like everyone else, and the last thing I would want to do is hurt your feelings." I knelt down and covered her soft hands with my rough and calloused fingers. "I should have been clearer about the importance of this job. People's lives depend on my finishing it—including yours. You are an integral part of my equation, and I need your help. I have to put my feelings for you aside until I know we're safe from a very nasty and powerful man. Do you understand what I'm saying?"

"Yes," she said, taking my hand and putting my fingertips to her lips. "I'm hearing you say you have feelings for me. They are the same ones I have for you."

The softness of her skin on my fingers shot pleasure through my hand and up my arm, immediately finding the pathway to my dick. Her heavy brown eyes waved me over with every slow blink of her lashes, begging me to give them a reason to close.

"Jack," she whispered, moving my hand to her cheek, "why won't you kiss me? Show me there is something more than my imagination between us."

All protocol was instantly thrown out the window. I smoothed the dark strands of her hair between my fingers, and our lips came together. Though she was an aggressive conversationalist, she was the complete opposite when our lips touched. Her upper body relaxed into my embrace, as I tried to control my yearlong, pent-up animal instincts.

Not wanting this to escalate into something she would regret, I pulled away. I enjoyed the smile that swept across her face. I wanted to make my feelings for her clear, so I gave her more truth.

"You're the first woman I've kissed in almost a year—since my ex-wife, anyways. I'd forgotten how wonderful that feels. I hope that won't be the last time you let me kiss you."

She fanned her hands across my cheeks and this time, *she* pulled my lips into hers. For a moment, I felt like a normal man in a situation that occurs a thousand times a day. Whether by saying my name or by giving me another first kiss, Francesca had the ability to momentarily erase my hyperplane surroundings. She gave me the gift of normality.

"Thank you," she whispered.

"For what?" I asked, smiling like a school boy who had just copped his first feel.

"For being honest and trusting me enough to let go. You're more normal than I gave you credit for, and probably more than you give yourself." It was as if she had been reading my mind. "Okay, let's get to work. What's next?"

We spent the next several hours going over every detail of what she should expect at the bank the next day. It wasn't safe for Francesca, Sena, or myself for me to be anywhere near the building, so Francesca would have to pull this off mostly on her own. I couldn't be in the bank holding her hand, even though there was no other place I rather would have been.

Attendance was required at my own meeting tomorrow, and I knew at least one of the interested parties would not be pleased by my arrival. We were moving into the sweet spot, and each step needed to mirror perfection if we wanted to reach the glory hole by tomorrow night.

"Let's go through everything one more time," I instructed my wilting student.

"No more times, Jack. Please, let's order room service and a bottle of wine. My brain hurts."

"If you don't get this right, your brain *is* going to hurt—not from memorization, but from the bullet lodged in your skull. One more time!" I exclaimed.

We switched places: I took her seat in the chair, while she paced the floor. Her body was erect with confidence, and without hesitation, she answered my questions as if she had been studying for this exam her entire life.

"What time do you get to the bank?"

168

"Eight-thirty AM."

"What do you do when you get there?"

"I wait on the southwest benches until I see Sena Demir walk past. I'll know it's her because of the pink scarf around her neck. I follow her inside the bank."

"Excellent. What happens when you get inside?"

"I go to the booth beside her and fill out a deposit slip for Carmela's account. Once Sena has checked her phone, I wait for her to write out the account number. I take the blank slips underneath the pile with me. I never look at her. I never talk to her. I make my own deposit and walk back out."

"During the time Sena is in the lobby, the branch manager will most likely come out to personally greet her. They don't like their multimillion-dollar clients to wait. What happens in that situation?"

"I watch for the manager, and if I see him approaching Sena, I discreetly place a pad of paper on the nearest table. He watches her write down the account number and tears the sheet off the pad. I take the pad and put it safely in my purse. No matter what, I make a deposit, so I don't seem out of place."

"What happens if you're standing next to Sena at a booth, and someone follows in behind her?"

With a big smile, she said, "I give them this," magnifying her ample cleavage, "or this," turning and rubbing her ass, just the same as she had done to me the first night we met.

I laughed as she put on a display for me, causing the suffocating seriousness in the room to evaporate.

"Last question. Where do you go after you leave the bank?"

"I go to the Sheraton Hotel, by the ferries on Lake Zurich. I check in with my new identification, under the name Carmela Mancini."

"Excellent, Francesca. I have no doubt you'll do a fantastic job tomorrow. You've put in a lot of work, and I'm very proud of you. I don't want to overload you with too much information at once, so when we meet at the Sheraton, I'll tell you about the next, and more complicated, phase of the plan."

"And my reward?" she said in an excited voice.

"Yes, and your reward."

"I'm ordering room service now," she said, waving the menu in front of me. "I'll order for both of us."

My willpower against her is becoming useless.

ANNIE

As I tossed and turned in my empty bed, my mind raced with the anxiety of what was to come. Restlessness didn't have to accompany a crisis, but it was usually associated with one. I felt as if I were a child counting down the hours until Christmas morning. I couldn't force Kessler out of my thoughts. He hadn't made any attempt to contact me since Louisville, and I thought I understood why, but assumptions had never turned out well for me. How could it be that men and women are so similar in physical form, yet emotionally, we are almost two different species?

Kessler and I had grown up with the advice and love languages of two opposite-spectrum women. Because his mother had fiercely loved his father, and then ultimately lost her heart with his death, she had taught him that the anguish of emotional misery was a casualty not worth the risk. I couldn't imagine any mother not wanting her son to experience the joy of finding the one common thread that crosses every race, species, and language barrier. Since I wasn't a mother, I could only sympathize with the immeasurable love she must have had for her son. The strongest emotion she had felt for her child was the same one she withheld from his future. Through loving default, where intimacy was concerned, Kessler's mom had kept him a child.

The love surrounding my upbringing was entirely the same, but the teachings were channeled differently. Even though I too had experienced the devastation of heartbreak, I was grateful for the memories of my parents. My grandmother had worked tirelessly to explain the fickles of love, and she showed me that the positive always outweighed the negative. With her arms constantly around my neck, and through a steady stream of encouraging words, she had planted within me the seeds of intimacy. By the time I was in high school, I had no doubt that I was worthy of love.

Kessler possessed all the abilities of love. I had seen them. His attention to detail and overwhelming compassion had shown me the man inside of him, who was desperate to break free from the child of his past.

For the most part, the roots of our past are a good thing. They keep one foot on the ground, allowing the rest of us to float in all of life's possibilities. Kessler's roots ran deep, spanning farmland and bayou throughout southern Louisiana. He bled birthplace pride. I wouldn't have fallen in love with him if he didn't.

Unfortunately, the roots of our past can also be defective, and perspective is our only hope. My prayer tonight: Kessler would sever the one dead root still clinging onto him, and he would allow himself a chance to be loved.

Both of us could have spun our Jack-and-Carlie situation in either of our favors, but if we didn't recognize the ultimate prize, we wouldn't end up together. I had already forgiven Kessler. His worldwide punishment was more severe than anything I could dish out. What I didn't know was whether Kessler could forgive himself. If he continued to revert to the boy who wouldn't work through the hard times of a relationship, all of our heartache would be for nothing.

JACK

S tepping onto the balcony, I watched the end of another Swiss day in silence. Soft wisps of orange colored the base of the sky, as the sun continued to exit behind the serrated mountains. Tiny flickers of light made their nightly debut throughout the city, like windblown flames, and the aggressive traffic of twilight swept up the remaining daylight minutes.

The beauty of Zurich was not lost on me, and juxtaposing it to Francesca created a mirror image. They both contained jagged and sharp edges that guarded their core, and from afar, both city and woman had picturesque artistry fit for a frame. You had to get up close to see the crazy. Undeniably, they both had curves that would entice you to keep looking around every next corner, pleased with what you discovered. Finding Francesca in Zurich was certainly no coincidence; this was her city.

Before the food arrived, she pulled the down comforter off the bed and began meticulously straightening out the corners, pulling it tightly across the floor for the makings of a picnic. In only a short time, I'd learned to keep my questions until the end of the program. I liked watching her surprise me with off-the-wall antics, and my attraction continued to grow with each eccentricity.

I watched her walk back and forth across the comforter, until she was satisfied with the result. She noticed me watching her, and did that sexy little tilt of her head, before coming out to the balcony to see what I was doing. As she slid the door open, a blast of wind tousled her long dark hair in every direction, covering most of her face. I couldn't help but laugh, because a more graceful woman would have pulled off an effortless transition, never losing her sex appeal. Francesca easily laughed at herself, aware of her oddities. The moment was actually more intimate than a heavily seductive one.

"Come on, Jack. I made us a carpet picnic," she encouraged, grabbing my hand and gently pulling me inside. "I don't know what you like, so I ordered fondue. There's a little bit of everything, and I think you can find something to make you happy."

"I think I already have," I confessed, completely breaking my own rules of romance.

She had been clear about sex, and I wasn't going to spoil the mood by offending her. But then, without hesitation, she slipped her hands inside my shirt. She lightly ran her nails across my nipples. Goose bumps immediately spread throughout my chest, causing a skin erection. Every part of my body was turned on. Her hands wrapped around my sides, and she waited patiently for me to kiss her again.

Her breath was warm, as I slipped my tongue inside the candy center of her mouth. Her breasts pushed firmly against my chest, and her bare foot began sliding up the inside of my pant leg. Once I felt my actual erection begin to grow, I ended our kiss, embarrassed by my lack of control. I expected her to move toward the blanket on the floor, but she stood comfortably in my embrace.

"This is nice," she whispered, resting her head on my chest.

"Yes, it is," I replied, lacking the suaveness to say anything else.

She looked up at me and said, "Let's eat."

Francesca arranged the food for easier access, while I poured the wine

.

"This is the only bottle tonight," I said, tapping the bottom against my palm. "Don't try to talk your way into another. You need to be sharp tomorrow morning, and this won't help our cause."

She didn't answer, and only rolled her eyes at my boring instructions.

I'd never had fondue before, and I was pleasantly surprised by the taste. Switzerland is known for its many gourmet cheeses, and the freshly baked bread added a nice touch. I especially enjoyed when it Francesca baited my skewer, swirled the bread around the cheese, and fed me a bite, cupping her hand underneath the bread to catch falling droplets.

We talked about our exes and growing up as orphans, chatting as friends, with little sexual energy invading our conversation. By the time I looked at my watch, it was already ten o'clock.

"We should probably clean up and call it a night," I begrudgingly but sternly said.

"Yes, Jack Allen, you're the boss."

"No, Francesca, I'm not the boss. We're equals, okay? I don't want to be the boss of someone ever again."

She replied with a smile.

She sat on the floor and handed dishes up to me, while I put them back on the cart the waiter had left us. After clearing a space, I sat back down, stretching my legs and propping myself onto one elbow to finish my glass of wine.

"Why did you choose the name Carmela for my identification cards?" she asked.

I let out a nervous chuckle and said, "Because that's what I started calling you in my head after the first time I saw you, but before I knew your real name. I guess it was just easy to remember, and when dealing in fake names, the simpler the better."

"But *why* did that name come to your mind?"

I let out a long sigh, knowing I was walking a fine line. I chose truth again. I was getting good at telling the truth. "Carmela was the first name that popped into my head. When you sat down across from me at the financial aid office, I couldn't take my eyes off you. And, that's a big deal for me, because I'm usually very focused. Your obnoxious leg-crossing and irate temper were like a train wreck, fascinating me in a strangely sick way."

"Hey!" she exclaimed, punching my shoulder. "Italians are passionate about everything. A tantrum means we deeply care."

"I'm just being honest. It's what I do now." I gave her a wink. "But you redeemed yourself with the Italian card." I paused before finishing my thought. "Your hair and your skin—especially your skin—are soft and smooth, like waves of warm caramel, and like nothing I've ever seen before. The name just seemed to fit."

An awkward silence finally found us. We both looked toward the door.

"That's the nicest compliment I've ever received," she confessed. "Ask me to stay, Jack. If we are telling truths, I want to stay here, with you. You said it yourself: I've never met anyone like you, and I don't know how long this will last. I'm not asking for you to love me. I'm not a stupid woman, but I want to know you, Jack: in every way. So, ask me to stay, because I will say yes."

I reached over to her and stroked her cheek. "I know you're not stupid. I would never think that about you. I want you to stay—please believe I do. I know something is happening between us. I can feel it. You have to understand, my life has been lived in a certain manner for a long

175

time now, and I'm not used to making rash decisions. I'm struggling with what my heart wants and what my mind is telling me to do. The only reason they differ is for your safety. I can't... no, I won't let anything happen to you. Sex fills the heart, but it complicates the mind. My mind needs to be crystal in order to protect you, along with my heart."

Her eyes filled with disappointment as she stood up. "I understand, Jack. I'll be going then, but don't worry about tomorrow. I'll be ready. I can see myself out."

I walked her to the door, but just as soon as I opened it, I slammed it shut.

Wiping my brow with the palm of my hand and completely disregarding my better judgment, I changed my mind.

"Don't leave. I haven't wanted you to leave since the first day I met you. Stay with me, Francesca."

I grabbed her waist and pulled her body against mine. Her hands found their way under my shirt again. Her lips were strong against my mouth, as I slipped my fingers into her hair and cradled the base of her head in my hand. The warmth of her tongue gradually found mine, while tiny breaths of longing passed between us. For good reason, I had kept closeness with a woman an arm's length away, and tonight, I was afraid that if I didn't cut myself off, I would devour her. I knew sex was off the table, but I still wanted her to stay.

"I have to stop now, or I won't be able," I whispered. "Please don't take this any other way than that I'm exceptionally turned on. *You* turn me on, Francesca. Will you still stay?"

"Of course, Jack. Of course, I want to stay."

She hung her dress up in the closet and pulled one of my T-shirts over her head. Watching her walk across the room, back over to me, filled me with hope. After tomorrow, there was a chance that I could live a normal life. Tonight, I had proven to myself that I was capable of love.

ANNIE

We spent the morning outside in the warm Tennessee weather, sunning ourselves by the heated pool. Most of the girls had brought books to read, but they easily switched back and forth between reading and joining one of the multiple conversations going. Our personal lives seemed to fade into the background whenever the rare opportunity for relaxing togetherness arose.

Like a ten-year-old on summer break, Tori kept jumping into the pool off the top of the waterfall. Watching her circle back around again and again, it dawned on me: I'd never taken the same plunge. So I raced her to the top, and we jumped the twenty-foot drop together. The jump liberated me.

It was a splendid metaphor for the last year of my life.

After Jack had "escaped," the prospects of my future were dim—until I arrived in St. Croix. Meeting Kessler had felt exactly like standing at the top of the waterfall: the scenery was beautiful and the sound relaxing, but the courage to jump, even twenty feet, had eluded me. But once the switch inside you flips to courage, the *only* thing left to do is jump. When I'd decided to walk off my ledge and into Kessler's arms, the free fall had exhilarated me—just has he had—and the plunge into the water had rewarded my bravery. In St. Croix, I jumped *to* Kessler; here in Tennessee, Kessler and I needed to jump together.

After showering, we ate a lunch of Mama D's leftovers, lovingly packaged in 1970s avocado-green Tupperware and hand-delivered by the chef herself. I was surprised she didn't try to gather up our dirty clothes and wash them as well. She was the ultimate Southern mama.

As we filled up on cold chicken and fried okra, the front gate bell rang. I checked the oven, and it read two o'clock. *Right on time.*

I had been harboring Hope's surprise to the girls, mostly because I didn't know what I should be expecting. I turned to Leslie and gasped, "Hope sent something over for all of us, but especially for you!"

Everyone ran to the front doors, while I opened the gate for a large white delivery van. As I walked outside to greet our guest, my heart raced, and I couldn't help but hope that Kessler would climb out of the back seat. When the possibility struck me, unstoppable tears began to fill my eyes. I knew my hope was a long shot, so I dug deep and forced them away. If it hadn't been clear to me before, that moment made my longing for Kessler transparent. I missed all of him: the sound of his voice, his hands on my skin, his body asleep next to mine. Tonight could not get here fast enough.

Six people climbed out of the van. Two began walking toward us, while the rest started taking clothing racks out of the back.

"Hello," I said to the gentleman in charge. "I'm Annie Whitman."

"Excellent, just the gal we're looking for. I'm Stephen, and this is Millie!" He introduced himself with flamboyant hand gestures and a high-pitched voice, continually touching the thick nose bridge of his light tortoise Ray Ban eyeglasses. "We're your glam squad today!"

"I'm sorry, our what?" As I asked the question, as several racks of clothing and numerous boxes of accessories poured out of the van.

"Your glamour attendants. Millie and I are Hope's personal stylists, and she's rented us out to you ladies this afternoon."

"Oh. My. God!" Leslie screamed, while boob-deep in a large container. "These are vintage Prada!" She had already begun digging through the shoes with ravenous lust in her eyes, and she held up a pair of black suede ankle boots.

"Now," Stephen ordered, completely changing his lovely-to-meet-you tone of voice into more of a tiny-drill-sergeant demand. "Show me inside. We obviously have a lot of work to do," he matter-of-factly stated, while rubbing the split ends of my hair together with his fingers.

I held the door open for what seemed like twenty people (even though I'd only counted six). Boxes and clothes filled the living room, while tiny Stephen with his thick glasses and super-skinny jeans barked orders at his staff. In less than fifteen minutes, the couture army had transformed the living room into a high-end clothing store. Separate makeup and hair-styling stations overflowed with more products than a Paul Mitchell kiosk. I was blown away; we all were.

"You and you go here," he said, pointing to Jenna and Claire while checking his clipboard, looking very official. "You're here," he added, pulling Tori to the kitchen island and sitting her in a chair. "You next," he finished, directing me to the last empty seat.

The chatter continued to grow through the excitement, until the house definitely sounded full of people. I was in awe of Stephen. His confidence and leadership were the opposite of what his slender stature would suggest, as he directed people to every station and multitasked the hell out of everyone. Just his hairstyle alone—shaved on one side, bob-length flowing brown locks on the other—could only be worn by someone who owned his shit and apologized for nothing.

The staff scurried about the downstairs, pairing outfits by size and piecing together accessories, while a row of blow-dryers and curling irons heated up the granite countertops. Every two minutes, Leslie let out a screech or moan as she held up another shirt or dress, poking her head out from between the clothing racks. Her couture cherry had been popped by her first full-blown clothes-gasm.

Two people worked on each of us at a time, one doing hair and the other applying makeup. Once the head-styling was underway, Stephen focused his attention on the clothes.

"No, no, yes, no." He quickly edited pieces without even seeing them on us, like a Gucci wizard with a crystal ball.

"Alcohol!" he yelled to the lowest on the totem pole. "Get those drinks in here!"

Quick as a whip, someone appeared with drinks in hand.

Claire was finished first, and holy smokes, she looked gorgeous! It's amazing how much better you look when you have absolutely no input on yourself, and you let a team of professionals overtake you.

"Clothes whore!" Stephen yelled across the room to get Leslie's attention. "You're up!"

I about fell out of my chair laughing when Leslie popped her head through a waterfall of dresses. She obviously knew he was speaking directly to her.

The house was full of people drinking, laughing, and completely enjoying themselves. Even though I hated having my hair styled, a stint in a salon chair was a small price to pay for this big piece of heaven. And just when I thought our afternoon couldn't get any better, the ringleader walked in.

"Hey, y'all!" Hope yelled as she came in through the back door. "Looking good ladies!" She greeted Stephen with a Hollywood kiss, kiss.

All of the girls pounced on her with a million thanks, buzzing like bees with the mixture of champagne and adrenaline.

"Well, honey, whatcha think?" she asked Leslie, resting her elbows on the kitchen counter while cradling her face.

"Either I'm dying, or I'm already dead," Leslie replied. "I don't know how to thank you."

"Oh, it's nothin'. Happy to do it. Just make sure you have an amazing time tonight!" Walking over to me, she asked, "How ya holdin' up, honey?"

"This is so great, Hope. Thank you for doing this for us."

"I had to make sure you looked your best tonight. You never know what will happen." She one-arm hugged me so she wouldn't mess up my hair.

"I'm nervous to see him. I know I shouldn't be—he's the same man he's always been—but I am. Hot flashes keep giving me the sweats, and my palms are cold and sticky. I don't know what's wrong with me." I rubbed my hands together in an attempt to dry them out.

She leaned down next to my ear and whispered, "You're in love, baby. That's what's wrong with you."

"Have a drink with us, and let Stephen yell at you for a while," Leslie hollered over the roar of the blow-dryer.

"Sorry, girls, tonight is not my night," Hope said, giving me a wink. "I've got a few errands to run. The limo will be at your gate at six o'clock sharp. Y'all swing by and pick me up. We'll head downtown early to beat the traffic."

Everyone continued talking over each other and yelling out opinions on one another's outfit choices, as if they mattered. We'd quickly under-stood that Stephen was the final authority on our public presentation. Apparently we were a reflection of his work, and none of us had the balls to fight him. Besides, we all looked like we had stepped out of a maga-zine. I couldn't remember feeling this beautiful—not since my wedding day.

JACK

Darkness still hovered over Zurich and my hotel room when I startled awake. Opening my eyes with a warm body next me was foreign to my nature, but it was a memory I fondly recalled. I had longed for a normal life for some time now, and this morning was a solid start.

The promise of money was on the table, and I'd sent Francesca to the bank with plenty to steal. But, she had come back, and she kept coming back with each of her promises fulfilled. A year ago, I would have been skeptical of the intentions of a hotheaded bombshell; I never would have let myself even set foot on the road I'd already traveled a ways down. Francesca hadn't given me a reason not to trust her, so I did.

Throughout the night, she kept finding her way over to my side of the sheets. We had purposefully fallen asleep at opposite ends of the bed, in order to control our obvious want for each other. But I found her tucked inside my curves, with her back against my chest, quietly breathing. The dark sheet was folded over her hip, and her white lace panties peered out from under my gray cotton T-shirt, which she had fallen asleep in.

I listened to her silent and even breath as her chest rose and fell, keeping in time with mine. Softly wrapping my arm around her waist, I pulled her body closer. I laid my head in the pillow of her long hair, and inhaled the provocative scent of an Italian woman. Channeling every ounce of maturity I had, I begged myself not to stroke her arm, cup my hand around her fleshy ass, or lean over and kiss the lips that spoke the words of a double-edged sword.

I won't fuck you, Jack, continued to roll back and forth through my increasingly salacious thoughts. Her reasoning, which had led to me lying next to her but not inside of her, conflicted with my primal thoughts. Francesca's words collided with her seductress signals, and as is the case with most of the men in the world, that collision left me confused.

She stirred between the sheets, bringing her knees close to her chin and unavoidably pressing her ass right into my midsection. She sweetly moaned and stretched her arms, resting her hand on my growing erection. This was absolutely more than I was equipped to handle; her almost-naked curves encouraged devious actions.

As I slid my arm out from underneath her neck, she turned toward me and opened her eyes.

"Where are you going?" she asked.

Sitting up, while roughly rubbing my knuckles into my eyes and praying for the pain to erase the bluing of my balls, I confessed my unruly thoughts.

"I can't do this, Francesca."

"Do what? What's wrong?"

"This!" I blurted out, extending my hand along her outstretched body. "I can't lie next to you and pretend not to stare at the lace that covers the part of you I want to see most. Do you want to know where I'm going? I'm going to the bathroom to jerk off my ridiculous hard-on, while picturing you taking off my T-shirt and wearing those fantastically arousing panties!" Regrettably, I had yelled out of my sexual frustration.

She smiled like the victor in a war, and slyly said, "I can help you."

Running my fingers through my hair and wanting to rip the strands out of my head, with a huff, I fell to my knees on the bed. "I don't understand you. You don't want me to kiss you, you *do* want me to kiss you, you want to stay the night with me, but you explicitly tell me you aren't going to fuck me. If you want to help me, help me understand you."

She pulled the covers down to the foot of the bed and crawled across the sheets on her hands and knees, like Tawny Kitaen in a Whitesnake video. Stopping just out of my reach, she spread her knees apart, resting her weight on the heels of her feet. Slowly, she pulled her shirt off. The most perfect breasts escaped their cotton confinement. Never in real life had I seen such copious tits, which held the perfect circular shape of smaller ones, easily rivaling any four-page spread in *Penthouse*.

Now wearing only see-through lace panties, she put her arms around my neck and pulled herself onto my lap.

"Shhh," she whispered as I started to protest. "When I said I wasn't going to fuck you, I meant I wasn't going to double-cross you, Jack. Isn't that American slang?"

I only nodded, while tracing her bare spine with my fingertips.

"Besides, I'm expecting *you* to fuck *me*."

With that confirmation, I grabbed her waist and flipped her on her back. She let out an excited startle, and I immediately drove my tongue into her mouth. Through the fury of undressing me, she egged me on with whispering questions and requests.

"What are you going to do to me, Jack?"

"Everything."

I was overwhelmed with options, like a shark in an open-water feeding frenzy. Wanting to touch all of her body parts with all of mine, I slowed myself down to hear her beg me for it. I knew that all the erogenous zones needed to be fully covered for this to be considered amazing sex, so I started with her collarbone, sweeping my lips and fingers across her shoulders. She moaned in soft agreement. Her nipples were already tightly at attention as I kissed and swirled my tongue around their pebbled hardness, desperately kneading and clasping my fingers around her skin.

As much as I wanted to reach the climax of this love making, I steadied myself. I was a pupil of anticipation, methodically working her into delirium. Her hands found my hair as I kissed her honey colored stomach, working my way to the promised land. I grabbed the lace between my teeth and glided the lingerie down her thighs and over smoothly shaven knees. Using her toes, she kicked them all the way off. The lace launched across the room.

As she arched her back with anticipation, I clutched her ankles and pulled her to the edge of the bed. Her knees hit the sheets, and I couldn't help smiling as I relished my first taste of a woman in almost a year. The delicacy of a woman is a pleasure you never forget, and sliding my lips over her glossy wetness made me feel every bit a man.

With a matching smile, Francesca slid off the bed and onto my lap, digging her knees into the carpet as the delicate skin of my erection disappeared into physical elation. Our lips smoldered together, and my hands tucked firmly under her corpulent backside to support her weight. She domineered my manhood, toying with my ecstasy and slowly raising herself up so that only my head was inside of her, then lowering herself back down onto my shaft, allowing every one of my nerve endings to experience the tight suffocation of her warmth. With tenacity, she whispered slurs of swollen body parts and pleasure centers, begging me to flip her again.

This time, Francesca kept all of me inside her, and although I tried to hang on or just keep up, it wasn't long before I had to let go. Finally, I had reached the glory hole.

ANNIE

T he limo arrived promptly at six o'clock, and true to the dealings of a group of women, we were running late. Women, as a gender, have been known to keep people waiting as long as they please, and these girls were no exception.

I say *we*, but I meant everyone except me. I was ready an hour early, and pacing the house. I checked my outfit—a white eyelet, one shoulder shift dress—about a thousand times in the floor-to-ceiling mirror on my closet wall, which was a hard task to accomplish with four other girls coming in and out, hogging the lighting.

Stephen had left me explicit instructions to wear the tri-colored slingback Lady Peep Louboutins, explaining that sexy exuded from those platform heels. I'd nodded in agreement at his expertise, and then waited for him to leave so I could pull on my boots. There was no way in hell I would last an hour in those shoes, much less avoid breaking an ankle. For the women who slip on those heels like a pair of Birkenstocks, I commend you. You are much more refined than I.

I had never thought of myself as anything but a city boot girl, but after I relented to trying on a pair of Luccheses, I'd never looked back. My only pair of honest-to-God cowboy boots were vintage destroyed goatskin, with hand-tooled patterns that recalled the craftsmanship of expert tannery hands. Once I learned of the steps and details needed to customcraft a boot of that detail, I had been swept away by the romanticism and passion needed to bring such art to life. My admiration for architecture had been hand-crafted, especially for me, on a gorgeous pair of boots.

Plus, Kessler had bought them for me. He had reeled with pride that he'd worn boots his entire life, and that in his forties he had finally been able to pass his love along to a complete novice. It had made his week.

When I first brought them home, he had instantly wanted me to put them back on. The customary look in his eyes changed to a sparkle; in a bedroom confessional, he divulged his fantasy. Jack hadn't ever asked me to dress up for him or engage in kinky role-play. Not to say that he wouldn't have been onboard if I'd spearheaded something, but I think we got too comfortable in our traditional roles to risk embarrassment in front of each other.

I didn't want to get pigeon-holed into a-vanilla-housewife-who-always-says-no role with Kessler. So when he asked me to bring his fantasy to reality, I thought, *What the hell. I'll give it a go.*

He didn't ask much of me—only a slow striptease (I slapped his hands when they got near the goods) to some old Alabama, while keeping the boots *on*. I was horrified at first. I was not a stripper, nor did I possess the skills of seriousness required to turn someone on just by taking my clothes off. But once I realized that he was engrossed in the situation, I let my inhibitions go. And I broke in my new boots.

When Kessler saw me in my boots tonight, I hoped that was the memory that would come to his mind.

Excited chatter dominated the ride downtown. As the limo came to a stop in front of flashing camera bulbs, Hope gave us some advice.

"Squeeze your knees together while you're getting out of the car. Those jackasses aren't trying to get a picture of your face. Vagina shots make more money than faces do. They don't know if you're famous, but since we're pulling up to the front, those leeches can't take a chance on missing a money shot."

Everyone leaned in, listening intently, and my dress immediately started pitting out.

"When you get to the end of the carpet," she continued, "turn to the right. We'll gather together in front of the first step-and-repeat to get our picture taken. After that, they'll pull me aside and ask for individual pictures. Y'all go on ahead inside, and I'll find you. And you," she pointed her finger at me, "don't answer any questions. Someone will inevitably ask me about Kessler. You just keep your mouth shut, or they'll make you look like an idiot. This isn't the place to defend him."

I nodded my head, as terror ripped through my insides. When Hope had told me she'd gotten us good seats to the show, I didn't know they required this kind of an entrance. Grace had always been a character for me to play, usually within the same allotted time frame as Cinderella. Thank God I had my Fairy Godmother with me tonight, holding my hand, because I easily could have turned into a pumpkin.

"All right, let's go have some fun!" Hope exclaimed as the suicide doors swung open.

Knees pinched, chest out, bottom tucked, I repeated to myself, while clenching my teeth in the fakest lock-jawed smile.

Immediately, the insanely bright flashes began going off, and voices shouted Hope's name. The rest of the girls walked the carpet flawlessly, following Hope's instructions to a T. I, however, became hot and nauseated. And I could pinpoint the exact moment the blood drained from my face.

"Hey!" someone shouted at me. "That's her! She's Kessler's girlfriend!"

Oh, crap.

The questions from the black-lensed jury came faster than the diarrhea I was forcefully holding in my puckered ass.

Don't let me shit myself in front of these people. Please, God, have mercy on me.

"Are you still together with Kessler? Who was the woman in the picture? Did you move out? Who are you wearing?" they repeatedly yelled, blinding me in the blaze of pictures.

I was grateful for the distraction from the man who kept yelling questions about my outfit. Even if I could have talked, I didn't have any idea who had created my dress. No one could have known that the press would recognize me. It had never crossed my mind that anyone would have an iota of interest in me. As I continued to smile, Hope shook her head, reminding me to keep my mouth shut, and then she expertly turned me around so they could get some shots of my dress. I followed her lead and did a small twirl, thinking that now would have been a good time to have my ass waxed shut.

When I saw the girls waiting inside the front doors, my abdominal pain subsided. They were my light at the end of this terrifying tunnel; they always were.

As we waited inside for Hope, everyone assured me that I had done a fine job of faking grace on the red carpet. Collecting myself, I walked over to the T-shirt booth. I smiled at the buzz of conversations—different groups of women were discussing the hotness of both Wade and Kessler. A few months ago, the comments might have bothered me, but tonight, I had to agree. The line to buy items with Kessler's face on them was ten deep.

This is what Leslie was talking about. These people have grown up with him, and as far as they're concerned, he is a part of their lives.

Hope laughed when she finally found us.

"You did good, sugar. Worked it like a pro," she said, slapping my arm. "Only one problem."

"What? What did I do, or not do?" I was terrified to hear the answer.

She lifted up her phone and showed me a text from Stephen. "Boots? Where are the Lady Peeps? And for God's sake, her dress is Stella McCartney! WTF, Annie!"

"Was that national? How does he already know about the boots?" I was praying I wasn't on syndicated television.

"Calm down," Hope said, still laughing as she put her arm around me. "The local news was outside. Your celebrity hasn't reached past Nashville yet. Let's get drinks and then head inside."

We found our seats, which were in the third row on the right section of the outer banks. Hope had told me that she always sat in the same vicinity, so Wade would know where to look for her. The floor was standing room only; that section was for the hardcore fans. She didn't mess around down there.

The instant the arena went dark, the crowd was on their feet, and undeniable electricity activated the entire coliseum. At a deafening volume, the band fired up with a song off their first album.

We heard Kessler's voice before we actually saw him. With the lights still down, he sang the first verse offstage, seducing the fans a little longer. Right before the first chorus, white lights suddenly illuminated every inch of the arena, blazing like a thousand suns, and Kessler Carlisle swung out onto the stage, hanging tight to a thick knotted rope.

I knew right then: this was a night I would never forget.

JACK

O ur smiles and sleepy breath matched one another's, and I was quite sure my dick had never woken up this satisfied. Over the last several months, I'd grown to pity that his only fleshy contact was the palm of my hand. During the early morning hours, we had both gotten to experience the full-bodied warmth of a woman, and she was better than either of us remembered.

The muted light of the debuting sun seeped in through the window, braiding its way into the fibers of the carpet. If exceptional life moments were stamped into a book like the countries in a passport, the ink from this occasion would have taken up an entire page. I glanced around the room, taking note of all the small details of this morning, just in case I never felt this way again.

When my tendency to overanalyze—one of my character flaws—began to compete with the revitalized glory of daydreaming, I reluctantly inched my body away from the heat of my naked companion. Thinking Francesca was still asleep, I tried to pull my arm out from under her waist, only to feel Chinese finger cuffs preventing my escape.

"Ah, no, Jack," she whispered as our fingers entwined each other's. "Don't end this night with me yet."

Leaning my lips into her neck, I softly replied, "I have to, because it's morning and we have work to do. But I'm hoping to find a woman who matches your exact description waiting for me in a Sheraton hotel room this afternoon."

She smiled at the invitation and turned over, exposing her fantastic breasts.

"I know that you know exactly what you're doing right now," I said, "and as much as I would love to bury my face in your beautiful skin, I can't risk losing my head. I'm going to take a shower. Why don't you order us some breakfast? With coffee, please. From my experience last night, I trust you know exactly what I like."

I hurried to the bathroom and stepped into the cocoon of warm water flowing from the showerhead. It seemed as though, having enjoyed the taste of Francesca, my dick was like the worst kind of junkie. One hit wasn't going to be enough.

Sorry pal, but this morning, you get the palm again.

I swiftly stroked my cock, reminiscing how my morning started.

Today was going to be crucial in the takedown of John Savage. I couldn't bust into a corporate board meeting full of cum and thoughts of a naked Francesca.

***

Bracing mountain air blew through me, splitting the tails of my trench coat around my legs. The glacial morning weather invigorated my already-brisk pace, helping me focus my thoughts on the quick speech I was about to give.

Maintenant Nouvelle used to be one of the big six European power players in print publishing. When the shift to online newspapers began, the company's geriatric leaders had refused to succumb to the digital age, forgoing enviable change for illusory superiority. They had held tightly to their unchanging position dedicated to a print-only newspaper—and they'd successfully run their multimillion-dollar company into the pro-verbial ground. Now, a new and nepotistic generation of board members had acquired majority shares, offering their predecessors false promises of a lucrative comeback. In the meantime, they were discreetly seeking a buyer.

The funnel of the class system can be found all over the world. Rich is in neighborhoods across the globe, and wealthy is in every country. But, opulent is a minute percentage of the world's population; the ones above a feature on the *Forbes* wealthiest list. The company I planned on double-crossing was the latter.

Company buyouts don't happen overnight, and in Maintenant Nouvelle's case, it had been a two-year process. Luckily for me, I had caught wind of the takeover at the exact time that my plan to extinguish John Savage was coming together. A struggling newspaper was a perfect piece to add to my puzzle.

Pushing through the revolving doors could be intimidating to a nov-ice, but having played numerous parts over the years, I approached it as the act of just another character in disguise. The hustle of the morning commute noisily transferred to the starkly white tiled floors and echoed throughout the three-story lobby. I approached the visitors' desk, where an impeccably dressed elderly woman looked me over from the top of her bifocals. The name on her tag read Astrid.

"*Oui?*" she arrogantly asked, as if helping visitors weren't her actual job—as if I were interrupting her morning routine.

"I need a visitor's pass for Maintenant Nouvelle, please."

Her immediate eye roll was blatant and purposeful, relaying her disgust for my primary language. She sat erect, coldly continuing her silence and boasting her pitiful attempt at power.

"I'm sorry, but I was under the impression that the space directly below a gargantuan "'Visitors' Desk'" sign is where visitors are to check in. Am I mistaken?"

She let out a long sigh and a short *detest*, which sounded more like a loogie than an actual word. She leaned toward me in a condescending manner.

"*Quelle est la nature précisez de votre entreprise?*" she questioned in perfect French.

"The nature of my business is actually not of your concern. And I don't think someone of your unhelpful candor should be working at a help desk. I'll make sure you're the first one fired," I said through a delightful smile.

She sat silently, as the spark of confusion began to morph into understanding.

"That's right, Astrid. I own the paper, which makes me your new boss—or your old boss, depending on how you look at your situation. Whenever you're finished being smug—and by the look on your face, that could take a while—you can clean out your cubby. *Au revoir*," I added, reaching over the desk and grabbing a visitor lanyard off a silver hook.

I held my card over the scanner, entered the elevator, and, with the push of a button, sent myself to the top floor. After stepping off the elevator, I didn't need directions to the main boardroom; I just followed the noise. The yelling in several languages became louder as I made my way to the back of the building.

The buyers, Le Droit, and the sellers, Maintenant Nouvelle, had only had a small amount of time with the information that a third party had swooped in and bought the business during the early-morning hours. Publicly traded companies can amass billions of dollars, but like every pendulum, those fortunes can change. The risk could mean a loss of percentage shares, and ultimately, a loss of control of the business.

After only a moment of inspection through the glass partition, the disarray of skinny-suited men erased any doubt that I would be anything other than successful today. Chaos breeds the neglect of rational thinking, allowing unstable emotions to result in hurried decisions. I was banking on instability with these board members. In under eight hours, I had singlehandedly ruined two years of ligation in my hostile takeover of Maintenant Nouvelle. I pushed my way through the cold glass doors.

Waiting for silence, I stood stoic at a corner of the expansive rectangular desk. One by one, the voices ceased, as eyes and anger became fixed on me.

"*Qui diable êtes-vous?*" the lone man standing asked. He was wondering who the hell I was.

"Ladies and gentleman, my name is of no importance to you. The only thing that concerns you is what I can offer you. As of this morning, I own 51 percent of the shares of Maintenant Nouvelle. By the room full of red faces, I can understandably see how upset you all are, but unfortunately, the deal is done. However unreasonable you might consider this acquisition to be, overall, I'm not an unreasonable man. By now, you must realize that everything comes with a price. Had you not dragged your feet over the last two years, nickel-and-diming Le Droit, I wouldn't have had the opportunity to stand before you today. Let that be the main lesson you carry into the next deal. I appreciate your time, and I look forward to bringing mainstream America into the longevity of this company. *Au revoir*," I slid a white business card across the table with only a phone number on it.

This was the ego-stroking side of my job, which I always loved. Blindsiding pompous and unsuspecting victims brought me immeasurable joy. The slow-moving cognizance that appeared in their faces was like a time-lapse video of a flower in growth. It built with each small thought, until *BOOM*, the flower bulb opened—as did the realization that they were fucked. I had added the threat of the paper being Americanized to light an extra fire under their asses. No self-respecting Frenchman wanted to be duped by an imbecilic and egotistical American. I was counting on that.

As I made my way down the catwalk hallway and onto the empty elevator, I held my laughter through the continuous wave of heads popping over cubicle walls. The elevator doors began to shut, when a hand cut through them, and a stereotypical American woman stepped in. Our eyes silently met as the doors closed. I noticed her smile in the reflection of the metal. She seemed like she wanted to talk.

When the elevator lurched and we began to move, without ever looking directly at me, she said in perfect English, "I don't know who you are, but that was genius."

The doors opened on the bottom floor, and without another word, she simply walked out.

JACK

I was back in a set of elevators, but this time, I was heading to a new hotel room. When financially fucking people over, it's best to keep moving. This move had brought me—no, us—to the Sheraton.

The Sheraton was a boutique hotel in the Financial District, at the northwest end of Zurich. The glass elevator located on the corner of the hotel allowed for a spectacular view of Lake Zurich. Swiss law prohibited buildings from exceeding six stories in most parts of the city, with exceptions made for government or historical property. The flat roofs and rows of balconies enhanced the uncommon view of the sprawling lake, which sat at the foot of one of the largest mountain ranges in the world. Nestled in the midst of bistro eateries, specialty shops, and the giants of the banking industry, the Sheraton was our utopian abode for the next two days.

I knocked on the door, and after a brief pause, I heard the scraping of chain locks against metal hinges. Francesca swung the door open and forcefully pulled me inside, shaking a blank sheet of paper in front of my face.

"I did it!" she squealed, jumping into my arms and kissing my face all over, as a mother would do to a child.

"Let me see it," I said, panicked with hope that she was right.

A blank sheet of paper had never made me happier—or richer, for that matter.

"Tell me what happened, and don't leave anything out."

"Okay," she said, calming herself with the details of the morning. "I sat on the southside bench and waited for Sena. I worried, because the crowd got bigger for the festival, and people quickly filled the sidewalks. But thanks to the pink scarf, she was easy to find. I followed her into the bank, keeping my distance—just like you told me."

"Good, Francesca. Good job."

"There was a man in line behind her at the deposit counter, but I pulled the neckline of my wrap dress down so far, I think my nipples were showing."

"Lucky guy." I smiled, knowing how pleased that unsuspecting man had to have been. "What next?"

"I whispered to him what a hurry I was in, and of course, he let me go in front of him. I mean, look at these," she instructed, pulling her dress apart and exposing her partners in crime.

"I get it, and yes, they're magnificent. But, can you stay focused on the story, please?"

"Yes, okay. So, Sena filled out her deposit slip, and immediately the branch manager came into the lobby to greet her. She followed him back through the corridor and disappeared down a closed-off hallway. I grabbed all of the leftover deposit slips, just to be safe, and put them in my bag. After that, I made my own deposit into the Carmela Mancini account that I set up yesterday. I stopped at the nearest coffeehouse and copied the password down." She held up a small slip of paper, which had our future written across it in black ink.

I held the blank deposit slip directly under the light of the desk lamp. The paper was perfectly indented with the password to John Savage's sixty-million-dollar account.

KESSLER

The murmur of the crowd grew thick as showtime neared. Hoots and hollers accompanied each roadie who ventured out on stage to check the instruments one last time. We liked to keep the crowd waiting, to build up anticipation. But, just like a woman, if you kept them waiting too long, they'd turn on you. I needed this crowd tonight, a lot more than they needed me.

My roadie, Randy, hooked up the belaying device, locking the D-ring securely in place. Normally I wouldn't have taken these kinds of safety precautions for something as simple as swinging on a rope, but this wasn't my tour, and I didn't get to call the shots.

"Did you check the seats again?" I asked Randy.

"I looked, but they're still empty, boss. I'll radio will-call and ask if the tickets have been picked up yet. Try not to think about her, and focus on hanging tight to this rope. If you let go, the harness with catch you, but there's a good chance the force of the jerk will break your back. Just be careful," he pleaded.

"I know what I'm doing when it comes to this." I pulled the straps tight. "It's the rest of the world that gets confusing."

The band started their intro, as cold sweat trickled down my already-wet back. I climbed to the top of the ladder, perched myself on the wooden platform, and waited for my cue to come in.

Whether she's here or not, I'm gonna sing like she's sitting in the front row.

I sang the first verse in darkness, and right before the chorus hit, I dried the sweat from my hands. Holding the rope in a death grip, I took off in a short run, and then swung across the forty-foot stage. The rush of an almost-free fall awakened my excitement, as well as the crowd's. They went crazy with that kind of an entrance.

Now, singing and swinging are hard to do, and as perfect as I wanted to sound, I think I probably missed some notes. The crowd didn't seem to notice, though, and the arena echoed as fans sang each word in flawless harmony.

Since this was my last show of the tour, we'd decided to mix things up. Our normal routine would have started with my set, then Wade would have come out to do his set, and finally, we'd do some songs together. Tonight, we were doing a run-and-gun concert, switchbacking the stage with one another. The intensity of this kind of show elevated the atmosphere for all of us.

After my elaborate entrance and one of my songs, it was Wade's turn.

"How y'all doing tonight, Nashville?" I yelled to the crowd, waiting for Wade's cue in my earpiece.

That question always made me laugh. I'd never done a show where the crowd didn't respond with anything less than lunacy. They loved that question.

The intro to Wade's song began, and I exited stage left as a hole in the floor opened, ejecting Wade from an underground springboard. He wasn't roped to a safety harness, and I was sure he was going to break his ankle, flying straight up into the air and landing on the hard soles of cowboy boots. That man was a beast.

This part of touring was so damn fun. Swinging through the air or shooting up from the floor, acting a fool on stage or riding the wave with the crowd—all of the bad parts of the road were erased in these first few minutes of a show.

When the third song started up, I ran back out. Wade and I were doing this one together. I was covering every square inch of the stage by running back and forth, up and down the catwalk, when Wade grabbed me and pulled me to the far right side. Knowing Wade, I braced myself for a bucket of ice water or some awful prank, but the exact opposite happened. He positioned me at eight o'clock and started kissing his fingers and pointing to a specific location in the crowd. Confused, I shielded my eyes from the blinding stage lights. I could only see a few rows out.

Wade got right up into my ear and screamed, "They're here! Annie is here!"

I turned and smiled at him, letting him know that I'd finally seen her. Even though I could barely make her out, just knowing we were in the same room filled me with hopeful anxiety.

We finished our song, and I took in a deep breath to calm myself. I'd heard Wade's advice the night before, and like usual, he was right. A gesture was nice, but small. What I needed was a display.

I had stayed up the first half of the past night trying to decide what to do. Once I'd figured it out, I was too excited to sleep through the rest of it.

JACK

T he wall of windows in our hotel room overlooked the already-crowded streets. Tourists were spending the day partying, while locals scrambled to finish last-minute preparations for the annual spring festival called Sechseläuten.

The winter months could be brutal and dragging in Zurich, and each year the city commemorated the end of winter and the beginning and promise of spring. The history of the festival dates back to archaic times, when the first days of summer working hours were celebrated in taverns across the city. Ordinances strictly regulated the length of working hours in that era. During the winter months, the workday in any shop lasted as long as the daylight hours, but during the summer months, the law stated that work must end when the church bells tolled at six o'clock. Sechseläuten is a Swiss word that literally translates into, "The six o'clock ringing of the bells." The changing of work hours was considered a celebratory event. Not only did the warmer weather bring better spirits among the people, but it also brought the opportunity for more money.

The climax of the festival was the burning of Böögg, the Swiss version of the bogeyman. Nightmares ride indiscriminately through the minds of all children, in any part of the globe, and along with Americans, the bogeyman also visited the younger generation of sleeping Swiss. The burning ritual in Zurich was comparable to Halloween, Mardi Gras, and the Fourth of July all rolled into one holiday.

Through the open windows of our hotel room, the steadfast hammering of the final touches on Böögg pounded in unison. A week before the parade, a crew of locals began resurrecting him, starting with a thick wooden base. As the week progressed, they continued adding height to the foundation, surrounding it with flammable hay. On the tip-top of the upside-down cone structure, workers secured a frightfully robust snowman, complete with jagged teeth and a smoking pipe. It was all in preparation to blow him up.

The morning of Sechseläuten kicked off in elaborate fashion, with children in costumes at the forefront of a ceremonious parade down the main street. The costumes represented the nightmarish fear they hoped to drive back into winter's night, leaving the summer months to run free of the bogeyman. Hundreds of participants partook in this Swiss tradition, while several thousand stood on the sidelines, celebrating the end of darkness and the beginning of light. After the parade, the crowd gathered in the city center to blow Böögg, the evil lurking snowman, to smithereens.

Francesca enjoyed watching the children run in the luscious grassy square, and I couldn't help admiring her natural beauty as the wind blew the hair back from her face. Admiration quickly turned to lust, and soon I was drawing the shades while undressing myself, my patiently waiting cock in hand.

I'd never been with a woman like Francesca before. She whispered her desires in my ear, inviting me to experiment with her body. Her confidence and fearlessness not only turned me on, but they also made me obey. The role reversal was a tranquil change for me.

For the first time in years, I could fall asleep quickly. With the sound of the breeze gently blowing through the open window and the murmur of the crowd below, the white noise of life lulled me to a state of relaxation that I hadn't known I had the ability to attain. After tomorrow, life was going to get a whole lot easier.

***

I was already awake before my phone rang. Eight hours of sleep for me were like sixteen for a normal person. I tried to savor the moment of resting well and knowing I wasn't alone. The thought crossed my mind that Francesca would take her money and end the relationship. I hoped she would come with me, but I wasn't counting on it. Whatever she decided to do after we finished this job would have to be okay with me. I didn't have any other choice. But, I did have hope.

"Yes," I answered into my phone.

"The board has come to an agreement," he said in broken English. "Can you come back to the office this morning?"

"I have no reason to come down there. Surely you can run the business without me. You've done such a fine job so far," I said condescendingly.

"We would like to make you an offer, one you can't refuse."

"I can't make it today, but I'll be there at seven o'clock tomorrow morning," I replied. I hung up.

Exactly as I'd planned.

I woke Francesca with soft kisses, encouraging her to get moving.

"This is the day I've been waiting for, Francesca! Are you sure you're ready?"

"Yes, Jack. Of course I'm ready."

"Let's go over it one more time, okay? We can't make any mistakes today."

"I understand. We can go over it again, but I want a shower and coffee first. No negotiations on that," she demanded with a smile.

JACK

"My stomach is tingling, and I'm starting to get nervous, Jack," Francesca admitted as we started the four-block walk from our hotel to the bank.

"Sit down," I urged, guiding her to a sidewalk bench. Putting my arm around her shoulder and exhaling a deep breath, I said, "When you're doing something for yourself, it's easy to overanalyze the details. Even when you have the best intentions, you still might screw the whole thing up. Self-service never extracts the most possible good out of a situation—call it divine intervention or karma, but I think all the laws of the universe come together to purposefully prevent good from happening. I've found that when your mindset is purely selfless, good intentions tend to lead the way, opening infinite possibilities. The bigger we think, the more global the possibility. Is what we are doing illegal? Absolutely. But that's the wrong question to ask. If you pull this off, will you have the ability to change lives indefinitely into the future? The answer to that question is not only yes, but yes a million times over. The children you have yet to meet are the ones who will benefit from our actions today. They are the ones you need to think about when you walk through the bank doors. I promise that the confidence will arm you. It will shield any negative thoughts."

She stared at me in silence, dropping her eyes to the concrete. My temples began sweating at her lack of words and the possibility that I would need to adapt the plan.

"If you don't want to do this, I'll understand, Francesca. I don't want to force you to be Rana Demir, even for a short time. The fact that you've been so willing and so warm to me is something I'll never forget. You helped me open myself not only this world again, but more important, to a woman. You've already gone above and beyond for someone else. I have no doubt that karma will reward you greatly."

Without looking up from the sidewalk, she asked, "Would you stop talking, please? I'm trying to get into character. Rana Demir needs silence."

I laughed, pulling her close to me and kissing her forehead.

Grabbing her purse and throwing the chained strap across her body, she stood up and flattened the bottom of her dress. "Okay, *vado*."

"Wait! One more time through, where does the money go?"

She sat back down and began counting her fingers as she talked. "One million gets deposited into Sena Demir's personal account, another million to Carmela Mancini, and also a cash withdrawal of twenty grand. The rest of the money gets split up, transferred between two separate accounts in the Cayman Islands." She held the paperwork with the Cayman account numbers, along with John Savage's top-secret password.

"What's the most important part of this process?" I quizzed her one last time.

"I must wait for the confirmation codes. If I don't have the codes, all of this is for nothing, and I'm still broke."

"Excellent, Francesca. The entire process shouldn't take longer than an hour. Just don't ever panic. If you believe this is your money, then they will, too." I took her face in my hands and kissed her hard on the lips.

She advanced down the alley dressed like a high school principal, but she worked her walk like a high-dollar hooker. Each passing pedestrian gave her the attention of either a head turn or a full-blow catcall, and she never once flinched. I didn't attribute her confidence to my speech. You can't teach authority; people are born with that.

My fate, as well as that of countless others, depended on Francesca's ability to perform, and I was banking on her being a clutch player. Left with only nerve-wracking time, I stretched my legs—along with my anxiety—amid the expanding horde of people in the city square. Law enforcement had already barricaded most of the Financial District, allowing pedestrians to move freely of their own accord.

As I shuffled along the long stretch of six-story buildings, sidestepping costumed children giggling through homemade masks, a sense of regret came over me. We had tried and failed in the most painful way, but Annie and I were never to be parents. Though I certainly enjoyed watching my niece and nephew grow, the attachment was incomparable to the bond with your own child.

I had been unable to reach Jamie by phone, and my suspicions didn't need further verification. I was almost positive that he had been eliminated. My hope for Liz was that she had followed the same path as Annie and refused reconciliation.

Why am I thinking about this? Those days were a lifetime ago.

With my hands deep in my pockets, I walked off the past and concentrated on the present. John Savage's money *had* to get wired into those accounts this morning, or the Maintenant Nouvelle acquisition would falter from insufficient funds. Using seventy million of my own money, I had secured an authoritative position with the down payment, but I needed fifty-seven million more to acquire ownership. If the deal went bust, Francesca and I would live an insignificant amount of time longer. The suits would find us, and they would most certainly kill us. No one can run forever. Not even me.

I pushed the negativity aside and went back to studying the elaborate, old-fashioned costumes of the children lining up for the parade. Feeling a little out of place in regular clothes, I scanned the onlookers to see if I stuck out like a typical tourist.

Good, I'm not the only one. That guy went overkill with the suit, I thought, catching his stare. He immediately looked away.

Was that intentional?

Unnerved, I headed towards a pretzel vendor, constantly scanning and now fully aware of my surroundings. I ordered a salted big mouth and moved to the side of the cart to wait for my food. Another plain-dressed gentleman stepped up behind me. He placed his order with a thick Boston accent.

The shift was immediate: I went into work mode.

Scanning… scanning. Another gray suit at nine o'clock. That's two, which eliminates a coincidence. "Homeless" man talking into his wrist at three o'clock. Pretzel Boston hasn't moved. Four men so far, obviously here for me.

With three drum beats and the ear-piercing blare of the horn section starting up, the parade was off, and so was I. Doing my best spin move (and dropping my pretzel), I busted through the front doors of a smoke shop, leaving my trackers to scramble and scaring the hell out of two stoners behind the register desk. I pulled the heavy Zig Zag display down in front of the door to buy myself some time. Rolling papers exploded across the ground, scattering in all directions.

"Back door?" I yelled to Cheech and Chong. "Back door, *hintertür!*" I screamed again to their unregistering faces. "*Polizia! Polizei!*" I hollered, not knowing what language these locals spoke. "Cops, goddamnit! Cops are coming!"

That they understood. With wide eyes and only a slight head jerk, Cheech motioned toward a narrow hallway cluttered with shipping boxes. The distinct sound of glass breaking arose with each box I overturned; I was probably destroying a recent shipment of new bongs.

The emergency exit led outside into an empty but marching-band-deafening alleyway. Music filled the city.

I need a vantage point.

Grabbing a metal pipe that vertically ran the length of a building and yanking on its end to see if it would support my weight, I began the climb. I wedged hand over hand between the pipe and the brick wall, shimmying myself up—until the burning pain of electric voltage seized my muscles. Homeless Man stood underneath me, tasing my ankle; a jagged line of blue and white sparks plunged into my skin. The immediate atrophy denied my hands their proper grip on the pipe, and I began slipping toward the ground.

Fortunately, with the jolt of my electric seizure, my foot collided with his face. As blood spatter attached to the exposed hairs on my leg, he looked up, but not directly at me, blinking several times at the sun. My foot smashed the bridge of his now-broken nose, and it was obvious that my image was intermingling with blurry and watered vision. For good measure, I kicked him again. This time, I heard his jaw crack, and I saw the whites of his eyes exposed as his head hit the pavement.

Years had passed since a situation of this magnitude had presented itself, and I was surprised by how easily I slipped back into an aggressive role. Disciplined killing was strategically straightforward, as far as muscle memory was concerned. The mind and body connection went back into full-swing immediately.

John Savage found me, and I need to get to Francesca before someone else does.

Pretzel Boston swung the back-entrance metal door open and let off a round of shots. I jumped over the lip of the building and flattened myself against the rooftop. With the pause in gun fire, I got up and ran. As I hopped over the slivers of space between each building and sidestepped randomly smoking chimneys, I blocked the pain of my dragging left foot.

The last twenty feet of rooftop had recently been covered in heavy black tar, and orange cones blocked off the fresh asphalt.

The Swiss take these longer working hours seriously. It's only the first day of the festival, and they're already working overtime.

With my ego in check and Pretzel Boston closing in, the figure eight was my only escape. My shoes immediately sank into the heavy substance, and I had to leave them behind. I stepped off the six-story ledge and landed into a dumpster filled with broken bottles and rotting trash. The impact of the fall sent my knees up into my chest, and it sent the pencil drill, which was stashed in my front pocket, deep into my right thigh.

Adrenaline kept the pain at bay and gave me an idea. I pulled myself out of the dumpster and the drill from my thigh. A perfect oval of blood soaked into my pants. I circled around the back of the building and climbed the fire escape. Repositioning myself at the top of the ladder, level with the roofline, I hid from John Savage's goon behind a blue and gold awning. Pretzel Boston carefully inched his way closer to the building's edge, trying to keep his balance and his shoes as he squished through the asphalt thickness. With his attention focused and his gun drawn in the opposite direction, I reached over the handles of the fire escape, and stabbed the spinning pencil drill directly into his Achilles' heel.

No weapons left. I'll have to fight him. I'm too old for this shit.

Stepping onto the roof, I promptly felt my legs sweep out from under me.

Freshly laid rooftop tar pillowed my fall, but it also enveloped everything attached to me. The black and viscid goo suctioned my jacket like quicksand and covered my graying hair, extinguishing the possibility of my using fists to fight back. Pretzel Boston hovered over me with his hands on his knees and a *fuck you* smile across his smug face. He seemed pleased that he was about to add another notch to his belt. I squirmed uselessly. My clothes were fully embedded in the tar; I had been immobilized. Squinting from the direct sunlight, I studied his fat and sweaty face. He resembled a cartoon character, with wide-set eyes and crooked teeth.

There's no way he's from the program. John Savage is hiring street thugs to kill for him.

As my mind streamed last-second regrets, his foot hit my exposed ribs. I thought of Francesca, and I realized that her life was most likely coming to an end along with mine. The second kick came up underneath me. With the force of his foot connecting to my backside, I was quite sure that he had lost a toe in my asshole. My feet lurched upward, the entire posterior side of my clothing making a universal ripping sound. I was glad that Gail had left Switzerland when she did; otherwise I never would have lived down this ridiculously humiliating death.

The last blow came to the side of my face, and the force of his Beretta across my cheek scalped the back of my head. Where hair had recently been attached to my skull, now those hairs were stuck to the roof.

In the slow movement of time and the flittering glimpses of speckled unconsciousness, my last thoughts were of Annie. I wished her all of the happiness she deserved, even if it was with Kessler Carlisle.

Oh fuck, now the last thought in my life is going to be about some country music wanker. So help me God, I've most definitely lost my edge. I deserve to go out like this.

Pretzel Boston moved to adjust himself out of the glare of the sun, and I instinctually sat up. Then, I realized I was sitting up. He had unknowingly dislodged my clothes from the tar and inadvertently freed me. As a last-ditch effort, I reached up to grab his weapon—at the same time that the shot was fired.

I waited for the pain of my last breath, but instead, I felt the crushing weight of Pretzel Boston crashing into me. Confused but thankful, I scanned the rooftops for the shot that had saved my life. A small tripod was set up directly across the street atop another row house, and popping up from behind it was a petite woman who wore her hair in a massive red bun.

Gail!

Her figure crouched back down behind the scope of the tripod. She held her index finger in a number one position.

I had only counted four men earlier on the street below, but there easily could have been more on the way. Her "one" finger signified that another man was heading to the rooftop. I was sure that the remaining suit had gone in search of Francesca. Over a half an hour had passed, and the money should have already been in an account, which meant Francesca was on her way back to the hotel to meet me.

Gray Suit was now only Gray Pants—he had ditched his top layer to reveal a young and chiseled chest, advancing toward my location. Lowering myself onto the top-floor window ledge and smashing the nearest window with only my socked foot, I swung through the broken glass into a midcentury laundry room. The dark and dingy rectangular room housed a row of top-loading washing machines and an equal number of dryers. Several connecting two-by-fours held powdered detergent and bottles of bleach, with a few other bottles littering the corners. The red EXIT light glowing above the only door in the room showed me my one way out.

Opening the ancient exit door, which led to an equally archaic stair-well, I attempted to make a mad dash, but I was pulled back by a younger-generation version of myself. The concrete floor greeted my tailbone and sent a jolt of pain screaming up my spine. Gray Pants covered me. His salty skin wrapped tightly around my neck, squeezing out my breath like a boa constrictor readying for his next meal. I plunged my hand into an abandoned box of detergent cowering by the foot of a washer, and came up with a handful of blue and white soapy granules. Reaching behind my head, I violently smeared the potent soap into every available orifice of his face. His grip released as soon as my finger found the soft tissue of his eyeball, and he let out a pain-filled scream. His gun skittered across the floor.

My body ached as I stumbled to my feet, feeling every bit of my forty-four years. My strength was no match to the physical advantages my pseudo-younger self had. I would have to beat him with my intellect. As he stretched himself toward his freedom, the black Glock just out of reach, I furiously uncapped a jug from the floor. I poured the liquid that I hoped was bleach over the top of his head; he let out another cry as the chemicals drained into his open mouth.

This guy certainly exhibited the standard training from the program, and he was determined to use every ounce of fight left in him. Even though his eyes were squeezed shut, he pointed the pistol in an assumed straight line, and rapid fire ensued. The ricochet of bullets sent us both to the floor. Two exited through the broken window, one lodged into the side of a washing machine, and the last came to rest inside my shoulder.

A decade had passed since I'd been shot, but the pain was exactly as I remembered.

Blind, crippled, and out of ammunition, Gray Pants was also out of options. With his back leaning against an open dryer and his face resting in perfect position, I repeatedly slammed the heavy commercial door on his neck.

The motions of assassination were automatic until, upon stopping the dryer door, I realized that he was almost decapitated. I immediately threw up. Detergent was smeared across his neck and face and blood ran from his bleached-soaked eyelids. I saw him as an actual person, instead of just an assassin. This man couldn't be more than thirty years old. Because, he had chosen a life with John Savage, he had ultimately solidified his death.

"I'm sorry," I said, pulling a blanket from the dryer to cover his lifeless body.

I quickly rummaged through the rest of the machines and I found enough clothes to outfit myself. Grabbing another abandoned bottle of bleach off the floor, I stood over the filthy freestanding laundry room sink. After rinsing out an old metal bucket with warm water, I added a slosh of bleach. As I leaned over the sink, I pour the bleach water directly into the hole in my shoulder. The pain seized my limbs and watered my eyes, yet it was manageable because I knew I would be walking out of there alive. I grabbed my wallet and a stowaway pack of Zig Zags out of my shredded and bleach-soaked clothing on the floor, dressed my wound, changed into fresh garb, and took off down the staircase. I needed to find Gail and, hopefully, Francesca.

KESSLER

The monstrosity of tour shows was planned out to the last minute and the last detail. Convoys of semi-rigs arrived in each city four days early, and eight hours of construction were required to orchestrate a three-hour show. Any diversions from the script were seriously frowned upon. Tonight, I wasn't just diverting; I was detouring in the most grandiose way. I could give a shit about the script, because tonight, I was putting on a display.

As the band played an instrumental version of the next song, I gathered everyone together in a huddle, quickly shouting out my plan. Wade threw his head back in laughter and gave me a hug, slapping my back and following that up with a high-five. The band softly played on as Wade exited stage left. I approached the standing microphone.

"Is everyone having a good time tonight?" I yelled, trying to keep my voice steady as the crowd went wild. "I want to thank everyone for coming out and supporting us, especially since I've made some poor choices over the last few weeks."

The arena got eerily quiet as I paused to collect my thoughts.

"I know y'all have seen me in the media lately, and I just want to apologize to everyone I've let down. For the fans who have been with me from the beginning, I know how disappointed you must be. I'm truly sorry for disgracing our relationship. To my newest fans, I want to assure you, this isn't the way I usually conduct myself. I promise, if you stick with me, I won't let you down again."

They wrapped me up with hollers of support and more homemade signs that assured me: we were in this together.

"Over the last few months, but especially over the last week, my life has taken a turn for the worse. You see, I lost the woman I love."

More silence from the crowd.

"Now, for most people, falling in love is the best thing that could ever happen to them, and I would have to agree. I'd never been happier. But along with falling *in* love, you risk the chance of falling *out* of love, and I let that possibility scare me into doing some pretty stupid things. The woman I fell in love with is here tonight, and I owe her the biggest apology of all. Let's see if we can get her to come up on the stage." I was sweating buckets of fear that she would say no.

The audience helped me out with cheers of excitement. I stood on the right side of the stage and faced the blurred figure of the woman who could make my life better by taking another chance on me. Annie made her way toward the security guards, and they lifted her up, gently placing her on the corner of the stage. As soon as she began walking to me, my mouth went dry. Covered in sweat, my T-shirt clung to me like a wet paper towel. My hands began to tremble, and my heart pounded inside my chest. But, a smile was unstoppable when I noticed her boots; she had worn those for me.

I met her mid-stage and reached for her hand.

"Hey," I said, trying in only seconds to burn a lifetime of her image into my mind.

"Hey," she replied, a little terror mixed into her smile.

Her eyes were the color of warmth, and her face was the picture of home. I immediately recognized the physical aspects of her longing, because my body was an exact match. I wanted to grab onto her and pick her up in my arms, beg her to forgive me, and make the promise that I'd never leave her again. We stood awkwardly-still in front of thousands of screaming people who were egging us on to make something happen.

I led her to the middle of the stage, and grabbing the microphone, I introduced her.

"Everybody, this is Annie," I said. The crowd welcomed her with heartfelt hollers.

She surprised me by doing a small curtsy, while dipping her head and waving to the people in the first few rows.

"Annie, this is everybody!" I laughed with her, relieved that this was already going much better than I had expected. But guilt kicked me hard when I stood back and studied her. Desperate love overwhelmed me, and I had to clear my throat a few times to find my voice again.

Microphone in one hand and Annie's hand in my other, I asked, "Would y'all mind if Wade sang our newest song? We wrote this one together, and y'all will be the first ones to hear it."

Wade walked out from left stage with his guitar in hand. He went directly over to Annie, kissing her on the cheek while Randy placed a stool at center stage.

"I'll go backstage and wait for you," Annie said, pointing toward the scaffolding.

"Please stay," I begged, not letting go of her hand.

She looked unsure of herself and her situation, completely out of her element standing on stage. I liked how nervous she was, and I like it even more that I was able to make that go away. I nodded to Wade, and he started to play the song I had written for Annie in the Savoy Hotel.

"Dance with me," I said, putting her other hand in mine.

Her eyes quickly darted in all directions. "Here? Now?" She looked embarrassed, and exactly the same as the last time I had asked her that question, which also happened to be the last time we made love. The memory engulfed me.

"Yes, baby. Dance with me."

ANNIE

K essler and Wade ran all over the stage. This performance was nothing like the ones I had been privy to at the Soggy Bottom in St. Croix. Enamored and full of butterflies, I immediately fell in love with Kessler all over again.

Watching Hope watch Wade on stage, I understood the advantage they had over other couples. His voice boomed through the speakers, as thousands of people sang his songs in unison. His commanding presence was undeniable; just slinging a guitar over his shoulder was a gesture that could easily entice a woman to fall in love.

Wade moved to our side of the stage, and when he found the person he was looking for, his face lit up. He grabbed Kessler and pulled him aside, while kissing his fingers and pointing to Hope, who was screaming, "I love you, baby!" even though he couldn't actually hear her. When Kessler turned my way, his smile almost made me cry. His face looked as though he could finally breathe again, and his arm cradled his stomach as he gave Wade a relieved look.

After they had finished their song and had a group huddle, Kessler stepped up to the microphone. I got why he had been so miserable without any live performances to look forward to. Who wouldn't love to have a special connection with twenty thousand people at the same moment? No matter what he said to the crowd, they ate up every word, grateful to be involved in the conversation.

I'd been to plenty of concerts before, but none where I was in love with the lead singer. This certainly put an interesting spin on the night.

As if he were a preacher at a podium dolling out advice on the afterlife, people instantly quieted before he spoke. By choice, Kessler was an incredibly private person, and when he made a very public apology to his fans, I could not have been more proud of him. Standing on the stage in the first place took balls, but humbling himself—in what would only take seconds to become a viral video—took heart.

"Over the last few months, but especially over the last week, my life has taken a turn for the worse. You see, I lost the woman I love," Kessler admitted.

I lost my ability to breathe Hope and Leslie grabbed onto each of my shoulders; my hands immediately covered my mouth.

"The woman I fell in love with is here tonight, and I owe her the biggest apology of all. Let's see if we can get her to come up on the stage," he said.

"No!" I pleaded to my friends, shaking my head in my hands. "I can't go up there! Please don't make me do it!"

A spotlight magically found me. The girls stood up from their seats to allow me to pass by, pushing me forward until I got to the stage. The security guards smiled at me as if they had already known who I was and had expected this as part of the show.

Being in a seat in the arena was exciting, but standing on the stage as forty thousand eyeballs judged me was nothing short of paralyzing. My list of all the things not to do cycled through my head, and my feet refused to move. I focused on Kessler, who nonchalantly stood at the microphone stand, his hand lazily perched on the top. He flashed me a smile—the same sexy signature smile—full of happiness and confidence, which took me all the way back to that first night in St. Croix.

He moved toward me, and the knowledge that I was only seconds away from closeness with him gave me the extra push I needed to meet him halfway.

"Hey," he said, reaching out and taking my hand, his smile stretching to both of his ears and his dimple causing me to melt.

"Hey," I replied, unable to find any other words.

He looked so good to me—all of him, in every way. When our fingers entwined, the power of our chemistry surged through my body. I wanted him to hold me close, our cheeks pressed together with his breath heavy on my neck. I wanted to hear my name escape his lips as he pulled me close, holding my face in his hands before kissing me. I felt our entire lifetime together in this one single moment.

I followed him to the microphone and faced the crowd.

"Everybody, this is Annie," he said as the bone-white lights illuminated the arena all the way to the back row. The floor shook underneath me, vibrating my feet inside my boots.

My nerves dissipated, and I grasped the balance between entertainer and fan. Bowing to the crowd, grateful for their warmth, I started to relax. Wade came out with his guitar and gave me a kiss on the cheek. I'd missed him being next door since he had gone on tour. The night began to feel like a family reunion.

"I'll go backstage and wait for you," I said into Kessler's ear, pointing to the area behind the curtain and seizing the opportunity to taste his sweat on my lips.

"Please stay," he urged, begging with serious eyes and a firm grasp of my hand.

I was unsure of what I was supposed to be doing out there. Kessler took both of my hands in his and said, "Dance with me."

A memory of what felt like a thousand years ago transported me back to our bedroom, back to the beginning of what I had thought was the end of us. It was the last time we had held each other, and once he was gone, it was a night I had taken for granted.

"Here? Now?" I asked, suddenly embarrassed.

"Yes, baby. Dance with me," he whispered, wrapping his hands around my waist.

He pulled me to him, but stepped back when I didn't relax in his arms.

"Don't look out there." He motioned toward the audience. "Look right here," he whispered, directing my eyes to his. "Everyone else will fade away."

With my head resting on his chest and his booming heartbeat rhythmically tapping my cheek, I pulled myself closer into him. He gently rubbed his chin on the top of my head, as Wade sang in the background. Kessler was right—everyone did fade away, all twenty thousand of them. I was finally in his arms again, and I would have given anything to stop time so I could stay there.

He leaned down, and his breath found my ear. I longed for the softness of his lips to cover my mouth, for the people to disappear, and for Kessler to say all the right words that would prove how much he really loved me.

He held onto me, swaying with the music, as Wade sang the chorus in the background.

If you can't see it on my face,
Then write it on my grave,
'Cause all that matters in this world,
Is that I was loved by this girl.
Annie, baby,
I begin and end with you.

With widened eyes, I pulled away, shocked to hear my name in the song.

The ocean blue of Kessler's eyes fixated on mine, and with hardened seriousness, he took my face in his hands.

"Annie," he began as I inhaled my name from his breath. "I'm so sorry, Annie," he repeated, our eyes heavy on each other.

"I know you are, Kessler, and it's in the past, so let's not go back there. Let's just go forward," I pleaded. I closed my eyes, sinking back into his embrace.

He gently kissed my lips, and sparks surged through me with lightning speed, awakening every part of my body. I'd waited so long to be in this moment, and I didn't want to hold anything back. Wrapping my hands in his hair, I brought his lips back to mine and plunged my tongue into the familiar warmth of his mouth. The lights cut to darkness, except for one lone spotlight holding bright on us. The crowd boomed in the background.

Both of us smiling and holding onto each other, Kessler suddenly let go. He dropped to both knees. At the eruption of the crowd, I looked to Wade for a reality check, to make sure I wasn't dreaming. He put his hand over his heart as a nonverbal blessing.

The sixty-foot screens flanking each side of the stage were filled with the image of us.

He pulled the arm of a small microphone down from behind his ear, and again took hold of my hands.

"Annie," he began, his words echoing through Bridgestone Arena. "I've been miserable without you. I can't eat, and I don't sleep, because all I care about is getting back to you. Lord knows I don't deserve you, but I need you. I desperately need you in my life. You make me want to get up every morning and be a better person than I was the day before. I'm not saying this won't take work, because it will, but you're worth the work. A life where we're together is worth the work. I'm in love with you, Annie, probably more than you'll ever fully understand, and I don't want to do this life without you. I begin and end with you, and you deserve a man who knows that." He pulled himself up to one knee as he took the hook bracelet off his wrist and held it out to me. "Marry me, Annie, and be with me always. Me and you, baby."

Barely able to see through my tears, I sat down on his raised knee and wrapped myself around him, my body shaking from uncontrollable sobbing.

"Yes!" I said, barely audibly, over and over again.

When he stood up, carrying the weight of us both, I didn't let go. I just hung onto him, my arms tightly wrapped around his shoulders and my boots interlocked around his waist. The lights came back up over the arena, and the fans went wild. But, I kept my face buried into the strength and safety of the man who made me love so hard, I couldn't let go.

Wade came over, congratulating us with slaps on the back. I was still clinging to Kessler, who walked us backstage, behind the curtain.

"Baby, please look at me," he said.

I finally dropped my boots back to the floor, and we grabbed hold of one another, our fingers locked into each other's hair, furiously kissing and repeating, "I love you, baby." I had no doubt that we meant it.

As he wiped the mascaraed tears from underneath my eyes and smiled an all-encompassing smile, he said, "I have to go back to work now, but promise me you'll be here when I'm done."

"I promise," I repeated, still sniffing up the rest of my tears. "I'll always be here."

After kissing me one last time, he bounded back out, sliding on his knees across the stage and hamming it up for the crowd. He popped up at the microphone with his fist in the air and yelled, "She said yes!"

JACK

As I made my way back to the Sheraton, bellowing tubas drowned out the chitchat among the patrons in the crowd. Francesca and I were supposed to be having celebratory sex in our hotel room by now, but instead, the image of her lifeless body crept through my mind. Pre-vomit salivation coated the inside of my mouth with each gruesome thought. I continued an eye-searching sweep of the rooftops for Gail, but she seemed to have vanished from sight.

I pushed my way through the forward-advancing crowd. Every face began to look the same, and the anxiety of suffocation among the hordes of people bore down on me. Like an antelope in a stampede of buffalo, I had only one focus: to emerge out of the masses and into the direct breeze of fresh air.

As I rounded the last suffocating corner, I saw her running toward me. Complete terror froze her face in a silent scream. Her once-polished dress was now mangled; shards of fabric chased after her. I reached out to the small duffel bag slung over her shoulder, trying to get her attention to tell her I was here now, I would take care of her, but startling her instead. She screamed at my touch and clawed her nails into the soft and bruised skin of my face, her bangle bracelets jingling in my ear.

"Francesca!" I yelled. I searched for any sign of recollection in her eyes. "Francesca, stop! It's me, Jack." The band drowned out my voice.

Her arms, covered in raised red and pink welts, accounted for how she had spent the last hour. My furnace of anger ignited as more cuts and bruises became exposed on her delicate caramel skin, and my eyes turned a similar color to her markings. Revenge seethed inside of me.

Her glossed-over look faded, as recognition took charge of her walking coma.

"Jack?" She was like a lost child, stopping passers-by in search of a recognized family member.

"Yes, Francesca, I'm here. You're okay now. I've got you."

She fell into my arms, the weight of her legs suddenly too much to bear. Tiny convulsions came over her with the onset of shock.

"You're hurt," I said, continuing to look her over. "I'm sorry. God, I'm so very sorry," I repeated, angry with myself for minimizing the danger of the plan and, once again, putting another woman in harm's way.

"I'm okay," she stated without confidence, taking in a deep breath and holding her face to the sky.

My heart hurt for what I had put her through. She wasn't Gail, and she wasn't trained for this type of mission. I'd found her at a financial aid office, for God's sake. How could I have been so self-consumed? I had lured her into the crazy of my world on the promise of five thousand dollars, knowing that someone of her financial status wouldn't say no. Whether I'd meant to or not, I had played her, ultimately toying with the safety of her life. Now that we were a target, and this was only the eye of the tornado; the second round of destruction was coming. I was sure of it.

"It isn't safe here. We have to go," I urged her, gently taking her battered arm in my bloody hand.

"Go where, Jack? They are everywhere!" she screamed, trying to hold back tears.

"How many came at you?"

"There were two men waiting for me in our hotel room. They know who you are, and now, who I am, but those aren't the only men looking for us. The smaller one kept talking to someone else on his phone, taking directions from a third party." She was trying to keep her hysterics to a minimum.

John Savage! That son of a bitch is dead, by my hands, and the image of my face will be the last thing inside of his head besides a bullet.

"How did you escape? Where are those men now?" I kept my voice steady and my panic subdued.

"They're dead, and they got what they deserved. I don't want to talk about it further."

"They're dead? Okay, we're going to be okay. Just let me think a second. We need to get to the airport and charter a plane. Not that you have much of a choice, but will you go with me?"

She vigorously nodded her head, and an inkling of a smile touched the corner of her lips. I stroked her cheek. Her features softened as her hand found my hip. Her eyes told me that she would have gone with me even without the threat of danger.

The Sheraton sat at the pinnacle of four intersecting main streets, all of which were now inundated with people. Shadows from the skyscrapers of the most influential banks in the world cast darkness onto the streets below, a constant reminder to keep moving. As the sun moved behind the clouds, turquoise-stained, copper-plated steeples seemingly rose from the ground to make their presence known, taunting our existence. Our short-spanned mortal duration was laughable compared to the age of the stones that made up those feats of architecture, as well as the shadows they'd cast for hundreds of years.

I didn't ask Francesca if the transfer was successful. I didn't want to add to her stress, and honestly, I was scared to know the answer. If it was no, then this day had all been for nothing. If she had managed to pull off a prodigious yes, then we needed to find a place to sleep tonight, and I had already seen enough of this city. One more night was one too many.

We moved toward the lake, in the opposite direction of the crowd. Almost everyone in the streets was headed to watch the finale of Böögg. Cheers of explosive encouragement echoed through the alleyways, and the climax of the festival surged through the pedestrians, who were like children overdosing on sugar.

Francesca's hand was almost embedded in mine, and the protection and responsibility I felt for her were nearing matrimonial. So when the gunshot went off, I immediately pulled her into the cover of my body, ready to take a bullet for her.

Heads turned in all directions, and confusion took center stage. Was Böögg beginning to burn and was the finale starting, or were mischievous children lighting cherry bombs in an abandoned trashcan? The naïveté of civilian life would never escape me. Those were gunshots, and I was sure they were meant for us.

"Run!" I yelled, pushing Francesca out in front of me, trying to shield her from more harm. "There!" I pointed. She glanced back, making sure I hadn't deserted her.

We moved toward the blaring horn of the Lake Zurich ferry, warning passengers that they were about to miss their ride and, ultimately, the best view of Böögg.

"Hurry," I yelled, dodging the high heels Francesca had taken off and thrown over her shoulder, and then realizing how fast she actually was when her stilettos weren't holding her back.

The infuriating pain in my shoulder screamed with every jarring motion of my feet hitting the pavement. I was quite sure that the bullet was purposefully worming its way to the core of my body, ripping and shredding all muscles in its path. The blood was now free-flowing, and my shirt was becoming soaked once again.

We ran across the boat ramp, the loose metal clanging and bending with every step, like a swinging bridge at a tourist trap. Cars filled the wide-mouthed bottom of the ferry, securely stationed in exacting rows. The upper deck was filled with excited spectators, each holding an oversized camera and taking pictures of others in various poses. Had the enormity of our situation been lost on me, I would have taken a moment to capture the spectacular view, with a mirror image of the mountain range reflecting in the Picasso blue rippling glass of the water. Yellow-coned rays of light scattered around the top deck, supplying the warmth to fight the constant hilltop breeze

The final horn blew as I spotted two men jumping the last section of the swinging bridge, both nearly escaping a swim in the sixty-degree water. The first man to climb over the railing swished his coat-tails behind him so as not to trip on the extra material, but he managed to expose his pistol to an unknowing crowd.

"Can you swim?" I asked Francesca.

"I grew up in southern Italy. Of course I can swim."

"The water here is much colder than where you grew up swimming. Your body will immediately display the first signs of shock. You'll panic, and breathing will be difficult. We have to stay underwater for as long as possible, making our way back to the shore. If we jump, can you handle the swim?" My voice was stern as I spoke.

"As long as you carry my bag"—she pulled it out from underneath the shoulder strap of her small duffel—"I can make it. But I don't know how long I can hold my breath."

Taking the bag from her, I rested the strap on my healthy shoulder. It dawned on me that I had never questioned where the bag came from. "What's in here?" I asked, thinking the answer would be the personal items she was escaping with.

She looked at me like I had *idiot* written across my forehead and let out a disgusted haute. She put her hands on her hips.

"Money! What else would I be running through the city with?"

"Ours?" I asked, shocked. Francesca was more of a badass than I had given her credit for.

"Of course, ours. And a little from the hotel corpses, too." She said it with a no-shit tone of voice.

I unzipped the brown canvas carryall, revealing scattered bundles of one-hundred-dollar bills, as well as her purse. The new bag she had bought for today's adventure was now scuffed, and the shoulder chain no longer attached. A light bulb idea exploded in my head. I reached into the cargo pocket of my stolen pants and pulled out a packet of Zig Zags.

Despite knowing Francesca only a short time, I knew she would have straws in her purse. I hadn't seen her drink anything over the last week that didn't come through one of those red and white striped straws first.

The crowded ferry bought us time, and I dropped the bag onto the wooden deck, pulling a handful of Francesca's signature straws out of her purse. Carefully extracting a thin rolling paper from the bright orange Zig Zag packaging, I said, "Hold the ends of the straws together. I'm going to make us a snorkel."

Mustering up enough spit to properly wet the paper was almost impossible; adrenaline sucked the moisture from my mouth. I carefully taped the paper to the straws and interlocked the ends together. I realized this was a long shot, but it was better than another gunshot. Thinning ourselves out, we moved through the crowd to the back of the ferry, to the farthest spot from the stairs. Hissing and crackling popped in the distance, as snakes of fire shot from the base of Böögg.

"Hold onto the straws until you get in the water. Once we're submerged, stick an end in your mouth. Do not come up for air!"

Francesca nodded, the same terror in her eyes as when I had found her on the street.

"My bag will fill up with water and act as a weight, keeping us from floating to the top. Hold onto my hand, and I'll get us back to shore. Don't let go of my hand!" I squeezed her palm into mine. "As soon as the explosion starts, jump out and away from the boat."

"What about you? You don't have a snorkel," she said.

"I don't need one. I've done this before."

No sooner had I gotten the words out, than a series of bombs exploded in the city center. It sounded like an air strike in Baghdad. Every face turned toward the firework show, and Francesca and I made our exit from the top floor of the ferry.

A thousand needles stabbed my skin as the water rushed over me and filled every available air pocket in my clothes, the cold hollowing my lungs. Upon opening my eyes under water, I saw Francesca thrusting and struggling about. Her feet kicked wildly as her arms made butterfly circles around her head, and I knew she was in a full-blown panic. I grabbed her arm, as the fully soaked duffel began its weighted descent to the bedrock bottom of the lake. Our eyes met through the crystal clear water of Lake Zurich. I tapped my finger to my lips, motioning for her to put the homemade snorkel in her mouth. She nodded and closed her eyes, taking in a much-needed breath of life security.

We hovered stalely three feet under the water, as the dense sound of the distancing ferry motor depreciated. At the signal of her thumbs up, I placed her hand on the shoulder strap of the duffel and swam like hell with my one healthy arm.

Flashbacks to my time in underwater training reminded me to focus on the shoreline instead of the pain in my shrinking chest. With every double swallow, tiny oxygen bubbles entered my lungs, satisfying my hunger for air a little longer. My swimming hand sliced through the water, creating hundreds of bubbles that rushed past my ears like angry ants running from a smashed hill.

Our feet simultaneously touched the smooth rocks of the shore. I gulped at the air, pacifying the burning pain of asphyxiation, and I began to consider a fix for our next problem: hypothermia. As we dragged ourselves out of Lake Zurich, the small amount of clothing we wore, now soaking wet, felt like the weight of another person. I pulled Francesca over to me, stumbling on loose rocks, desperately trying to connect our bodies, and we paused momentarily to enjoy the air in our lungs and the life left in our bodies.

A voice startled me out of my daydream.

"The very last thing I said to you was, 'Don't be a fool.' How in the hell do you explain this one, Jack?" Gail was leaning over the water lying flat on her stomach on a boulder. Her red curly hair dangled around her smile.

ANNIE

Security brought the girls backstage to watch the rest of the show. After many hugs and even more tears, I felt like I could finally breathe. Ever since had Jack come back into my life, my entire existence had been off-kilter. My feet couldn't find the right balance—neglecting one side of myself to fix the other—ultimately, I kept getting myself unraveled. With Kessler's bracelet on my arm, the horseshoe pointed toward my heart, balance was restored.

At the end of the final encore, Wade and Kessler spent forty-five minutes signing all things random for anyone who hung behind for an autograph. Hope and the rest of the girls floated in and out between backstage and the green room, encouraging me to let Kessler do his thing while we celebrated with drinks. I couldn't leave, and I didn't want to. With Kessler's supposed retirement from touring, I didn't know if I would ever see him perform in an arena of this magnitude again, and I wasn't going to miss one second of it. Plus, I'd made a promise, and I was going to keep it.

Wade came off stage first, straight into the arms of his wife, and the make-out ensued. True to form, they couldn't keep their hands off one another. Now, I understood why.

Once Kessler began his exit off stage, his eyes never faltered from mine. He held my gaze, while the smile on his lips became bigger with every step closer to me.

Without a word, he swept my body up, along with my breath, and I locked the toes of my Luccheses around his waist. His arms tucked under my backside for support; sweat rolled down the hills and valleys of his muscular and taut skin, eventually disappearing into mine. We started down a narrow corridor. I didn't know where he was taking me, but I didn't care as long as we were together.

His roadie, Randy, stopped us as we approached the door to his dressing room.

"Sorry, boss, but reporters are waiting for you outside the green room. They want to know about a possible comeback."

"You can tell them I just had one, and they'll have to wait. I'll be busy for a while."

He walked me across the threshold of his dressing room and locked the double-set doors, carrying me over to the gray tufted sofa. He sat me down in his lap. Gently kissing every inch of his face, I felt his jaw tense up.

"Did you mean what you said out there?" he asked. "Will you really marry me?" He spoke with a shy but paranoid tone.

"Of course I did! I love you, Kessler."

"I'm sorry, baby. I'm so damn sorry for everything," he whispered, shamefully turning his face to the wall.

"Kessler," I sighed, trying to comfort him. "I made mistakes, too. Let's not rehash the last few months by pointing fingers or placing blame. We have a clean slate and a second chance. The past is in the past. Me and you, baby. The only words you need to focus on are *happy wife, happy life*. And even though I'm not you're wife yet, I'm not the happiest I could be either." I slowly unsnapped each button on his shirt, coaxing a smile, along with a healthy amount of his sweaty chest.

Straddling his lap, with the heels of my boots sinking into the couch, I playfully asked, "Do you like my boots?"

"Oh, Lord, I almost died when I saw you standing across the stage in those sexy boots. I knew in that moment that you were coming back to me. Thank you for looking through my bullshit and seeing the real me."

Cradling his cheeks in my hands, I looked deep into his eyes and said, "I love you, Kessler, and nothing will ever change that. But, right now, I need *you* to see *me*."

I slowly guided his hands underneath the bottom of my Stella McCartney dress, resting my fingers on his and taking my time to turn him on. We made several passes around the strings of my thong, and I teased him with feels under the lace of my panties. A moan escaped his parted lips when he realized how wet I already was. He closed his eyes, opening his legs farther to make room for his expanding erection.

"Kessler," I whispered. "Don't look away, look right here," I teased, motioning his eyes to look at mine.

His smile slowly faded as my dress went over my head, and he licked his lips, like a predator salivating over potential prey. When his face came toward my breasts, I playfully stopped him with my hand in his hair.

Hopeful excitement widened his dilated eyes as I stood up and seduced his weakness over my naked skin.

"Holy shit, baby. Yes!" he exclaimed, cheering on my lack of inhibition.

Leaning myself just out of reach and turning my back on him, I bent down in a slow and pornographic motion, sliding my thong beyond each leg. Once again, I left my boots on.

My newly waxed (and properly healed) Brazilian was more than Kessler Carlisle could handle.

Ripping through the remaining snaps on his shirt, and back on both of his knees, he pressed his chest pressed against the back of my thighs before his lips did the same. The warmth of his tongue found the heat of my centermost flesh, as my lips swelled with painful pleasure. He pawed at my ass, leaving one hand to continuously run the length of my leg, and even pausing to fondle the inlay of my boots.

"Touch me, Annie. I need to feel your hands on me," he begged. I turned around to face the rock-hard eye of his delicate frame.

I wiped my longing away from his lips and led us to the velvety softness of the back of the couch. Before I could offer any suggestions, he laid me over the sofa, tapping the insteps of both of my boots with his and instantly spreading my legs farther apart. My fingers held firm to the large circular buttons sewn into the fabric of the couch, as Kessler eagerly guided himself into me. Our skin suctioned together, and the thickness of his erection swallowed up the space inside of me. Hovering over me, he ran his lips across my shoulders, while short throaty breaths announced every deep thrust of his manhood. Wildly scanning my back, his hands searched for leverage; finally finding my hips, he dug in. Frenzied rapture held us together, connecting our bodies, inside and out.

Suddenly he pulled away and turned me around.

"I want to see your face," he breathed out in partial words.

Perching myself on the thick frame of the back of the couch, I squeezed his sides together, using my legs as a vice. We panted out broken words of affection while multitasking different parts of our bodies. My toes curled with the onset of an orgasm. Kessler wrapped his arm around my waist as he pushed himself deep inside of me, collecting every bit of ecstasy and leaving all of himself behind. Unable to see through the blinding pleasure, I squeezed my eyes shut as my pulse thumped in my ear, and the blinding pleasure of my all-encompassing orgasm released me from a full-bodied grip.

As I still hung onto his neck, our eyes said all the loving words our voices couldn't find. With a look of the most serious kind of pleasure, which only sex could bring, Kessler erased the frustration, heartbreak, and longing of the last few months in one back-bending moment.

"The best ever," he whispered, smiling like a schoolboy as we slid over onto the couch and came to rest on the newly desecrated cushions. "Just lie with me," he said, pulling my waist into his. "Right here next to me, so I can feel your skin and hear you breathing. I don't want to let you go yet."

I studied his face, and I was filled with more love than I had ever imagined for myself. Something was different about Kessler. His eyes were deeper, his touch softer, and his words more sincere. He was a changed man. I knew right then that he would always give me the best of him.

JACK

I left Francesca to pack our newly purchased clothes for our upcoming flight. I had given Gail explicit instructions for protecting Francesca, but she only rolled her eyes at me as if to say, *No shit*. She walked me out to the street, where I waited on a taxi. As she stood with me, I was sure a lecture was upon me, and I was right, but in the most wrong way.

"You like this one, don't you?"

"Yes," I answered honestly. "She's smart and crazy, easy on the eyes, and she never even flinched when I told her the truth about me."

"I need you to admit that I'm right, all the time, about everything," she gloated.

"Okay, I'll submit. But, what specifically were you right about this time?"

"Oh, lots of things, but mostly about what you said concerning Francesca. I'm happy you found her, Jack."

"You like her already?" I was surprised that Gail would immediately approve of my relationship with a woman like Francesca.

"No, I haven't known her long enough to like her. What I do know is that you think you have found a beautiful woman, here in Switzerland, who is crazy enough to accept you for who you are, and who is satisfied with the little you have to give her." She smirked her way through the absolute rightness of her speech. She was basically repeating herself from a few weeks ago, when she had told me that a woman like Francesca was out in the world waiting for me. "I told you before, you could thank me later. It's later, Jack."

"Well played, partner. Are you staying in Switzerland, or are you coming with us? You're always welcome on any adventure of mine."

"That's a nice offer, Jack, but I'd only be a third wheel where you're going. Zurich is dripping in eye candy, but also in cold, and after the mistral Missouri winter last year, I can't take another day of cold weather. Not one damn day. I need to feel the sunshine on my face, and soak a little color into this drab Midwest skin. I've already rented a house near the ocean. I'm headed that way now." She twirled a loose curl of red hair around her finger. "I love you, buddy. Take care and don't be a fool, but thoroughly enjoy this next adventure."

As she got into her own taxi, she turned around and waved through the back windshield. The image of her wild red hair slowly faded into the city, eventually disappearing down the throat of morning traffic.

***

Firm and fast-paced, I charged through the revolving doors of the final piece of my master plan to end John Savage's life. The white tiled floors of Maintenant Nouvelle smelled strongly of a harsh cleaning, and they shone like the sun-caught sparkle of a diamond. I whipped out the visitor's lanyard I had neglected to replace the last time, and I blew past the visitors' desk, making a mental note that Astrid, the unfriendly and unwelcoming slave to that welcome desk, had been replaced by a softer version.

Centering my cardinal red power tie on the pitch-black breast of my takeover suit, I smoothed my clothes, along with my mind, in the reflection of the upward-moving elevator. As I made the familiar walk to the cold double doors, an American woman stood watching at the entrance of her cubicle. Discreetly, she smiled at me and gave me a silent cheering nod. I recognized her as the young woman who had slipped in with me the last time I'd taken the elevators down.

"Gentlemen," I began, my voice entering the room before my body. All eyes from both parties—the sellers and the former buyers—focused on me. Chatter immediately ceased. "I understand you have an offer to make me. Who would like to begin?" I pushed a supple leather chair away from my assigned seat at the conference table. I chose to command authority by continuing to stand.

Two rows of sickly and pasty faces turned to the mediator of the meeting, who stood to match me.

"I speak for Maintenant Nouvelle and Le Droit," he said, "when I say that we are dedicated to and flexible regarding, working out a solution to this buyout. Years of arbitration have compiled to get to this point, until two days ago, when it seemingly all fell apart. The gentlemen of Le Droit came to play today, and they would like to make you a deal."

"Excellent," I said, retrieving the chair and sliding myself to the table as a sign of willingness.

The mediator sat as well. He folded his thick fingers over a thin manila folder.

"Well, sir, what will it take?" he asked. "For how much are you willing to sell your percentage of shares?"

"How much are you offering?" I snidely replied.

Each ass in every seat shifted with the words of my question, causing a symphony of squeaking leather and rolling chair casters. The men farthest from the doors, toward the back of the room, were obviously lower on the food chain, and they had little weight in the matter. Those were the noisiest of the lot. The suits sitting at the head of the table and closest to the doors barely made a sound. They never once strayed their flared nostrils or angered eyes. These were the men in charge, and they were most certainly the ones with the most to gain or lose in this meeting.

"I realize you are American, sir, and may not be accustomed to the fact that financial matters aren't handled this way in Switzerland," the mediator condescendingly said to me.

"Hmm, no, sir," I replied, matching his tone. I paused for effect. "I think that *because* I'm American, and *because* I currently own 51 percent of shares, *this* financial matter *will* be handled my way, whether *you're* accustomed to it or not. Otherwise, this meeting is over. Now, what's the offer?"

He glanced across to the head of the table. A balding head angrily but submissively nodded.

"Ahem," the mediator coughed, reluctantly opening the folder as though it were filled with pictures of murder victims he was being forced to study. "Le Droit is prepared to offer you the fair price of eight million dollars for ownership of your shares."

"Eleven million," I immediately countered.

His eyes again connected with those of the final authority, and I noticed a faint smile escape the corner of the balding man's mouth, matching a slight eyebrow raise. The deal was as good as done.

"Ten million dollars, and that's our final offer," the mediator argued. He slid over the folder with the paperwork for me to sign.

"Done," I obliged, signing my name, and adding the appropriate banking information for an account deposit.

The men stood and roared with approval, shaking hands and slapping backs. Arrogant jubilation danced throughout the room. They assumed they had gotten one over on the American, buying him out at such an imbecilic low price. The mediator step forward to congratulate me on my new financial status, but I bypassed him and headed through the glass doors.

On my way to the elevators, I poked my head around the corner of the American woman's cubicle, and found her eating a peanut butter and jelly sandwich at her desk. Her elbow-to-elbow space left only enough room for a laptop, a metal desk set, and a small but familiar yellow-fringed American flag.

"Working through lunch?" I asked, startling her enough to make her drop her sandwich on the floor.

"I was, until you scared the crap out of me. It doesn't matter." She sighed, looking up at me. "It will take years working at this paper before I get a shot at a newsworthy story. They aren't rushing to promote the American. I'm used to working through lunch."

"Are you ready for a newsworthy story?" I asked, testing her integrity.

"Of course I am. Traffic jams and bus schedules aren't what I would consider hard-hitting. I'd be happy to cover cat videos, just for a change of pace."

"This is for a proper lunch," I said, placing a crisp one-hundred-dollar bill on her desk. "And this is your next story," I added, pulling an over-stuffed accordion folder out of my satchel. "I hope you find it more exciting than cats."

With the final piece in place, the puzzle was finished.

The outside breeze blew through me, and I took off my suit jacket to let the air chill my soaked armpits. In one hour, I had made ten million dollars from a company I'd never wanted to buy, using money that wasn't mine. The only thing left to do was get the hell out of this country.

The taxi pulled up to the curb and Francesca jumped out and into my arms. She smelled of sweet perfume and looked good enough to eat, starting with those delicious red lips.

We got into the cab, and she pushed herself into the crook of my waist and intertwined our fingers together, exhaling a comfortable breath from the back seat.

"Where are we going?" she asked, unfazed by the strangeness of the fact that we were only now talking about our next destination, on our way to the airport.

"We're going to the United States. Louisville, Kentucky, specifically."

"I don't know this place. Is it nice?"

"Not the part we're going to, but I've made a promise to someone, and I intend to keep it. Did you send the money order?"

"Yes, Sena Demir should be a millionaire by Tuesday afternoon."

"What about Carmela Mancini's account?"

"I closed it before picking you up, and I dropped my final payment to the University of Zurich in the mail. The outstanding balance has been paid in full." She giggled like an actual schoolgirl.

"Excellent. I'm so proud of you, sweetheart."

She turned and looked up at me with questioning eyes.

"I know," I said. "Jack Whitman never would have used the word sweetheart, but he is forever gone, and Jack Allen might talk like that. I'm just trying it out." I leaned down and lost my heart and lips in the comfort of Francesca.

ANNIE

The delightful buzz of the alarm clock woke me well before it was time to get out of bed. Not that our days ahead were rigid with exacting structure, but recordings did start promptly at two o'clock. Kessler and Wade were in the production stage of their song "'I Begin and End with You.'" The collaboration with Wade was so effortless that Kessler had decided that my song would be just the first of an entire album yet to be written. The record would be filled with songs written with his favorite artists, and with those he had always wanted to work with.

He was excited to wake up in the morning, to push toward a final product that was his idea, his music, recorded in his studio, by his final authority. His eyes seemed a deeper shade of blue with every song he wrote.

Since his afternoons were happily taken up with work, his mornings belonged to me.

The ease and comfortable silence of our warmed bodies cocooned together under the sheets reminded me each day of where we came from, who we were now, and, together, who we would grow to be. I'd gotten good at perfecting hindsight in order to be mindful of the present, making the most of each day and knowing that tomorrow had a mind of its own.

Watching his breath rise and fall beneath his skin was like begging without words. Slipping my leg between his thighs, I pulled myself as close as possible to his warmth.

"Hey, baby," he whispered, his smile cut short by a yawn.

"I bought coffee and some of those pastries you like from downtown."

"You did?" he excitedly asked with equal amounts of surprise and gratitude. "That's so nice, baby. Thank you."

I fluffed and propped his pillows, doting on him just enough, but leaving him to get situated while I went downstairs to grab our breakfast. As I piled the plates and drinks on a serving tray, Kessler's voice rang out, startling me into cursing.

"Oh my God!" he kept repeating at full volume. "Annie, get in here! You've got to see this!"

I shuffled into the bedroom at the topmost speed that carrying a tray would allow, only to find Kessler wide awake and sitting up on his knees in bed, the sheets entangled all around him. His eye sockets—staring directly at me—and open mouth were equal in size; his finger pointed to the television, encouraging my attention to the news report.

My reaction was the same as before, but this time the location was different. Running across the screen in red letters, once again Kessler's name was followed by "Breaking News." The on-scene reporter prefaced the story from a microphone-littered podium, painstakingly rehashing Kessler's recent sex scandal.

I sat down next to him and grabbed his hand, as the whore from the hotel took her place at the podium. She smoothed out a folded sheet of notebook paper on the hard surface, and gave a painful glance to a busty Italian woman with bright red lips standing next to her. She began to read:

"My name is Carlie Sexton. Earlier this month, I sold pictures of myself and Kessler Carlisle in compromising positions to a number of media outlets. I am admitting now: the pictures I sold were staged, and I never had sex with him at the Savoy Hotel, or anywhere else for that matter. The only act we shared on the night in question was a kiss, but he was too intoxicated to even know my name. He continually called me Annie." She paused and gave a pleading look to the Italian woman, who sternly nodded her head. Carlie Sexton began again.

"This isn't the first time I've siphoned money out of a man. Although, this *is* the first time I've gone public with my indignities. I've blackmailed several men over the years, most of whom were married. I've been the cause of broken homes, all for a few bucks, and my rap sheet is full of petty crimes. I have little desire to be a productive member of society, and I feel as though I'm entitled to continue taking from unsuspecting victims, while adding nothing good to this world." The volume of her voice lowered as she added an eye roll to her last statement. "I apologize to Mr. Carlisle, and I especially apologize to his fiancée Annie, for trying to destroy her fairytale forever."

"No way did that just happen," I said, astonished that anyone would apologize in the first place, let alone completely degrade her existence and show her worthlessness to the entire planet.

I kept waiting for Kessler to freak out, yell and scream at the TV, or revel in in his innocence, but he sat quietly with a smirking smile, silently nodding his head in agreement with what he had just heard.

In my heart, I'd already known the truth about that night, but I have to admit that hearing it confirmed was certainly delightful. I fell into the down comforter with both hands glued to my forehead, my mind spinning in disbelief. Trying to replay everything she said, I could only focus on one statement.

Kessler lay down beside me, propping his head up on his elbow.

"You said my name that night? You wanted me there, not her?" I asked.

He looked down at me with the only eyes I ever wanted to stare back into, and said, "I've always wanted you, Annie. From the first night I met you, I've never wanted to be anywhere but with you."

Butterfly wings fluttered hard in my stomach, causing an avalanche of chills to spread over my skin.

"Why are you so calm? Aren't you going to say something about that press conference? You're acting like you read her speech before she gave it."

"No," he said, smiling at me. "I've never read it, but I'm pretty sure I've heard it before."

"Am I missing something?" I asked, confused by his vague statement.

Holding the hook bracelet between his fingers and sliding it up and down my wrist, he said, "Not anymore, baby. You have everything you'll ever need right here. Me and you."

JACK

Francesca's head rested underneath my chin. My shoulder cradled her temple, as a fountain of long auburn waves flowed down my chest. Her hand was wedged between my crossed thighs. Through dark sunglasses, we silently stared beyond the wall of hangar windows, waiting patiently for our jet to pull out onto the tarmac. The suction of the glass door, which breathed in and out with the entrance and exit of each employee, continued to give me false hope of an early exit from Kentucky.

A small metal television saturated our silence with a twenty-four-hour news channel. The woman behind the check-in desk commented on each story with a, "Lord have mercy, such a shame, and you know, that's right."

I watched the TV from the reflection in the windows, and as soon as "Breaking News" flashed on the screen, the receptionist turned the volume up and radioed other employees. The news anchor spoke hurriedly into the camera, revealing fragments of information to her audience and solidifying her first place in breaking the story.

"We're going live to Washington, D.C. where our correspondent is collecting facts."

"Thank you, Robin," the correspondent responded. "I'm here on Sixth Street, in the Capitol Hill community, at the private residence of the vice president of the United States, John Savage. As you can see"—she stepped out of view, while the camera zeroed in on a stately, red brick brownstone—"a crowd of reporters has begun to set up camp for what could be the biggest news story of the decade. Reports surfaced late last night, citing sources out of Switzerland of all places, about the VP's involvement in felony activities. There are a number of allegations in this report. Among the most damaging offenses are: theft, racketeering, mail and Internet fraud, blackmail, and the concealment of at least two illegitimate children. But, the most serious accusation is murder."

The roar of the twin engines fired up, vibrating the ground under me, as the anchor at the station began questioning the correspondent.

"Can you go into detail about any of the charges against the vice president?"

"First let me clarify, these are still accusations, and no official charges or arrests have been made concerning John Savage. The gist of what we are being told is that during his time as an agent, and all the way through to his tenure as director of the CIA, John Savage used government-mandated missions as a means of personal gain. Allegedly, there are specific accounts that he targeted nonradar cells without government knowledge or approval, basically going on a crime spree and leaving innocent victims in his wake. Obviously, government officials deny knowledge of any of these events, but proper documentation of proof has been submitted. We are awaiting verification. As far as any illegitimate children, we have only found the paper trail of a bank account, from which an un-named woman has collected several hundreds of thousands of dollars over the last eighteen years."

The camera again closed in on John Savage's picture-perfect brown-stone. A wall of officers stood guard at the black iron fence, prohibiting reporters or looky-lous from getting too close. Crepe myrtles lined the yards on either side of the house, littering the rooftop shingles with fiery pink flowers. The arched picture window was framed as the focal point of the home.

By now, the small airport waiting room was crowded with employees, all trying to stay informed or get caught up on the story. Francesca and I sat silently. We already personally knew the facts of the case. The jet gleamed in the sun as an attendant pulled down the staircase for board-ing. Standing up, I turned to face the television, and I took Francesca's hand in mine.

The camera footage showed sheer curtains hanging inside John Sav-age's picture window, thin enough to let the light shine through but still masking specific features. A figure paced back and forth beyond the cur-tained barrier. My gut told me those were the panicked footsteps of a felon. I relished the sickened terror running through his worthless spine, and knew of only one way for him to escape it.

As the news crews transmitted live footage to a national audience, the figure came to a stop at the center of the window. In one fluid movement, he reached to his head and fired a gun. The force of the discharge blew back the curtains, and the glass became covered in a splatter of thick crimson substance, as if someone had thrown paint on the large arched pane.

This one's for you guys. Rest in peace, Jamie and Riley.

Francesca and I exchanged a glance, as the attendant motioned us outside.

"Ready, sweetheart?" I asked, squeezing her hand, not giving another thought to John Savage or the chaos that rallied around his property.

Nodding her head, she asked, "Where are we going this time?"

"Panama. I know of a senator hiding a large bank account, who's grossly misjudged the loyalty of a rogue patriot."

EPILOGUE
SIX MONTHS LATER

ANNIE

C ome on, baby, please? Just a quickie before we head out," I begged
Kessler, pulling on the drawstring of his shorts and trying to guide
him into the bathroom.

"Woman, we've got people standing on the dock, waiting for me to
help them aboard. You're seducing me at least once—sometimes even
twice—a day now, and quite frankly, I think you might secretly be trying
to kill me."

"Could you think of a better way to go?"

"Now that you mention it, no, I can't," he said. He leaned down to
kiss me, but quickly pulled himself back into the responsible partner role.
"You need to get your fine ass on deck and help me get these people settled. If you do that, I promise I'll get you real good tonight, after everyone is asleep. Deal?" He smiled and slipped his fingers inside the back of
my swimsuit bottoms to cop a feel.

"All right, deal," I agreed as I started up the galley steps to the deck of
Sue, Kessler's beloved boat, a tribute to Johnny Cash.

The sky welcomed us with sunshine, and the sea with smooth waters,
as I helped everyone get settled aboard. Wade was already half-drunk, so
Hope had spent most of the morning hiding herself from his numerous
sexual advances. Hutch hopped over from the deck, still as agile as a deer,
and still part of my chosen family. My nephew and niece, Max and Mia,
sat comfortably together, while their lifejackets seemed to swallow them
whole.

"Thanks for having us this week," Liz said, pulling me in for a sisterly
hug.

"Have you heard from Jamie yet?"

"No, but I was pretty hard on him and insistent upon divorce. He told me he was still going to go to Montana to learn how to be a husband, thinking his efforts might change my mind. I haven't heard from him since. I don't know what to tell the kids. They ask about him every day."

"I don't know either, Liz. What I do know is that St. Croix has a way of giving you answers, even if you don't know the right questions to ask. Just hang in there, and they will eventually find you."

"Do you know her?" Kessler asked me, pointing to a slender woman slowly making her way down the shoreline toward the boat.

"I believe I do," I answered. I walked down the dock stairs and onto the sandy shore.

I knew exactly who she was before I saw her face; her hair gave her away every time. I waded into the water and waited for her to approach me. A year ago, I wouldn't have given her the time of day, but knowing what I knew now—about people and relationships—I was actually happy to see her.

"Annie," Gail shyly said. Her eyes held mine for only brief moments at a time, continuing to dart her gaze toward the sand.

A hole of uncomfortable silence began expanding around us. She looked as though she wanted to say more, but we had time for that later.

"Get over here," I said, taking her arms and pulling her to me in a bear hug.

"Annie—," she started again, but I cut her off, waving my hand across my face.

"I don't want to hear it. You did what you had to do, and the past is the past. We're good. Besides, you were a part of helping me find Kessler, and for that, I'll always be grateful."

"Thank you," she whispered. "Speaking of Kessler, look at you. You're gorgeous! Love looks very nice on you."

"What about you? What are doing here?" I asked.

"I'm out, Annie, for good. No tricks, I swear. I had to get out of Missouri and get lost, and since you did well for yourself in St. Croix, I thought I'd follow your lead. I rented a house down the beach a ways, and I'm staying indefinitely."

"How wonderful! If you don't have any plans this afternoon, we'd love to have you on the boat. We're about to shove off now."

"I'd like that."

As we walked up the dock stairs, Hutch stood at the top to greet us. Well, to greet Gail anyway. I saw the immediate spark of fire in his eyes as he watched her approach.

"Hello there," he said, taking Gail's hand and bringing it to his lips. "And who might this young lass be, Annie?"

Laughing, I replied, "Francis Hutchinson, meet Gail Adams, my friend. She's a Midwest girl like myself, and she's going to join us on the boat this afternoon."

"The Midwest sure does grow lovely ladies. This must be my lucky day. Let's see what kind of trouble a couple of us gingers can get into," Hutch baited Gail, raising his bushy eyebrows and mimicking Groucho Marx. "May I escort you aboard, mi lady?"

"Oh, Lord," I laughed, rolling my eyes but hopeful for a possible love connection. St. Croix did have a way of helping people find each other, even if that way was disguised by chance.

As we settled in, rolling out to sea, I stood between Kessler and the steering wheel. His arm wrapped tightly around me, while his hand hung loose on the wheel.

"Construction is moving along quickly," I commented, pointing toward the shore and the almost-finished school complex. "They finally put up the sign. Allen Education Center is the perfect name, and a lot of kids are going to be very happy about this boarding school."

"Speaking of kids," Kessler crooned, gently rubbing my constantly expanding belly, "we only have three months left, and we still haven't picked out a name for her."

I wasn't worried about deciding on a name. A lesson I'd recently learned about life was that what we needed would come. You may not get what you were expecting, but if you open your eyes, you'll see that what's in front of you is exactly what you need.

I had spent years wanting a baby, and with the ability of hindsight, I understood why I hadn't been able to have one until now. The name would come to us at the right time, just as Kessler and my daughter had come to me, even when I didn't know I needed them. What's meant to be will always find a way.

Other novels by Karyn Rae

The Achilles Heel

Acknowledgements

First and foremost, thank you to everyone who has shown support by buying and talking about my books. Without y'all, the next book and then the next would never happen, so thank you.

I'd like to thank my editor, Grace Labatt. You are cunning with meticulous detail, and you are exactly who I needed to make my novels worthy. Thank you so much.

To Samantha March, for her kindness, availability, and honesty.

To my parents, who have given nothing but continual support to my pursuit of a writer's life. Thank you for always asking about my projects.

My in-laws, who tell everyone about my books, thank you for being proud enough of me to push my novels on unsuspecting victims.

To my beta readers: Alli Ritchey, Christi O'Riley, Samantha Halsey, Abbe Montgomery, Tara Horn, Lisa Rau, Nancy Vosters, Jessica Britten, Aimee Jeter, and Melanie Rich. Thank you for not being annoyed by my constant draft-revision emails.

Thanks go out to Tommy Varebrook for schooling me on all things law-enforcement related. Thank you for taking the time to guide me, even though you had a new baby at home. I appreciate your help, buddy.

Big love goes out to my mentor, Christi Nies. You already know my love and respect for you are immeasurable, but I needed to solidify my gratitude in print. To the moon and back, my friend.

And my biggest thanks go to my family, because I wouldn't have the words without you.

About The Author

Karyn Rae is an emerging romantic suspense author. Her debut novel, *The Achilles Heel*, was released in May 2014. She is a member of the Romance Writers of America and the Columbia Chapter of the Missouri Writers' Guild. She was nominated for Best Author of 2014 in the "Best of Columbia" issue of *Inside Columbia* magazine. Karyn lives in Missouri with her husband, son, daughter, and chocolate lab, Augusta Mae.

Find Karyn Rae on her website: www.karynrae.me

Made in the USA
Las Vegas, NV
28 January 2022

42474392R00146